the simpleton quest

OTHER BOOKS BY MWM

Scrapyard Ship Series
Scrapyard Ship (Book 1)
HAB 12 (Book 2)
Space Vengeance (Book 3)
Realms of Time (Book 4)
Craing Dominion (Book 5)
The Great Space (Book 6)
Call To Battle (Book 7)

Tapped In Series
Mad Powers (Book 1)

Lone Star Renegades Series
Lone Star Renegades (also called 'Jacked') (Book 1)

Star Watch Series
Star Watch (Book 1)
Ricket (Book 2)
Boomer (Book 3)
Glory for Space Sea and Space (Book 4)
Space Chase (Book 5)
Scrapyard LEGACY (Book 6)

The Simpleton Series
The Simpleton (Book 1)
The Simpleton Quest (Book 2)

the simpleton QUEST

an alien encounter: book 2

Mark Wayne McGinnis

Cover design by:
MWM

Published by:
Avenstar Productions

ISBN: 978-0-9992147-1-8

To join Mark's mailing list, jump to
http://eepurl.com/bs7M9r

Visit Mark Wayne McGinnis at:
http://www.markwaynemcginnis.com

chapter 1

Deep space — present day...

Captain Cuddy Perkins sat in the near-darkness and tried to quiet his turbulent thoughts.

The surrounding modern, egg-shaped, enclosure could hold up to four individuals. Three tiny indigo emitters blinked, providing just enough light for him to make out the nearby, hovering spherical drone that went by the name of Bob.

More and more often, Cuddy found himself escaping into the *Evermore's* wellness chamber. The chamber wasn't even on. No diagnostics were taking place—no rapid infusion of healthy Pashier DNA to alter his ecumenical genome.

Cuddy waited for Bob to say something. *Anything*. And eventually, it did.

"There is no dispute to your logic. What you have described correlates to some of my own observations... my sensory inputs. Keep in mind, as an artificial intelligence I was not designed specifically to interpret diagnostic issues. To interpret such categorically medical matters . . ."

"Yeah-yeah . . . got it! So what did you pick up on?" Cuddy asked, referring to his and the orb's most recent meeting on Primara with Tow, when they were informed what was causing so many beings on Primara to be sick. They'd brought the disease from Earth. Already, three of the gentle aliens had died in just as many days. *God!* The thought that they—*humans*—had something to do with that was horrifying. Cuddy squeezed his eyelids together . . . *damn*!

Bob continued, "In my evaluations of the affected, I monitored rapid fluctuations in body temperatures, telltale epidermal lesions, and constant itching. Later stages, of course, resulted in respiratory infections . . . and then—"

"Death." Cuddy sighed, finality to his tone. "You too saw it, that Tow was purposely evasive. Did his best to stave-off directly blaming me . . . our infectious, *human,* crew. Simply put, the Pashier are dying because of us . . . because of me!"

The orb hovered quietly for several moments before replying, "More accurately, due to Kyle."

Cuddy unconsciously tapped his foot on the deck as he contemplated the whole situation. *What twenty-two-year old still gets the chicken pox, anyway? How was it Kyle hadn't been vaccinated like every other little brat in America? Who would have guessed the Pashier would become so terribly infected by that mostly childhood human disease? With all the Pashier's technology, they couldn't combat such a common virus? Crap . . . things were so much easier*, he mused, *when I was incapable of thinking about anything more difficult than what was for breakfast on any given day or what I'd done with Momma's shopping list.*

"The buck stops with me. I'm responsible for this ship . . . her crew, Bob." Cuddy thought about that—his own words. The simple fact he was sitting here in the near darkness within this advanced alien ship was preposterous. It was also preposterous that he, no more than the village idiot of Woodbury, Tennessee would have been the first to encounter a marooned being, Tow, of a hunted and dying out race of aliens. He looked about the surrounding enclosure. The same enclosure, mere weeks earlier, that had made him whole—had made him intelligent. The others, Kyle, Jackie, and Tony had come along out of some sense of loyalty to him. He knew that. Brian, he was here because Jackie was here. In his own way, Brian was still in love with Jackie—just as Cuddy was himself. The five of them were now a part of this—whatever *this* was. A mission. A mission to save a gentle people that would surely go extinct without their help.

The drone softly beeped twice, then spun several degrees on its axis.

"If Tow were here he'd . . ."

"But Tow is not here," Bob replied flatly.

An image of his Pashier friend, his mentor, flashed across Cuddy's mind. Gentle, unassuming, Tow.

Cuddy looked about the confined space, where weeks earlier he'd undergone a life-saving treatment, which not only healed his physical wounds but also vastly altered his diminished mental faculties beyond anything imaginable—changing his life, the direction of his life—*forever.*

"Look, Bob, you need to keep at it . . . keep searching Interstellar databases, seek a solution . . . some cure." Cuddy's eyes roamed the sleek-contoured bulkheads. *Why couldn't this same wellness chamber provide the cure? Be the answer they sought?* But Cuddy already knew why—the embedded existing software for the amazing contraption wasn't capable of diagnosing, let alone curing, chicken pox.

"We should be back on Primara. Doing what we can to help them," he told the orb.

"You *are* helping, Captain. Retrieving heritage pods is fundamental to the survival of the Pashier race." Bob initiated several audible clicks to emphasize the point.

"Uh huh. You know as well as me that we're stuck here for diversion sake. Until Tow figures things out."

"Still, it is a crucial diversion," the orb emphasized.

chapter 2

Alone on the bridge, Cuddy let the music sway him. With Bob's help, Jackie had figured out the *Evermore*'s ship-wide entertainment system; enough to sync it to one of hundreds of playlists on her iPhone. He knew she'd selected this particular track specifically for him—to bolster his spirits. She often did things like that—was thoughtful that way. He didn't know the song, the female artist—but he liked it.

From where he stood, he could see out the forward observation window, as well as out the starboard and portside windows. But right now, Cuddy's attention was locked onto the emerald green world lying beyond—directly forward. Without turning around, he *felt* Bob's presence as *it* hovered into the compartment.

A Class B Planet, Captain Perkins.

The orb had spoken telepathically. Cuddy nodded, still uneasy hearing himself being addressed that way. Bob did that from time-to-time—chose telepathy over verbal communications. Cuddy looked at the Class B planet. The Pashier gave designations to planets based on their suitability for sustaining life—based on Mahli, their once beautiful, now wrecked, totally decimated, home planet. From memory, Cuddy knew the comparisons, which designated a planetary world either Class A, Class B, or Class C, were determined by the correlation of the world's existing volume of nitrogen to oxygen. If nitrogen was between 75% and 80% of the total atmosphere, then oxygen needed to be between 20% and 24%. The remaining percentage consisted mainly of argon. Other factors included gravitational properties; amount of water available—i.e., ice formations, lakes, and oceans—the list went on and on. Cuddy had it all stored methodically within his repaired, highly-organized, mind.

He took in the zoomed-in feed presented on the viewscape display. "Class B. Close to Class A; acceptable, but not really preferable for colonization. Or habitation, either," he added, basically repeating the on-display—scrolling, meta-data-type—info. The planet's temperatures were far too warm for his taste. Outside, the terrain was green and lush—jungle-like.

Bob said, "Good news. Yes . . . the heritage pod is indeed present and still viable."

Relieved, Cuddy assumed the controls at the forward console. With the *Evermore* in descent, he scanned the fast-approaching landscape then pointed to a distant rise. "It's over there . . . and that could be a suitable LZ."

Cuddy maneuvered the *Evermore* toward a slightly hilly landing area—one that overlooked a particularly dense section of jungle fauna. Bringing the craft to a gentle stop, 200 feet above the clearing, Cuddy felt a short-lived sense of triumph at finding this next heritage pod relatively easy. His mind flashed back to an earlier conversation he had with Brian Horowitz, MD—*self-described* as the most intelligent human being in the known universe.

* * *

Just days earlier, the five teammates banded together around the main cabin of the *Evermore*. The only two seated were Kyle and Tony. Kyle, Cuddy's older brother by two years, still appeared to carry burdensome guilt upon his slumped shoulders. All signs of redness and rash from his recent outbreak of chicken pox had mostly disappeared. Next to him sat Tony Bone, a well-known stoner, and hoodlum back in Woodbury, Tennessee. The town sheriff's son, he looked like he was hitting the bong again. Somewhere along the line, Tony had replenished his stash of weed. He'd be fine, just as long as he didn't have to return home to his oppressive, father. Tony and Kyle had been playing some kind of Pashier video game up on the *Evermore*'s 3D display.

"Hold up . . . let me get this straight. Out of the five of us, I'm the only one you've designated to stay back? Tell me your logic . . ." Brian asked Cuddy, with an accusatory stare.

Cuddy anticipated hearing those exact same words from this fifth member of their oddball, although strangely effective, team. Brian tended to say that type of crap a lot; in fact, all the time. *Tell me your logic. . . . What's your logic . . . I don't see your logic. . . .* There was nothing easy about Brian. The once-prominent New York City doctor, and Jackie's ex-fiancé, the man radiated entitlement and privilege. Cuddy had tried to like the guy—he honestly had. But Brian made it so difficult to do so.

Jackie said, "Come on, Brian. Who saved us and the Pashier last time? Wasn't it you who transported those Howsh ships . . . like . . . vast distances away from Primara? Far into space, with the simple wave of your hand?" Jackie gestured, making the same waving motion.

Placating Brian's colossal ego was *smart*, Cuddy thought.

"And come on, I know you want to look the way . . . *you know* . . . the way you used to look, right? God . . . you were so handsome!" she added.

Brian bristled at that. Slightly raising his chin, he stared down his misshapen nose at

Jackie. He *was* butt-ugly now, no other way to put it. Bloated and disfigured—but it had been his own damn fault. It had taken place weeks earlier—an attempt at one-upmanship with Cuddy. He'd figured out the amazing side-effects that would result from spending time within the *Evermore's* wellness chamber. The most enticing of all to him was the incredible improvements to one's mental capabilities. As human physiology synthesized into some kind of a human-Pashier hybrid, another capacity gained in the process was telekinesis—moving objects simply through one's mental focus and intention.

But the *Evermore's* wellness chamber was created specifically for Pashier crewmembers. Its ability to heal was derived from bombarding patients with healthy Pashier

DNA—deoxyribonucleic acid—the main genome constituent of chromosomes. Mostly the same self-replicating substance found in all living organisms on Earth and, *apparently*, throughout the universe. What was assumed to be an insubstantial and seemingly inconsequential gland within the human brain—called the para-hippocampal gyrus—remarkably comes *alive* when humans spend time within the chamber. While Cuddy's wellness chamber sessions were carefully monitored and timed by the alien Tow, Brian elected to go it alone. Clandestinely extending his time in the chamber to multiple, longer sessions. Like Cuddy, Brian was now a human/Pashier hybrid being. And though Brian's mental and telekinesis abilities were greater than Cuddy's—even greater, possibly, than any Pashier alive—the regrettable side effects from too much time in the chamber was apparent in his monstrously misshapen physical appearance.

"So what the fuck am I supposed to do here? There's absolutely nothing on this plebeian world that interests me. Nothing! And everyone's getting sick . . . all that scratching and hacking. I don't want to be around any of that," Brian said.

Cuddy said, "Come on, Brian, you're a doctor, for God's sakes. And Primara is beautiful. There're lakes and forests and pristine oceans. It's like Earth. You know . . . the way it used to be, before mankind tainted it. Look, Brian I've already spoken to Tow. You will stay with him and Soweng . . . both are still healthy. It's all been worked out."

Jackie said, "Only *you* can do this, Brian. You do realize, the wellbeing of an entire race of people rests in your hands.

You can protect them . . . in case the Howsh return. That has to mean something to you."

"Well . . . actually, no," Brian replied. "These people creep me out . . . they fucking glow in the dark. And would it kill them to throw on a stitch of clothing once in a while?"

"If you haven't noticed, Brian, so do you! Both you and Cuddy kinda glow," Jackie said exasperated, looking at Brian then Cuddy. "Come on Brian . . . you're just being obstinate."

Brian shrugged and feigned boredom. Jackie stepped in closer to Brian. She placed an open palm on his chest and looked up at him with tenderness in her eyes. Once again, Cuddy was reminded that the two of them had once been engaged to be married.

She said, "One more thing . . . during your stay here, you'll be tended to by *empath* elders, Pashier healers. They're not like the wellness chamber that got you into this state, but not as fast-working either. They'll help restore your physical appearance. I'm told they'll help your body accept, you know . . . better assimilate, your new Pashier DNA integration."

Jackie gave Brian's chest a few affectionate pats and turned away as he absorbed her words. She glanced at Cuddy and gave him a nearly imperceptible wink.

Over past weeks, while out on numerous missions, Cuddy communicated over the vast distances of space indirectly with Tow on an almost daily basis, via a nearly identical drone orb to Bob, only this orb, back on Primara, went by the name Rob. *Something like orb walkie-talkies.* All agreed that the crew of the *Evermore*—on their ongoing mission to retrieve other heritage pods from within the system—would return them to the new home world, Primara. That, and the *Evermore* would act as an early warning system; feeding long-distance scan information back to Rob and ultimately to Tow, relaying if any enemy Howsh vessels had been sighted.

"Fine . . . I'll stay for a while," Brian agreed reluctantly.

Apparently, Jackie still had a captivating effect on him. That was something Cuddy could certainly relate to. Cuddy thought about this amazing, beautiful woman—how they'd been thrown back into each other's lives, after a number of years apart. Now, they were at the precipice of a different kind of relationship. Though there'd been only one quasi-intimate moment between them some weeks earlier, even now it was all he could do not to think about it. Her lips on his . . . her hands on him. He didn't know what she wanted long-term—or, for that matter, what he wanted for himself. Only that he was a more than willing participant in their unpredictable, early relationship dance.

"Oh . . . one more thing, Brian," Cuddy said.

"What is it?" Brian asked, his patience clearly being tested.

"Watch Rufus for me? I don't think he's a big fan of space travel."

Cuddy gave the yellow Lab, sitting at his side, a few pats on his flank. He and Rufus had been through a lot together and Cuddy suddenly wondered if leaving him there was such a good idea.

* * *

Back in the present moment, standing at the controls of the *Evermore* and appreciative of the fact that Brian was light years distance away, Cuddy activated the vessel's landing struts and eased the *Evermore* lower into the surrounding dense foliage of the Class B planet. A thick flock of birds, or whatever the weird-looking flying organisms were referred to here, took to the air—screeching in protest as they flew upward and out of sight.

As the spacecraft came to rest upon firm ground, he shut down the ship's propulsion system.

"Atmosphere?" Cuddy asked.

"You'll find it a bit heavy . . . but certainly breathable," Bob said.

With the AI orb close on his heels, they exited the small bridge. The others were already assembled within the main cabin—close to the portside hatch. They'd all been through this same routine a number of times before. Cuddy made eye contact with his brother Kyle, then Tony. There was nervous anticipation on their faces. He felt it too. Jackie, as she always did prior to these excursions, had pulled her long hair back into a high ponytail. She wore snug-fitting jeans that accentuated her long legs and a pink tank top. Strapped over one shoulder was her tattered army-green satchel. Designated as the group's medic, now that Brian wasn't a part of the team. Brian was a licensed physician—unlike her, who'd been a pre-med student still in college—she carried an assortment of medical supplies as well as an assortment of other useful items in her satchel.

Making eye-contact with Cuddy, she asked, "Are we going to do this thing or not?"

"Let's rock and roll," Cuddy said.

* * *

Bob led the way deep into the jungle. With both articulating arms extended, the orb emitted white-hot plasma bursts—hanging vines and thick leafy foliage disintegrated into a misty black haze—Bob's own version of a jungle machete. Careful not to breathe in too deeply, Cuddy did his best to spare his lungs the lingering God-awful stench.

It took less than fifteen minutes for Bob to locate the Heritage Pod. They needed to hurry. Missions like theirs were always at risk.

Basically, the Howsh were the enemy of the Pashier; and thus, by default, they were Cuddy's enemy too. They were a race of vile, furry, aliens that for decades had been hell-bent on eliminating other beings within their home star system; mostly those who inhabited the neighboring planet of Mahli. The Howsh had been highly successful in exterminating the gentle, pacifist, Pashier. First, by bombarding the surface of Mahli with explosive weaponry, then, if that weren't enough, by dispersing into the planet's atmosphere a genetic, lethal disease, called the Dirth. What the Howsh had not counted on was the Pashier's unique capability to go into a form of hibernation—sort of a reincarnation-like transition. Cuddy found their wondrous and mystical transitioning a natural process—an enduring progression of life. The dying, or very recently dead, Pashier were guided into the opened leaf fronds of a heritage pod—an organic, plant-like organism. Its sole purpose in life, as far as Cuddy could determine, was to provide a safe, perpetual, existence for the many thousands of Pashier life forces. That is, until the same, *now in suspension,* life forces were again *reconstituted* at some future time. He didn't know how it all worked, but he found the strange alien evolution process miraculous and fascinating.

Hot and steamy, moisture dripped off the surrounding plant life.

"Um . . . where is the thing?" Tony asked, looking around. "There's no pod here."

"Why don't you give Bob a minute before spouting off?" Jackie urged.

Cuddy noticed Jackie, of late, was in a particularly foul mood, maybe due to fumes wafting from singed plant life. He reminded himself to stay out of her way as much as possible.

The orb slowly began to rise into the trees. Twenty feet up, it paused, emitting a series of clicks and beeps, then descended to the waiting group.

"The heritage pod is situated high up in the trees."

Cuddy strained his neck, staring up, trying to get a glimpse of it. "I don't see it. Are you sure . . . that it's up there?"

"They've never been placed in trees before," Kyle said skeptically. "This is weird. I'm not liking this—"

His words were cut short by a loud animalistic shriek. Startled, everyone crouched low and peered upward.

Suddenly, the jungle was alive with hulking black shapes moving up in the trees. Shrill squawks erupted from all around.

Above the noise, Cuddy heard Bob say, "*Spinktrolls*... indigenous tree beasts."

Furry and the size of small gorillas, they had long thin arms—maybe more like monkeys, in that regard. Their elongated faces reminded Cuddy of pictures of camels he'd seen in nature books. Hanging from vines and extended branches, they swung their big bodies through the trees, springing from limb-to-limb—from vine-to-vine. *Incredibly strong,* Cuddy thought.

As the blur of black shapes descended from the trees, Cuddy glanced around to the team—instinctively looking for Jackie. Crouching low to the ground, he found her huddled beneath his brother's outstretched arm. *Terrific*... she'd turned to him for protection.

As the first *Spinktroll* beast landed on terra firma, Bob complicated things further—informing him that a Howsh warship had just entered the planet's upper atmosphere and was heading in their direction.

chapter 3

Seven years earlier . . . Woodbury, Tennessee

Kyle, fourteen, Jackie and Cuddy, both twelve—bounded through the tall, waist-high, *Indian-grass*. Late afternoon breezes had caused a shimmering sea of tans and golds all around them, outward as far as the eye could see. Now late August, the southern enclave, known as Woodbury, Tennessee, was both hot and humid. A wake of disrupted *jewelwing* and *spiketail* dragonflies filled the air as the three ran farther and farther away from the Perkins' farm.

Huffing and puffing, Cuddy used his sleeve to wipe the salty perspiration from his stinging eyes. He was ready to walk for a spell. His head had started to hurt again for he wasn't supposed to be running around like this. He watched as Kyle and Jackie raced off ahead, leaving him far behind.

Getting lost out here could be a problem. Cuddy didn't

usually go this way—wasn't part of his daily routine. He knew how to get to town following the dirt road. Once he passed the old black folks' house—Elma and Rutherford—and crossed over the railroad tracks that went past the high school, the town sat just a little bit farther on. But way out here, Cuddy didn't know what lay ahead beyond the huge field. Momma said he wasn't supposed to go anywhere she didn't know about, and he was fairly sure she didn't know anything about this particular field.

Finally, he had to stop—the burning in his chest was just too much. Leaning over, hands on knees, Cuddy gulped in deep lungfuls of the thick, heavily scented, air. *Dang . . . they'd be long gone by now. Didn't even notice me lagging this far behind them.* Sure, that was pretty much normal behavior for Kyle—not to think about anyone but himself—but not for Jackie, Cuddy's best friend in the whole world. It had always been that way. Even with him being a lot stupider than other kids their age—*ever since the barn accident*—but she never seemed to care. Not one bit. Cuddy squeezed his eyes tightly shut. He knew he wasn't supposed to fib and he had a feeling he was fibbing to himself. Well, maybe things *were* different lately. Ever so long now, Jackie had been just like him; a skinny little kid with heaps of energy. But something was happening with her shape. Less bony angles and more curves. Sure, he'd noticed, but not as much as Kyle had, who stared at her a lot now. Sometimes putting a hand on her shoulder, or tickling her, or tackling her like she was one of his guy buddies. Cuddy didn't like that much. She was *his* friend, not Kyle's. He then thought, *maybe she'd be running ahead with me instead of Kyle, if it had been Kyle who'd fallen off the hayloft all those years ago.* The truth was, Cuddy knew he didn't simply fall; he'd been pushed. Pushed off by his brother.

Cuddy didn't want to think about that painful incident anymore. Feeling something on his tongue, he spit into his hand. Several dead gnats pooled in the hollow of his palm. Wiping his hand on his pants, he straightened up. Although alone in the field, he heard something. *A motor*? Turning around twice, he spotted wisps of black smoke in the distance.

By the time he made his way through the tall prairie grasses and approached the slow-moving tractor, and the man perched atop it, Cuddy had forgotten all about Kyle and Jackie—and about falling onto his head in the barn. But that was normal behavior for him. Ever since that bad day when he was seven, he wasn't able to remember things for long.

Cuddy smiled and waved. The man steering the faded-red tractor idled down the old machine.

"Are you daft? Good way to get yourself killed, boy." The old man wearing soiled overalls gestured to the swath of cut grass behind the mower attachment. "Whatcha doing out here, anyway?"

Cuddy didn't have a ready answer. Instead, he took in the old man's craggy face, the deep-set lines around his eyes and mouth when he removed his wide-brimmed hat, mopping-up sweat on his brow with a folded blue bandana.

Replacing the hat on his bald head, he leaned forward in the tractor seat. "Hey, you're that Perkins boy . . . ain't that right?"

Cuddy shrugged. "I'm Cuddy."

The old man, nodding slowly, with an expression that read, *yeah . . . I know who you are,* asked, "Lost?"

"I don't know. Maybe."

"Your dad . . . Carl . . . we were friends once when we were quite a bit younger than you are now."

That got Cuddy's full attention. He didn't know much about his father. Had no recollection of him. Momma didn't talk about him at all.

"Pa doesn't live with us no more."

"I know that. He's living in . . . Nashville, I think."

"My pa's alive?"

"Sure . . . alive as I am. Though not sure I was supposed to mention anything about that. I think it's best that you run along home now, boy, I got work to do. Your momma will be wondering where you've gotten off to."

Cuddy glanced into the distance—to the horizon beyond the field.

"People 'round here call me Slatch. Hop on up here . . . your farm's in the same direction I'm going. It won't be fast, but I'll get you back home eventually."

Cuddy considered what the old man proposed but something was nagging at him. He remembered watching Kyle and Jackie run far ahead of him and suddenly thought of Rufus, his yellow lab. He never went anywhere without Rufus.

"Can you see my dog from up there, mister?"

Slatch stared down at Cuddy for a long moment before he stood, steadying himself with one hand on the steering wheel.

"Did you try calling him . . . there's hundreds of acres for a dog to get lost out here?"

Cuddy cupped his hands around his mouth and yelled, "Rufus! Come on, boy! Rufus!"

Slatch, doing the same thing with his hands, shouted for the dog from high up. "Rufus! Here boy!"

They stopped and listened for a while. "Maybe you left him back at the farm?"

"Maybe," Cuddy replied, noticing Slatch was now leaning down, a hand extended in his direction. "Climb on up, we're burning daylight."

Cuddy strode up to the tractor. He figured the ginormous wheel was nearly twice as high as he was. Taking Slatch's hand, he felt himself hauled into the air.

"Sit here in front of me . . . careful not to fall off."

Cuddy looked around, taking in the view from such a high-up perspective. He felt the motor rev-up and the tractor wheels engage. The blades on the mower attachment whirled around and around, chewing up grass stalks as they rolled forward.

"Um . . . what's your name again, mister?"

"Slatch."

"That's right . . . Slatch. Do you think you can tell me about him some more?"

"Who?"

"My pa."

chapter 4

Present day . . .

Dropping down from above, the monkey-like *Spinktrolls* had become ominously quiet. Together, Jackie, Kyle, Tony, and Cuddy backed away, keeping their eyes on the approaching horde.

Kyle glanced at Cuddy, and asked, "Well, aren't you going to do something?"

"Something like what?"

"Like your *kinetic* thing. Just swoosh them away."

"If it comes to that, I will," Cuddy said.

Tony made a snorting sound. Grinning, he said, "What the fuck . . ."

Cuddy didn't see any humor in scores of wild beasts edging ever closer to them. Brazenly, several were approaching faster than most others. Then he saw what Tony was ogling at. He glanced at Jackie—she'd noticed too. Eyes wide, she covered her mouth with both hands.

Tony pointed. "They're springing boners. Monkey boners. The whole lot of them."

Kyle said, "Um . . . Jackie . . . looks like you have a few new fans."

"Gross! This isn't even a little funny." Scowling, she gave both Kyle and Tony a mean look then wrapped her arms snugly around herself.

"I think I saw the movie . . . *Beauty and the Beast*; this is like that, times a hundred," Tony said.

As one of the furry *Spinktrolls* drew a little too close to Jackie, Cuddy stepped forward—his hands outstretched. He used a rapid, shoving motion, which propelled the beast into the air. Arms and legs flailing, it flew backward thirty feet before disappearing into the dense foliage. Even out of sight, it continued to screech the same deafening noise they'd heard earlier. Fellow beasts now joined in, echoing a chorus of shrill cries.

At least that compelled them to back away somewhat, Cuddy observed. He brought his attention back to the tops of the trees, where he could see the organic outline of what he suspected was the heritage pod, though it appeared somewhat smaller than others they'd come across in recent weeks.

"Can you get it down from up there?" Jackie asked, not taking her eyes off her numerous, once-again-approaching admirers.

"Um . . . I think so. Can you guys distract the beasts . . . the *spinktrolls*?" Cuddy asked.

"So . . . what's up in the trees is more important to you?" she asked.

Surprised by her question, Cuddy shrugged. "No . . . of course not."

Tony said, "You know, I think they're more like lovers than fighters. More bark than bite. Go ahead and do your thing with the pod, Cuddy. Kyle and I will keep them busy." He picked a broken branch off the ground. Grasping it in both hands, he brought it up over one shoulder—like a batter waiting for his next pitch.

"And the Howsh ship?" Cuddy asked, giving the orb a quick glance.

"You have ten minutes . . . fifteen at the most," Bob replied.

"Why don't you go on up there, Bob . . . hover in the tree tops and zap away any vines or branches you see clinging to the pod."

Bob silently rose into the air. The movement caught the attention of the watchful *spinktrolls*—momentarily distracting them away from Jackie.

Bob slowed once high up in the trees—hovered there. Moments later, there was a series of bright flashes. As several branches tumbled to the ground, Cuddy raised his palms above his head. Feeling some initial resistance, he quickly found himself supporting the underside of the heritage pod. Psychically, he nudged its *heft* upward—up and off the tree branch that had been supporting it for years—possibly decades. More bright flashes then more branches and vines fell to the ground.

The heritage pod is now free of any encumbrance, Bob informed Cuddy.

Slowly, Cuddy lessened his mental resistance and the pod began to descend. From the corner of his eye, he saw the damn spinktrolls edging closer to them again.

Tony said, "Um … Jackie, maybe you should go back to the ship."

"Forget it! I'm not going back. That's ridiculous, not to mention sexist!"

"They're like … in heat or something," Tony added. "And as you can see, almost all are males." Tony swung his branch at an advancing spinktroll but caught nothing but air as the creature darted away at the last second.

"Males don't go into heat, dumb ass, females do … that's biology 101," Jackie said, nevertheless stepping a tad closer to Kyle. But, like Cuddy, he too was concentrating on the Volkswagen-sized heritage pod looming overhead.

As the pod lowered toward the ground, the more agitated and the louder the beast's screeches became.

"Guess they're getting a bit territorial 'bout us taking the pod," Kyle said.

With ten feet still to go, Jackie screamed bloody murder.

Cuddy lost all focused concentration. The heritage pod fell the rest of the way to the ground, making a mushy *thunk* sound.

In the blink of an eye, two spinktrolls were upon Jackie—dragging her off by her hair. Her hands clutched at her head, trying in vain to free herself. Her legs frantically kicked out, but couldn't make contact with her abductors.

Both Kyle and Tony took off, running after her. Kyle yelled,

"Can't let them reach the trees. They'll take her up where we can't get to her!"

Kyle leaped forward, his arms extended in front of him. One hand landed on Jackie's left leg and he managed to hold on, but now he too was being dragged off.

Using one clenched fist to punch the closest spinktroll, Jackie scream out, "Do something, Cuddy!"

Cuddy was already attempting to do just that. *Crap!* It wasn't like he was some kind of telekinesis expert at this point since he'd only possessed the mental ability for several weeks now. Try as he may, as badly rattled as he was, he couldn't maintain the necessary level of concentration. He watched as Tony threw himself next to Kyle, then grab ahold of Jackie's other foot. At least, they'd succeeded in halting any further progression into the jungle. But now, even more, beasts were flocking nearby to join in with Jackie's attackers.

Cuddy realized he'd been holding his breath. Expelling it, he did his best to breathe normally. He also tried to quiet his mind. Despite the craziness going on all around him, he thought about being back home and feeding the old nag in the barn. He thought about Momma and watching cartoons on Saturday mornings. But it wasn't helping. His mind was churning—horrific visions of Jackie being dragged up into the trees continued to bombard his senses.

Oh no . . . A spinktroll was now attempting to mount Jackie—his plank-hard, purplish member waggling back and forth mere inches from her horrified face. She screamed out, "Help me . . . do something, Cuddy!"

Paralyzed, he couldn't help her—couldn't get his mind in the right place. He just stood there watching. Jackie, on the verge of being molested by scores of foul beasts, and he was too scared, or too *something,* to do what needed to be done. His internal fury grew. He pictured tearing the beast's head from its neck and shoulders with the simple wave of his hand. Seeing it fly off, end-over-end, with crimson-colored blood spiraling-out in all directions. But that was only a mental vision. Wishful thinking. Three more aroused spinktrolls were now climbing on Jackie, clawing and ripping at her clothes.

Oh God... he closed his eyes, focusing on reining in his out-of-control thoughts—just as Tow had taught him. Finally, he was starting to concentrate. Cuddy opened his eyes and raised his hands. *Okay... I can do this.*

But Kyle and Tony were already on the move—both now back on their feet. Fearlessly, Kyle tackled one of the beasts—pummeling its elongated face with his fists. Tony, using his heavy boots as a weapon, kicked out, alternating between his left and right foot. He clumsily missed with both. Then, momentarily hesitating to get his body into the right stance—and looking more like a seasoned NFL punter—Tony strode forward and kicked out. He put his entire weight into it—into a kick that connected with the face of the closest spinktroll. The beast's head ratcheted backward with a decisive *crack!* Its neck was broken. The beast flew backward—hitting the ground—now a limp and lifeless carcass.

The other beasts became still. Their eyes leveled on

the dead spinktroll. In unison, they scampered away—disappearing into the trees without so much as a peep.

Kyle and Tony high-fived one another, hollering insults and obscenities toward the now eerily quiet jungle as Cuddy stood nearby, uselessly watching.

Jackie was still on the ground—her clothes in tatters. Becoming aware of her condition, she adjusted the torn fabric on her shirt to better cover her now-exposed chest. As they turned to face Cuddy, no one spoke.

Jackie glared at him and asked, "So how far are you going to go with this pacifist bullshit, Cuddy? Would you let the monkeys rape me . . . kill me? I thought I was more important to you than that."

"No . . . you have it wrong. I tried, honestly I tried . . . but . . ." his words spilled out, sounding hollow even to himself. He could see in her face that she didn't believe him and he felt ashamed. *I knew it . . . Tow chose the wrong person. What am I even doing here?*

Kyle offered Jackie a hand up, but ignoring it, she rose on her own, staring down in disgust first at her bloody hands, then at her ripped, soiled clothing.

Embarrassed, Cuddy turned his attention to the heritage pod. He noticed it was still pretty much in one piece—even after falling the ten or twelve feet. Like the other pods they'd recovered, the thing was roughly bell-shaped. Mostly in varying shades of brown, it was composed of large overlapping leaf fronds. Like it did the first time he ever saw one, back in the sub-deck of the *Evermore*, it reminded him of some kind of ginormous hive.

It figured, only now was he able to inwardly get centered—to concentrate—with apparent little effort. Using his outstretched hands, he mentally coaxed the pod upward —watching it slowly rise into the air as Jackie, standing nearby, clucked her tongue.

Bob said, "We better get moving. We have less than seven minutes before the Howsh ship arrives at these coordinates."

Bob helped him guide the pod as they headed toward their not-so-distant awaiting spacecraft.

chapter 5

Using their shared Pashire telepathy, Bob updated Cuddy almost continuously with data—providing spatial coordinates, velocity numbers, minute directional alterations—all of it. There was little doubt that the approaching Howsh ship's bridge crew, pinpointing them with their sensors, knew exactly where the *Evermore* sat, just outside the jungle they'd emerged from. The enemy would be equally aware there were four travelers, plus the orb, as they hurried along over the rough terrain toward the ship. They also would observe the heritage pod they were doing their best to transport quickly.

Above and beyond what the orb was informing him, Cuddy had done his own rough mental calculations. Determining the time frame necessary for the alien vessel—once it entered the atmosphere—to make a full descent to the surface and reach them before they took off, heading back into space. Hopefully, they could lose them with the *Evermore's* superior propulsion system, but it would be a race against time—one still too close to call.

Bob hovered out in front, guiding the pod using its two articulating arms.

"We're almost there... I got this, Bob. Go ahead and prepare the ship," Cuddy ordered. "Open the sublevel access hatch... power-up the emersion drive!"

"Yes, Captain. Note, the Howsh ship will be upon us in less than three minutes."

"Then best you hurry it up," he told the orb.

While Tony and Kyle still seemed to be on a macho-high from vanquishing the spinktrolls, Jackie remained quiet. She hadn't once looked at Cuddy. He felt her total disgust for the whole situation— for him. He contemplated trying to explain what had happened, but he knew it would come out like he was making excuses—sounding totally lame. A part of him wondered if his inaction was due to something other than not being able to concentrate. Maybe it really was a hidden reluctance to use violence. He didn't think so but didn't know for sure.

They reached the ship in two minutes. It took Cuddy another minute to get the heritage pod positioned onto the sublevel lift platform then elevate it up into the ship's underbelly.

The others were already seated, strapping in by the time Cuddy entered the bridge. Bob was at the forward console. He took in the viewscape display and saw the quickly-approaching Howsh ship. Realizing, unfortunately, that the alien ship was right on time.

Cuddy pulled up on the controls, raising the *Evermore* off the ground. Three consecutive plasma strikes struck the ship's outer hull, violently jolting those in the bridge to the point he had to reach out to the nearest bulkhead to steady himself.

"Shields are down to sixty percent, Captain."

"You better find something to hold onto, Bob," he yelled over his shoulder to the hovering orb. Cuddy increased their ascent—nearly redlining the *Evermore's* lift thrusters. Plasma strikes coincided with bright-red flashes of light being cast in through the windows.

Kyle, craning his neck to see out the starboard-side window, yelled, "I see it! They're coming around to take another pass at us . . . another strike."

"Yeah, well, we're not waiting around for that." Cuddy jammed the controls forward as far as they would go, engaging the*Evermore*'s big emersion drive. The sudden acceleration of g-forces forced him to tighten his grip on the controls. Feeling his feet start to slide backward on the deck, he heard a series of loud clanging noises coming from somewhere aft.

Kyle said, "There goes, Bob. You told it to hold on . . . guess it didn't listen."

Cuddy's attention was focused on the viewscape display. Represented as icons, he noted the *Evermore,* quickly moving up through the planet's atmosphere, and the Howsh ship still in pursuit—though steadily losing ground. He knew once they hit open space it would be all over for them—they'd never be able to keep up.

Cuddy's thoughts drifted to what their mission was *really* about. It wasn't about what was, or was not, going on between Jackie and himself. It wasn't about arrogant Brian back on

Primara. Nor was it about one more interstellar chase—evading one more Howsh spaceship. No . . . what it *should—must* be about was the heritage pod secured down on the sub-deck. About those hundreds, perhaps thousands, of life forces residing within that vulnerable pod. It was about bringing a race of people back from the brink of extinction. That was the mission they'd all signed up for. To accomplish what Tow and the others on Primara were incapable of completing themselves. To venture out into distant space and find all the hundreds of similar heritage pods—each strategically hidden where the Howsh, hopefully, could not easily locate them.

"Why are we slowing down?" Tony asked.

Cuddy refocused his attention on the viewscape display. Tony was *partially* right. "We're not slowing down, Tony . . . they're picking up speed."

"Then go faster, man!" Tony exclaimed.

Bob entered the bridge at that moment, hovering at Cuddy's side. There was a good-sized dent, clearly visible on one side of the orb.

"We're pretty much throttled-up all the way, Tony. They shouldn't be gaining on us. We have the faster ship."

Bob said, "My sensors tell me this craft has not the same configuration that's found on other Howsh vessels we have encountered in the past, such as the *Arm of Lia*. This Howsh ship, the *Mannia Han*, is a later generation scout ship. Faster. More powerful weaponry . . . far better armaments."

They watched as the enemy vessel moved closer yet. Although still not within range to fire off its big plasma guns, an attack was mere moments from happening—Cuddy was certain of that.

"So . . . we're sitting ducks? Waiting to be picked off?" Jackie asked, now also standing at the forward console.

Cuddy hadn't noticed her getting up. He didn't answer her—didn't have an answer.

"Is there anything I can do?" she asked. There was a note of kindness in her voice he hadn't heard of late.

The *Mannia Han* was now close enough for Bob to put her image up on the viewscape display. All sharp edges and angular design, the ship certainly gave the impression of swiftness. The aft backside of the vessel appeared thick and substantial—a robust propulsion system obviously evident.

"Fuck," Tony said. "We're like . . . in trouble here . . . aren't we? This could be it. Lights-out time."

"Shut up, Tony," Jackie said, without looking at him.

The *Evermore* wobbled as several bright-red energy bolts sliced through space in front of them.

"The enemy is firing," Bob said. "Shields holding."

"Thank you, Mr. Wizard," Tony said.

Cuddy stared at the viewscape image of the *Mannia Han* for a long moment—then closed his eyes. He mentally pictured the vessel's bridge—one not so different in size from the *Evermore's*. He pictured the Howsh helmsman, hairy and brutish, standing there—working the controls. Telepathically, Cuddy scanned the alien's thoughts. This Howsh didn't like being there. He felt nauseous. Was aware of a foul taste—perhaps something he'd eaten for lunch.

"They're gaining on us," Tony said.

Breathing in, relaxing, Cuddy stayed with the mental connection—but doubts were trying to infiltrate his thoughts. Then he picked up on another scent. It was Jackie's shampoo—strawberry. She was there, next to him. He felt her upper arm contacting his own. It was warm. He felt her eyes on him.

Cuddy said, "Okay . . . I can see them . . . the Howsh. There are six of them within the compartment. Looks like they're ready to fire off another round of energy bolts."

No one spoke.

Cuddy personally *experienced* the helmsman as he reached for the firing trigger at the top of the navigation control mechanism. Telepathically, Cuddy willed his furry arm in an alternate direction—knocking it off to the left. Then he mentally persuaded the alien to take a firm grasp of the throttle controls. He felt the alien's hesitation. His rising fear. Cuddy jammed the helmsman's arm all the way forward, nearly yanking the appendage out of the socket. The Howsh pilot cried out in pain as the alien ship lurched forward. Angry, the bridge officer behind started barking off loud commands. Scanning the unfamiliar control board, Cuddy found what he was looking for—a collection of touchpad controls that both configured and engaged the ship's Faster Than Light *(FTL)* Nav System. With a series of quick taps, still using the now highly distressed helmsman's right index finger, Cuddy set a new, light years away, course destination. With one final tap of a finger and one blink of an eye later, the *Mannia Han* was gone.

Cuddy opened his eyes. Peering down to his left, he found Jackie staring back at him.

"Now that's how you impress a girl. Not sure what just did . . . but it worked. Keep it up, Cuddy, and I'll forgive you for being such an ass earlier." She spun on her heals and left the bridge.

"Bob . . . set a course for Primara. I'll be down in the hold, checking on our cargo."

chapter 6

Howsh Command Ship, the Pintial

Lorgue Prime Eminence Norsh tuned out the chatter and noise—obligatory cheers from the rowdy crew and fellow *Pintial* officers, standing three-deep around the small arena's perimeter. This was stupid—was this the day he'd meet his match? Be killed? Surprised by a worthy opponent?

He circled the quadzone mat clockwise, never taking his eyes from his four scraggly, long-haired opponents. *Filthy cave dwellers,* he mused. His broad nostrils flared wider once he got a strong whiff of the foul-smelling foursome. He'd specifically chosen these four lowly, unrefined, scout ship pilots, because they were undoubtedly unaware of his exalted combat reputation within the quadzone. And although they too were like him—all equally *Howsh,* at least from a genetic perspective—all visual similarities stopped there. Lorgue Prime Eminence Norsh kept his furry skin trimmed to a ¼ inch nap. His physique was highly muscular and toned and he stood more erect than the four barbarian street brawlers. He'd been told that they were more than scrappy; that they were devious—*ruthless killers*. He was surprised he actually remembered their names: Gramal was the tallest. Sealth had something wrong with one eye—milky and it strayed off to the side. Banhown was thick and strong—and *could* be a problem. And then there was Topsen, the dominant leader, who showed some semblance of intelligence in his cold eyes.

The four had each done time within a constable's brig for one fighting infraction or another. Feared among their peers, each jumped at the chance to spar with the fleet's highest-ranking officer. He took pride knowing that not since Lorgue Supreme Eminence Calph himself, a known brilliant combatant, presumed dead by many after his disappearance some ten years earlier—had a Howsh officer so mastered the fighting arts of the ancients.

The four combatants circled in relative unison to Norsh's own footwork; each looking for that microsecond opportunity to make a move. Norsh hadn't expected to be so annoyed by their constant gnashing. A foul habit, they each chewed what was called their*galk*—a coughed-up phlegm *cud* secretion mixed with hair. Norsh watched as Sealth, the one with the straying-eye, hucked up a galk, then spewed it right smack into the center of the quadzone's pristine mat. Norsh angrily glared down at the disgusting globule, which was all they needed to wage their attack.

Two came at him fast from both flanks—while the other two came at him head-on—all charging in at once.

From an early age, Howsh cubs were taught how best to use their four sets of claws for self-protection from those that would do them harm. When extended, their claws were two-and-a-half to three inches long. The Howsh, those prone to fighting, spent long periods honing their individual claws to fine, almost needle-like, points. Norsh expected no less from the brutish foursome. He too took his nail-honing regime seriously—actually to a whole other level. Instead of simply filing his claws to fine points, he used a special powered apparatus, called a *Klish,* to add both posterior and interior razor-sharp edges that ran along the entirety of each claw. That often time-consuming and laborious process had saved his life on several occasions.

Norsh dropped to one knee just as one of the charging opponents, Gramal, the tallest one, swung for his head. Even before Gramal retracted his arm back—Norsh, with minimal effort, waved his extended clawed digits over his head in an almost backhand- waving motion. Now four thin almost imperceptible red lines trailed up Gramal's underarm, from elbow to armpit, then blood began seeping out. It was a strategically-placed attack by Norsh. With his tendons, muscle sinews, and two arterial blood vessels slashed, Gramal's arm was suddenly less than useless—it had become a hindrance.

Immediately, Norsh dove into a forward handstand, driving his powerful legs both up and backward. Years of fighting had taught him to gauge not only his opponent's relative stance positioning but their specific anatomical reference points, as well. In a reverse-scissor motion, he used both sets of his lower claws to rake across the exposed throats of his two flanking attackers. Far more violent—deeper—than his previous strike, the gaping fissures nearly decapitated both Sealth and Banhown. They were dead before dropping to the mat.

That left only one still-healthy opponent, Topsen, plus severely injured Gramal. Norsh had learned early on in life not to underestimate anyone in a match such as this one—especially not an injured foe. *Desperation bred unpredictability.* And while Norsh was weighing this bit of insight, at just seven point three seconds into the match, he instantly felt the piercing sensation of honed claws being dragged down the middle of his back. *Fucking Gramal!* The four, white-hot, agonizing gouges brought tears to his eyes, a strike that nearly rendered him unconscious. He rallied by doing the unexpected. He threw his arms up, while extending his legs downward, then did a high, up in the air, backflip, right over the head of the injured Gramal. Landing behind him, readying his right claw to strike, Norsh suddenly lost his footing—skidding on the copious amounts of blood and gore pooling in that section of the mat. Down he went. But Gramal was already staggering away. Norsh watched as he teetered, then flopped over sideways. He'd evidently lost too much blood to continue on.

Still flat on his back, Norsh, gazing upward, caught a blur of motion. Topsen was making his move. Norsh instinctively blocked the incoming blow—one coming as a downward strike from his left; and then, noting a second incoming blur on his right, he blocked that blow, as well. Suddenly, the tough street brawler was positioned directly atop Norsh, straddling him. A smart *Calinth-Rian*-move that almost always resulted in a win for the one who executed it. Norsh, not used to playing defense, was unaccustomed to being in such a vulnerable position. Mounted like a Howshian bitch. Perhaps this foul ingrate was the exception—a worthy opponent, he thought. He estimated the match was now at the twelve-second mark.

Calinth-Rian was immanent—dual deathblows driven into the top of his head—into his brain. Norsh's timing would be everything. At the precise second Topsen's extended open claws were hurling inward, right toward his cranium, Norsh made his move—a mid-flight spearing motion—his claws piercing both of Topsen's inside forearms. Bloodied, his claws now protruded out the tops of his enemy's arms. Both combatants stayed motionless for several moments—the two foes stared into each other's eyes. While Norsh was still on his back, his attacker's snarling face loomed inches above him. Still, Prime Eminence Norsh managed to jockey his legs beneath him, then maneuver them into a kneeling position. He slowly rose up. Topsen's harpooned claws—pierced four per side—were tightly constrained in Norsh's excruciating and unrelenting hold, rendering further movement impossible. At this point, they both knew the match was over. The reversal of power was complete. *Sixteen seconds.*

Forcing his arms out even wider yet only added to Topsen's agony. Norsh said, "You fought with cunning and spirit, scout pilot. But now you know what must come next . . . yes?" In one fluid motion, Norsh raised his clawed foot and drove it deep into Topsen's underbelly. Pulling it straight down, then out, he emptied the contents of Topsen's abdomen. Norsh retracted his claws and stepped back from the slithering mess of entrails on the ruined quadzone mat. He watched with total detachment as Topsen toppled over dead. *Twenty-one seconds—start to finish.*

Cheers erupted around the quadzone, bringing Lorgue Prime Eminence Norsh back to the present moment. With the battle now over, the pain returned with a vengeance. A medic, appearing suddenly at his side, placed something cool—an ointment of some sort—on his back that quickly anesthetized the pain down to a near bearable level.

Irritated with himself, he shoved the medic away, growling, "Leave me be!"

He wondered if he was losing his edge. *Which one had gotten the best of him—had nearly killed him?* He glanced around the quadzone—noting the carnage. Eventually, he was able to separate one form from the other three—*fucking Gramal.*

"Prime Eminence . . . a magnificent exposition, sire."

Norsh looked up to see Sub-Forgue Molth standing nearby just off the edge of the mat.

"You have returned . . . I trust your mission was a success. Another heritage pod eviscerated?"

Sub-Forgue Molth held his tongue for a moment then said, "I apologize. We were too late. The Pashier vessel was already leaving the planet."

"Leaving the planet . . . along with the heritage pod?" Norsh asked, barely containing his growing fury. Just seeing Molth's disgusting face, always enough to irritate Norsh, was now exacerbated by this show of total incompetence. Norsh tried not to look at it, there—between his brows—but his eyes were drawn to the mole, or wart, or whatever the disgusting *thing* was. It had grown in size—girth—since the last time he'd seen the officer.

"The *Evermore* returned to Primara. And, as you are more than aware . . . our warships cannot approach anywhere near that world . . . not without them being transported away, through their use of telekinesis, into far distant space."

Norsh rubbed his eyes as Molth droned on and on. He tried to ignore the growing pain in his back when it occurred to him that if it hadn't been for Sub-Forgue Molth's ineptitude in the first place, by not properly dealing with that foul band of humans, the Pashier could not have found refuge on Primara. He'd been deceived by the one called Cuddy Perkins . . . almost lost his command because of that one. Norsh had to mentally check his growing fury. No, if Sub-Forgue Molth had done his fucking job, the few remaining of that nearly eradicated race of Pashier would have been properly exterminated. Because he was doing his job so wretchedly, heritage pods were now being safely delivered to Primara from all corners of the galaxy. That meant more repopulating. Years of effort to contain the Pashier were quickly being undone. Fortunately, Norsh had petitioned the Imperial Howsh high counsel. They had agreed to build a new, far more advanced Fleet—state-of-the-art warships capable of dealing with the Pashier telekinetic powers—ones that were shielded and could also attack Primara from afar—from deep space. *They'll never know what hit them.* Finally, they then will be done with, the Pashier gone, once and for all.

Norsh couldn't stand to listen to Sub-Forgue Molth's voice—not a second longer. Glancing around, he interrupted a group of still-excited crewmembers, verbally recounting the match. "Give me your sidearm, soldier," he ordered.

The surprised ship's sentry did as asked—nervously handing the senior officer his weapon. Norsh casually took ahold of the handheld plasma pistol then aimed at the copious growth between Molth's still uncomprehending eyes. He shot Sub-Forgue Molth dead without giving it a second thought.

Norsh contemplated the situation with the seemingly immortal Pashier people. Then the band of humans who were assisting the Pashier—he would make an example of them. He stared down at the four slaughtered Howsh bodies. *Yes . . . an appropriate example.*

chapter 7

Seven years ago . . . Woodbury, Tennessee

Cuddy Perkins couldn't quite put a finger on it—why, suddenly, he had become so uneasy in this place. Fidgeting, he thought of Momma—she wouldn't want him to be here with a stranger.

There was an uncomfortable stillness inside the cabin.

He wondered if the old man, wearing stained overalls, lived here alone. *What had he said his name was? Stich? Swatch? No . . . Slatch.* He couldn't remember if Slatch mentioned a last name. His memory was terrible, due to the accident five years prior. Slatch had said the log cabin was over 200 years old *or was it 300?* That early settlers had built the rustic dwelling before America was even called America. Cuddy didn't know what that meant, but something so old—*well*—it must be something special. Something he'd want to see.

So quiet here inside. Cuddy began to make loud popping

sounds with his lips. The type of noise Momma would say *knock-it-off, Cuddy!*

He'd been told to sit on the couch. To wait and not touch anything. As Cuddy's gaze moved about the interior of the small timber dwelling, his eyes briefly lingered first on one item then moved to the next. Each object, albeit unconsciously, was giving Cuddy subtle insight into the old man's character who had brought him here—the worn recliner chair, with strips of silver duct tape securing its threadbare armrests; a snipped-open can of Miller beer, sitting on the small coffee table, half-filled with a pasty brown liquid. Cuddy then briefly recalled seeing Slatch spit out tobacco loogies while perched on his tractor. A TV was in the corner of the room, its two-prong metal antenna making a letter V above.

Off to the left, was the kitchen area. A glowing amber light indicated the rectangular-shaped hot plate was powered on. A small, lidded pot, sitting atop it, made soft burbling noises. A sweet, gamey smell, waffling out from the kitchen, scented the air in the oppressively small space. Cuddy wondered what, *exactly*, Slatch was cooking. He mentally pictured a squirrel, or some other small rodent, lying curled up beneath the pot's off-kilter lid.

Maybe I should go home now . . .

Cuddy glanced at the heavy wooden door, with its old rusted hinges and equally rusted oversized latch, then back to the dark hallway across from where he sat. He figured Slatch's bedroom, maybe a bathroom was that way. Slatch was back there. Cuddy listened hard but heard no sound.

He refocused his attention on the front door then back on the latch. Positioned directly to his left, Cuddy figured it was probably within arm's reach. Slatch had told him to sit there, not touch anything. *Did that include the latch?* Cuddly slowly extended his arm—then leaned even farther over to get a bit closer. The tips of his fingers came into contact with the cold metal. His hand wasn't oriented right to use the thumb lever. Instead, he pressed down on the latch using his forefinger. It didn't budge. It must be locked.*When had Slatch locked the door?* ¬He then heard a rustling sound coming from the back of the house.

A dim light suddenly cast out—partially illuminated the far end of the hallway. *Perhaps a door had opened?* Cuddy continued to stare into the murky darkness but something blocked his view. He realized he was looking at the silhouetted outline of someone—standing quietly in the semi-darkness. *It was the old man.*

"You have a problem doing what you're told, boy?"

chapter 8

The *Evermore* returned to Primara without further altercations with the Howsh. As directed, Cuddy piloted the *Evermore* to a remote, still uninhabited, location—an area of the planet he'd never been to before. Once landed, Cuddy told the AI orb to stay with the ship. Together, he and the others started down the gangway.

Cuddy was greeted with familiar excited barking just before the yellow lab shot up the ramp. Standing on hind legs, frantically wagging his tail, Rufus welcomed his master home. Lowering to one knee, Cuddy let his dog lick his face for a while. "Okay . . . okay . . . settle down, boy. I'm home now."

Brian too was there, waiting for them. Only Brian didn't look the same. Evidently, the *empath* elders, the Pashier healers, had indeed been proficient in restoring his physical appearance. Although still somewhat *strange looking*, he was no longer ugly. As surprised as Cuddy was, Jackie seemed to be bowled over by the transformation. Following an extended hug, she was all compliments and questions—*What had the sessions been like? Did it hurt? How do you feel now?* On and on the Q&A went.

Cuddy, Kyle, and Tony watched the two with equal, albeit growing, annoyance. Finally, Kyle queried, "Um . . . guess we should unload the pod now?"

Cuddy, staring at Brian and Jackie for an extended moment, nodded. "Yeah . . . let's do that." Once the sub-deck lift completed its downward progression, the trio carefully removed the pod's restraining straps.

"It's all yours, man. TK it away . . . ," Tony said, taking a step backward. Over time, TK had become the default idiom for anything to do with the usage of telekinesis.

Cuddy took in a steadying breath and then lifted his palms, inwardly summoning his mental TK ability to raise the small-car size heritage pod off the lift platform. Steadying the load at two feet above the ground, it hovered there then began to wobble. Kyle and Tony eyed Cuddy, throwing him uncertain glances. Cuddy was still feeling distracted. But he was reining in his mind—the wobbling was dissipating.

"What the hell you doing?" Brian barked behind them. "Just stop! You've already done enough damage transporting it here. *Fuck me* . . . look at that fissure along the side of the thing." Brian, elbowing his way past Cuddy, studied it. Then, casually lifting one hand, he maneuvered the pod—steady and true—away from the *Evermore* and into the open. Jackie fell in step beside Brian, as he moved the elevated pod toward a crop of tall trees in the distance.

Cuddy exchanged more glances with Tony and Kyle. Under his breath, Tony mumbled, "What a douche bag . . ."

Cuddy inwardly smiled. *Allow douche bag Brian to have his moment.*

"I heard that," Brian snorted, twenty yards out. But by the tone of his voice, he didn't really care what they thought.

* * *

Cuddy loved trees. Standing now beneath three towering leafy deciduous species—he contemplated how akin they were to Autumn Blaze Maples, the kind that would be thriving back on Earth. They definitely were a close *Primara derivative* of that same genome. He knew he was purposely focusing his attention away from Brian's non-stop self-narrative. The group was all there.

"Are you capable of concentrating for five minutes, Captain Cuddy?" Brian asked.

"Knock it off, Brian... and I *am* listening." Cuddy, resuming eye contact, gave him a sideways glance that said *my patience is quickly waning.*

Brian gestured to the newly positioned Heritage Pod, situated in the shade of the three leafy trees. He'd picked a good spot. *Of course, he had.*

"As I was saying... I've got this all figured out, and before any of you start whining, yes, I've already spoken to Tow." Brian hesitated long enough to level a displeased glance toward Kyle. "Sure... we might be on the verge of an epidemic here. It may become pandemic... who knows?" His expression suddenly brightened. "But with every new Shain ritual, the population on Primara grows. Hell, they're like gerbils running around now. Although if you ask me conditions around here are still pretty caveman-like. The good news is the Pashier are readjusting; regaining their dormant powers. Their TK is blossoming. Not anywhere near my level, but hey . . . it is what it is."

Tony pretended to shoot himself in the head.

"So what is this great idea of yours, Brian? And, please, while we're still young . . . okay?" Kyle said.

Jackie shot Kyle an annoyed expression. "Go on, do tell us, Brian."

"Up until now, the weight of protecting this world has sat firmly on my shoulders. Every time a Howsh warship attempts to enter into orbit here, I send it millions of miles out into deep space. And, it's tedious . . . ensuring that absolutely no one is killed in the process, well, that makes things even more challenging. It's getting *old*," Brian said, a flourish of drama in his voice. "High time the natives here start taking responsibility for their own welfare."

"Is this when you share your great idea with us?" Tony asked.

Cuddy too was ready for Brian to just get on with it.

"Look. Individually, one Pashier won't be able to send an invading ship away. I don't know if they'll someday develop, or rise up to my level of telekinesis, or not. But working together . . . working within an overlapping-type network, an adequate team of Pashiers strategically positioned around the planet . . . communicating between one another psychically . . . well . . . I think they can do the same as me. Can rebuff their enemies."

"You think there's enough of them here to make that overlapping-network-thing work?" Jackie asked.

Brian gestured toward the still-closed heritage pod, resting before them. "Once this latest pod is added, and a few hundred more essences released, it should do the trick."

"Are you sure you're not rushing things just a tad?" Kyle asked. "What's the hurry? By your own words, you're doing an adequate job all by your lonesome."

"No. I'm done playing God to these aliens. I have my own life to live. One that doesn't involve me patiently waiting around for the next spaceship to come wandering by. And Tow has a new mission for us, anyway. Something important."

Cuddy bristled at that. *Now Tow was giving Brian mission directives*?

"What mission?" Jackie asked. "Don't we have enough to do retrieving heritage pods from space?"

Brian shrugged. "Tow wants to speak to Cuddy first before he says anything more about . . . whatever it is . . ." He looked at Cuddy with ambivalence.

Jackie put her hands on her hips. "So . . . should we meet back here for the Shain Ritual of Awakening? In the morning?"

"Yeah . . . daybreak," Brian said, already walking off.

* * *

It was still dark outside. Witnessing a Shain Ritual of Awakening firsthand typically left Cuddy emotional, but today's early morning ritual was already affecting him more than usual. Part of him still worried the heritage pod had been permanently damaged due to his own negligence. He thought back to the train wreck of events on the green planet—how his focused concentration had been shattered when alien *Spinktrolls* attempted to abduct Jackie. Subsequently, when the pod fell hard to the ground, his eyes too noticed the jagged fissure on the pod that Brian so astutely pointed out to everyone.

Now, standing next to Tow as the pod's fronds began to unfold, Cuddy sent up a silent *thank you* to the powers that be. He wasn't religious; didn't know if there was one god, or even multiple gods, as some civilizations he knew believed. Or if there was some incredible higher power, watching over everything and everyone.

There in the pre-dawn darkness, he once again was witnessing the same breathtaking fountain of glittering lights—streaming upward from the unfolding pod fronds—shooting higher and higher into the air. He felt the now-familiar, swirling, comforting breeze all around him.

It took a while for the last few leaves to fully open before settling onto the ground. Looking up, a galaxy of starlight flowed above them—spanning out hundreds, even thousands, of feet—ascending ever higher and higher. The brilliance, sheer magnitude of it all, made it impossible for Cuddy to think about his own petty problems, including the ridiculous power play with Brian.

Then he spotted Jackie. She was standing alongside Kyle, on the far side of the opened pod. The shimmering lights, cast downward from above, gave her face a soft—angelic quality. *So beautiful.* As if sensing Cuddy's gaze upon her, her eyes lowered, searching around, before finding and locking onto his own. They held each other's gaze for a moment before she focused back on the spectacle taking place above her. Moments later, the first of the shooting star-like effects—raining down from the galaxy of lights above—reached the center point of the splayed-opened pod. In a flash, Cuddy saw the bluish glow of a Pashier female standing there. As always, at that same stage, she was naked and nearly transparent. She stood still for less than a minute before hurrying off—somehow sensing where she needed to go—what she needed to do. Then one-by-one—more and more life forces emerged from the pod, both male and female. Also Pashier children, arriving in groups of two or three, who were escorted away by an awaiting Pashier adult.

As the last ones appeared then left, Cuddy turned toward Tow. He was smiling; both palms pressed tightly on his chest—over his heart—moisture brimming in his shining eyes.

He gazed up at Cuddy and nodded. "Thank you, Cuddy. We all thank you . . . you have brought life and heartfelt reunion to this world . . . to our new home."

"It was a team effort. In fact, this go around, I was only a notch above useless."

* * *

As the crowd dissipated, slowly moving away, Cuddy heard distant coughs coming from more than one infected Pashier. With Rufus close to his side, he sensed something was amiss. "What troubles you, Tow?" he asked, but the alien didn't answer. He simply stared toward the hazy-blue horizon as they walked side-by-side into the early dawn light.

Cuddy knew he should be used to Tow's long silences by now. That and the fact that Tow didn't answer stupid questions.

Tow slowed his pace to admire something high up over the ridgeline. Whatever it was, it brought a smile to the alien's face. Pointing a thin finger, he waited for Cuddy to stop and also look.

Cuddy hunched-down his six-foot-three frame, low enough to follow the full length of Tow's extended arm and finger—similar to lining erup one's sight down a long-barreled rifle. "Okay . . . what am I supposed to be looking at?"

Tow continued to point—volunteering nothing.

Cuddy, straightening up, stared at the distant mountainous landscape, where the timber tree line gave way to jagged rock cliffs. "The crescent moons, right over the ridge? Is that what you're pointing at?"

Unlike the single moon viewable from Earth at certain times of the day, Primara had three moons: Timor, Dathan, and Horpris. Right now all three waxing moon crescents were visible at the same time—one an amber color, one yellow, and one blue. Cuddy remembered that the Pashier living on Primara commonly referred to them as the *jewels of wisdom, grace, and humility.*

They maneuvered around four large boulders and, at one point, had to turn sideways to squeeze through a narrow gap. Together, Tow, Cuddy, and Rufus followed along a meandering dirt path. Off to the right, a large open field revealed fresh, evenly spaced plow marks. The green tops of tiny heritage-pod sprouts peeked through dark soil mounds. Tow lingered around long enough to breathe in the scent of freshly churned earth. Continuing on, the path led to another clearing, where a large fallen tree rested on its side—probably toppled dozens of years before. The tree's once thick stout branches had been reduced to nothing more than irregularly worn rounded nubs. Where once coarse bark covered the tree's thick trunk, now only smooth, weathered surfaces were evident. In the not far distance, an azure lake reflected glints of light from Primara's closest sun-like star Sath.

"Let us sit for a while. I want to tell you a secret, Cuddy."

Cuddy waited for the alien to climb up on the fallen tree before doing the same, sitting down beside him. He was long past being uncomfortable around Tow's, and the other Pashier's, total nakedness. Their hairless bodies were beautiful, ethereal-looking and their nearly transparent forms emitted a distinctive bright *bluish* glow. Far brighter than Cuddy's own Human-Pashier hybrid glow. "What secret?"

"One of my favorite places on this new world. Right here . . . sitting on this old log. Having you here now, Cuddy, sharing this with me . . . well, that makes me quite happy."

Cuddy didn't like the way Tow was talking to him. It seemed—*patronizing*. Momentarily, he wondered how he even knew that word. But he knew a lot of things now that he'd never known before his time spent within the wellness chamber. *Stop, it doesn't matter,* he chided himself. What he did know was that Tow was incapable of acting in anything but a lofty manner, at least not intentionally. Yet there was a certain sense of *finality* in the way he was speaking. Like, in some roundabout way, he was saying goodbye *again*. With no further thought, Cuddy prepared himself for what the alien was about to say next.

"Tomorrow you will travel to Mahli... Pashier's home planet."

"Why's that? There's nothing left of it! The Howsh... they've destroyed it. You told me that much yourself."

"Much of it, yes. Even most of it... but not all of it," Tow said. "The Pashier are a technologically advanced race of beings. That is clearly evident when you witness the technology that comprises the *Evermore*. Once beautiful... highly advanced cities flourished across Mahli. And Cuddy, there is still Pashier technology hidden there. Newer... more advanced technology that is needed here to heal our recently infected Pashier."

Tow looked as though he were contemplating telling him something more.

"What is it?"

"Sometimes certain things come to me within the dream state and sometimes during my waking hours. Sometimes it is only a subtle nudge."

"So, you've had a nudge?"

"Yes... there is advanced technology we can use to help the sick. Somewhere within the city of Mahli exists another wellness chamber. A far more advanced model than the one you are familiar with on the *Evermore*. Every day, more and more of our people are succumbing to the disease, so your mission is of utmost importance. You must locate that chamber and quickly bring it back to Primara. Can you do that, Cuddy?"

"Sure . . . we'll leave today."

"I wish I could go with you, my young friend. As you know, none of us can leave Primara quite yet . . . not at this stage of our reemergence. While traveling to Mahli will be your new mission, Cuddy, I too have a mission of my own. In time, you will understand why I must leave here. Why I must venture to *the other side of Rah*."

"Wait. What are you talking about? You just said none of you can leave here yet."

"This particular place, I can travel to . . . I believe."

"And just where is this . . . that destination? What did you call it . . . *the other side of Rah*? What does that even mean, anyway?" Cuddy hated the idea of Tow leaving. He tried to think of reasons he shouldn't go. Nervously, he plucked at his shirt's sleeve cuff.

"The other side of Rah refers to a place few have traveled to willingly and later returned to speak about. It lies beyond where one enters the great space within a heritage pod. Some call it *Tanthian*."

"What is it like . . . like heaven?"

Tow's lips twitched. "Maybe. I will let you know."

"So you will come back?"

"I hope to." Tow place a hand on Cuddy's shoulder. "You will need my help in up- coming days, Cuddy. It is from the other side of Rah that I will be of most use to you, and to my own people. For now . . . let's leave further discussion for another time."

"Fine. But our leaving here puts Primara in danger. It's only a matter of time before the Howsh return. Without Brian around to fend off . . ."

"I believe we will be safe . . . for now." Tow looked up at the sky. "The other AI-orb, Rob, is up there now . . . constantly circling the planet. Constantly relaying back sensory data. Brian's network concept was a good one, and it is already in place. Even as we speak, key Pashier around the planet are reaching out to one another; working together. Are practicing combined telekinesis. We should know when the next enemy ship arrives. When it does, we will be able to send it away."

"And suppose there is more than one ship?"

Tow lifted his chin. "At some point, we must rely on fate. I cannot believe we have come this far only to be so easily annihilated by the Howsh. Now you must go, Cuddy. Travel to Mahli, bring back the new wellness chamber, and several other items I've listed for you. But you must make haste in leaving."

chapter 9

The small crew of the *Evermore* arrived at the outskirts of the Pashier capital city, Tripette, on Mahli. Prior to heading out on foot, Cuddy double-checked things with Bob one final time.

"You have asked me that same question in different forms on three recent occasions, Captain Perkins," the AI orb said.

Cuddy, securing the pack on to his shoulders, stared out the bridge-side starboard window. "I know that. But look at it out there . . . it's a—"

"Wretched wasteland," Kyle interjected, poking his head around the bulkhead and into the bridge. "And we're ready out here whenever you are. Can we go?"

Cuddy had witnessed Kyle's growing impatience over the last few days. Hearing there was a possible cure for the dying Pashier, he couldn't wait to get the mission started and over with. His feelings of guilt and remorse were ever increasing.

"We're coming," Cuddy said, not taking his attention away from the arid landscape outside the ship. He shook his head.

"I don't like this, Bob. What about the things we can't see... like the Dirth, or some other microbial infestation, or another harmful disease?"

"The Dirth is strictly a Pashier disease, Captain. Your human DNA ensures none of you will be infected."

About to turn away, Cuddy saw movement outside. Brian, now leading the others—Jackie, Kyle, and Tony—down the ramp. *So much for waiting for me,* he thought.

Cuddy and Bob exited the bridge and made their way to the starboard-side hatch. "I have no idea where we're going, so you'll be leading us, Bob. Lock down the ship then catch up," Cuddy instructed the orb over his shoulder, already halfway down the gangway.

By the time he joined the others, he wished he'd walked instead of run. The air outside was foul, far worse than what he'd anticipated—a harsh chemical smell to it. He wondered if Bob ever erred with his internal sensor readings.

Passing Tony, and then Kyle, who offered him a quick *no big deal* shrug, Cuddy—on coming even with Brian and Jackie—said, "In the future, please wait for me... we go as a team, Brian."

"Whatever. It wasn't as if you couldn't still see us."

Cuddy, hearing the almost imperceptible yet familiar hum, turned to see Bob approaching behind them. Hovering at head level—the orb quickly passed, then and took over the lead.

In the distance, Cuddy could see what remained of the ruined city. Even from where they were, a good mile out, he noticed standing buildings were mostly skeletal—completely ravaged. Only then did Cuddy fully absorb the carnage around them. What was once a meandering stream, off to the left, was now a thick, greenish, soup. The landscape was purplish-brown—scorched earth. *This planet's in really bad shape*, he thought. Even with that understanding, he saw it was already trying to heal itself. Tiny clusters, here and there of green, spotted the ground—base-level vegetation beginning to creep through the poisoned surface. He found that at least somewhat encouraging. *Tow would be pleased.* Then he heard it. Living on a farm most of his young life, he knew that sound much too well. Buzzing flies—or whatever was the Mahli-equivalent of flies. He didn't see them. Not yet. But he definitely heard them.

They entered the city proper in silence. While few of the decimated buildings still stood, albeit precariously, most had fallen; were nothing but giant mounds of rubble. Scores of Pashier remains lay scattered around the streets and sidewalks. Flies—like moving dark clouds above the still, lifeless forms. Though the smell was pungent, Cuddy figured the odor had been much worse—weeks, perhaps months, earlier. Those still lying here were mostly skeletons—signs of flesh long gone. Obviously, not everyone made it into an escape ship before succumbing, either to the aerial bombings or the Dirth. Worse, these poor souls were never assisted into a heritage pod. That made Cuddy sad—he wouldn't convey this one aspect to Tow.

Deeper and deeper into the fallen city they walked, the buzzing sound of countless hordes of insects increasing. "That sound is . . . so irritating . . . not to mention, gross," Jackie said.

They followed Bob down one street, then partially up another. The orb slowed, idling in front of a building whose upper half was decimated—.

"This is the central government science and technology building," Bob said. "Our destination."

"Not much of a building... looks like it was hit with a wrecking ball a few hundred times," Kyle said.

"If we've come all this distance for just this, we've wasted a trip," Brian said.

Cuddy couldn't argue with Brian on that point. He watched as the orb slowly moved closer to the building when suddenly a metal girder toppled down from above. It made a loud reverberating *clang* when it hit the ground.

"Careful!" Cuddy and Brian said to Bob at the same time.

The orb hesitated for a moment, then kept moving forward; entering the building's standing remnants of broken walls, shattered windows, and protruding, twisted, bent girders, before disappearing completely from sight.

"Might as well return to the ship... this is one giant cluster fuck," Brian said. He turned on his heels and walked away. Cuddy stayed put, noticing the others still remained.

In the near-distance, Cuddy heard Bob say, "In here. I have found an entrance."

Exchanging doubtful expressions with the others, Cuddy said, "All right... hold on." He told the others, "You don't have to go in there with me. But if you do, try not to touch anything. Um... try to tread softly."

"Yeah, you're a real twinkle toes," Tony scoffed.

Cuddy led them around mounds of debris then into the building through a narrow gap between two broken walls. The wreckage inside seemed even worse than outside. He roughly followed the same roundabout course he saw Bob take only moments before. Directly overhead, suspended by a single hanging cable, a girder slowly pendulumed back and forth.

Thirty feet on, Bob was waiting for them, at what looked to be a stairwell. No less than ten stairs rose up and made a ninety-degree-left-angle to a landing, before rising up another five steps. The steps ended—leading to nowhere.

"Come on, Bob! You can see from here there's nothing up there," Jackie said.

The orb lowered close to the ground. What Cuddy had first thought were dark shadows, he realized were open crevices. As Bob descended lower into the blackness below, after first switching on its forward spotlight, Cuddy could just barely see the outline of stairs.

Jackie followed close behind Bob. Halfway into the open crevice, she looked back at Cuddy. "Buzzing sounds are even louder down there," she said with a grimace.

"Don't be such a girl . . . either keep going or get out of the way."

Cuddy turned, noting it was Brian who'd spouted off. When he'd rejoined them, Cuddy had no idea, but he wished Brian had done what he said he was going to do—return to the ship.

As soon as Jackie's head disappeared from view, Brian followed suit. Then Kyle, then Tony, then Cuddy. It was almost total darkness below ground. But what Jackie referred to as insects buzzing—well, it wasn't so much buzzing as *something* else. Clicking. Still, definitely insectile, Cuddy figured.

Cuddy could see Bob's swinging headlight ahead, darting this way and that, as the orb made its way back to him. He heard the AI orb tell the group to stay put. Multiple complaints about being left in the dark began to spew out.

"We are fortunate, Captain Perkins," Bob said, drawing closer.

"Are you sure about that, Bob?" Cuddy said, still trying to think around the constant rhythmic *chattering* noise in his ears.

"Tow's directions were perfect. Indeed, this is the Tripette Science and Technology Building. What technology is not found stored within these walls, we will, nevertheless, find references to other, specific, locations within the city on where to look."

"Can you get some the lights turned on, Bob? There's no way we're going to see anything . . . or find anything . . . down here otherwise."

"Perhaps. Pashier structures each have their own internal power generation—unlike Earth which accesses power from a common distributed utility source. A grid. I believe I know where the subterranean sub-panel is located. If you will give me a few minutes, I will see if anything can be done." With that, Bob was gone. No faint departing audible *hum* this time. Nothing could be heard over the present, ongoing chattering sound.

In the distance, Jackie's voice echoed, sounding somewhat hollow, "Are you going to join us, Cuddy, or stay back there . . . all alone in the dark?"

Cuddy said, "On my way, but I just stepped in . . . Uh . . . something mushy."

"Someone should have had enough foresight to bring flashlights," Brian said.

"Thanks, Brian . . . nothing like stating the obvious," Tony retorted.

By the time Cuddy reached the others, his eyes had adjusted somewhat better to the dark. He noticed tiny openings high above them—streams of light catching on dancing dust particles filtering down around them. Jackie and Kyle were seated together on what looked like a bench. Cuddy noticed Kyle had one hand causally resting on her knee. Kyle pulled it away self-consciously. Tony was leaning against a wall, while Brian, resting on the ground, lay flat on his back. Cuddy personally didn't think that was such a smart idea but decided not to say anything.

"So . . . you have like a list? The one that Tow gave you?" Jackie asked.

"Nothing written down. I remember what he told me, though." She made a huffing sound.

"What?"

"Nothing. Just . . . when you were younger . . . after the accident . . . you couldn't remember anything. I remember once you forgot to put on your pants. Came out to the barn, where Kyle and I were shoveling horseshit, and here strolls in . . . little mister tightie-whities.

Everyone, including Brian, laughed at that. Cuddy didn't remember the reference. Analytically, Cuddy had studied the anatomical repercussions behind what happened to him when he was seven. The temporal lobes, located on the left and right cerebral hemispheres of his brain—where both the hippocampus and amygdala are located—became scrambled after his fifteen-foot fall directly onto his head, creating problems establishing new, long-term memories. Although what was filed away in his long-term memory bank before the head injury was still fairly accessible, new memories didn't endure longer than a few minutes to a few hours.

The tightie-whities incident, Cuddy figured, must have happened quite a few years after his earlier barn tumble, yet long before he spent time within the wellness chamber.

From above, came a series of click-clacks—like electronic relays opening and closing. When the lights came on, Jackie was first to scream out—quickly followed by Brian.

chapter 10

Not all the overhead lights had come on, but enough to take in the basement-level space around them. Brian was covered with insects; how he didn't earlier feel their presence, *whatever they were*, Cuddy couldn't figure out. Jackie, the first one to notice them, had pointed and screamed at the bright-yellow and purple *creepy crawlers*. Only then did Brian look down at his body. Dozens covered his shirt and trousers, perhaps had been attracted to his body's warmth as he lay prone on the cold concrete floor.

Cuddy realized the bugs, unseen until now, had long been skittering around them. A good four inches long, they were part centipede—possessing hundreds of tiny, constantly moving, legs—and part something else. Each owned three sets of elongated wasp-like wings. He hadn't seen any of them fly, which was one positive. He watched as they twitched and fluttered their useless wings—apparently the root of the annoying clicking sound they'd been hearing. He could almost feel the creatures' frustration—triple winged but unable to get airborne.

"Glithopedes. Mostly a seasonal insect here on Tripette . . . as well as several neighboring planets," Bob said. "Non-poisonous, but their sting is very painful from what I understand."

"What's with the useless wings," Tony asked.

"During this seasonal time, their wings are non-functional. That will change . . . soon. Any day, I suspect," Bob informed, hovering close to the floor while extending an articulating arm. "As long as they cannot fly, they will remain relatively docile."

A glithopede slithered up Bob's claw-like appendage. Not stopping there, it continued to crawl onto the orb's upper surface. Bob then rose to head-level to give Cuddy a closer, one-on-one perspective of the winged insect.

"Great, Bob's found a pet," Jackie remarked with a smirk. "Any other Tripette City surprises you want to tell us about . . . Bob?"

"If you will follow me, I will lead the way to the records conservatory."

"Terrific, now even the robot ignores me," Jackie muttered.

* * *

The records conservatory was as unimpressive as its name conveyed. Cuddy figured it was not so different from any number of similar government-type structures back on Earth. Though certainly more advanced, sleeker, it still was a utilitarian, unimpressive, office construct. Bob went right to work, accessing what looked like three different computer nodes. Display screens came to life as he interacted with each—going back and forth using their respective input devices.

Kyle asked, "What are we supposed to be doing? How do we help?"

"I think we wait for Bob to tell us. Maybe explain how to access the computers . . . the databases," Brian said.

"There are twenty-seven different Tripette City computer networks, yet only three remain operational. Fortunately, there was much overlap between them," Bob said, moving next to what looked like a printer station. Then, retrieving the output, the orb handed the single-paged sheet to Cuddy.

Jackie, peering over Cuddy's shoulder, said, "Cool! It's like . . . virtual. Like a tablet computer only on a sheet of paper."

"Not paper . . . *Transitine*," Bob corrected.

Cuddy used his finger to scroll down the sheet of items. The first listed was the all-important wellness chamber. "Huh . . . it's written in English!"

"Yes, that is what took so long. Needed to first construct a short translation program. You will note the articles Tow requested . . . the location of the chamber and several other items . . . and where in the city to find them. Also, the quantities that remain, although I do not believe this inventory completely reflects actual post-attack stock levels."

"That's a lot of stuff to find!" Jackie exclaimed.

Brian rolled his eyes at her comment. "Don't be stupid! Tow's seeking to heal the dying and rebuild a new world. I think he's entitled to ask for a few things . . . a few necessities."

Cuddy shouldn't have been surprised by Brian's antagonistic response, but to speak to Jackie that way—his only true ally—was indeed surprising.

"You really are a dick, you know that, Brian?" Kyle said, coming to her defense.

Tony jumped in. "You know where these sites are, Bob? Can you take us there?"

"Yes . . . we should go," the orb affirmed, as his *glithopede passenger* suddenly fluttered its wings and took to the air.

* * *

Bob was the first to exit the records conservatory. Cuddy watched from the doorway as the orb hovered through into the subterranean semi-darkness. Most of the overhead lighting was either still dark or irregularly strobing on and off. But at least the clicking sound was gone. Leaning farther into the gloom, Cuddy could now see why. The insects had taken flight—hundreds upon hundreds of glithopedes darting and swooping.

"No fucking way am I going out there," Tony sputtered, conviction in his voice, as Cuddy continued to track Bob's movements. The orb, going stationary, hovered some twenty yards out, almost completely obscured by the constantly shifting cloud of insects.

"Bob's waiting for us," Cuddy informed the others.

"Let him wait," Jackie said.

"Come on. Everyone stay close to me . . . it'll be okay." Cuddy quickly positioned his palms before him—one at ten, one at two o'clock. With each step, he parted a path through another swath of flying pests. "Brian . . . can you help out? Keep them at bay from the rear?" Cuddy asked, waiting for an answer. But none came back. Striding forward, he mentally focused—projecting an energy field around them. He'd never done this type of thing before, and wasn't completely sure it would work. The others crowded closer-in, as if huddling beneath an umbrella—protection from a torrent rainstorm. They proceeded on toward the center of the room.

"Good job, Cuddy," his brother said. "Um . . . just curious, but how long can you keep this up?"

"I think I'm okay . . . for a while still," Cuddy replied, though truthfully, he was already tiring. It wasn't the same as *lifting*, or TK-ing, something heavy. It was more difficult than that. Now his telekinesis powers were tasked with creating an air-tight bubble-like field around them, where even an instant lapse of concentration offered a gap for the bugs to find a way onto them.

"I don't see why we even had to come down here," Brian finally said. "It's not like we had anything to do. Bob could have come alone. Now we all have to suffer."

"Always the breath of fresh air, Brian?" Tony chided.

On reaching Bob then proceeding forward, Cuddy could see the stairwell just ahead. The strain he felt—all over his body—was increasing by the moment. A bead of sweat formed on his brow.

"Oh no . . ." Jackie said her voice barely audible.

"What is it?" Kyle asked.

"I think one of the bugs has found a way in."

Kyle asked, "Are you helping out, Brian, or are you making Cuddy do all the heavy lifting?"

Cuddy, chancing a quick peek over his shoulder, caught

Brian reading the sheet of *Transitine.* He glanced up, then around, and said, "Oh . . . yeah, sorry." Tucking the single sheet under his arm, he pushed his palms out before him, similar to Cuddy's.

Immediately, Cuddy felt relief—a weight lifted off his shoulders and back—now less than fifteen feet from the stairway.

Then, hearing a chilling scream directly behind him, Cuddy glanced back to see not one, but two, glithopedes stuck to Tony's face. With clawed fingers, Tony was frantically tugging to get them off.

"Keep moving, everyone. We're almost out of here!" Cuddy yelled, aware that Brian, once again, had stopped helping.

Tony was crying now—like a small child—fear and pain quickly overwhelming him. Kyle and Jackie, each taking ahold of an arm, kept him up on his feet. Climbing the stairs, daylight awaited them at the top. With each step, the cloud of glithopedes dissipated a little more, which was good. Cuddy, exhausted, was forced to release the protective energy field he'd formed. Now on the ground floor of the wrecked building, Cuddy lowered to his knees. Panting, he said, "Bring Tony over . . . next to me."

Kyle and Jackie helped Tony lie flat on his back. He'd quieted down some though his hands still tore at the imbedded insects.

Cuddy brought his face within inches from Tony's. In as calm a voice as he could muster, he said, "Hey Tony . . . listen to me. It's going to be all right. Bob said they aren't poisonous. Take your hands away from your face."

"No! I have to get them off me!"

Jackie, at Cuddy's side, stressed, "You need to do what he says, Tony."

Tentatively, Tony pulled his hands away and both Kyle and Jackie gasped. Cuddy studied what he was seeing. The two glithopedes had indeed imbedded themselves— countless tiny legs dug deeply into his skin.

As Bob hovered next to Jackie, Cuddy's irritation spiked. Where was Brian, he was the licensed physician here.

"I have limited data on the removal of insects, such as these, from their prey," Bob said.

"Prey!" Jackie spat. "You said their sting wasn't poisonous!"

Bob, spinning around on its axis, made a few beeps and clicks before answering, "Glithopedes are not poisonous. I apologize. Although nearly identical, I believe what we have here are . . . recent mutations to the genome." The AI orb extended a finger-like digit then said, "See . . . the purple and yellow coloring are reversed. The body on a glithopede is purple. See, both of these have yellow bodies. Perhaps a result of the Howsh bombings. The truth is, I have no idea what these creatures are capable of . . . or what they are currently doing to Tony."

Cuddy looked up and around. Still no sign of Brian. Tony was starting to hyperventilate.

"I'm going to try something, Tony. Hold on," Cuddy instructed him, bringing the tip of his right forefinger just above the elongated body of one of the bugs. Somewhere in his memory, he recalled hearing that imbedded ticks shouldn't be yanked out. Their heads could get stuck beneath the skin, causing an infection. These weren't ticks. But all those legs—perhaps their heads, too—he had no way of knowing. He had to manipulate it so this mutant bug would extract itself on its own accord.

He concentrated—bringing TK heat to the tip of his finger—then ever so slowly increased the temperature. It took a full minute before white whips of smoke drifted up from the purple, now turning brown, body. Suddenly, the mutant bug pulled its legs, as well as a tiny head—free and, fluttering its wings, flew away, leaving behind a bad smell.

Everyone exhaled a combined sigh of relief. Cuddy moved onto the second bug and, performing the same procedure, it took a bit less time for this bug to extract itself and fly away. Tony touched his face—probing his still-red, swollen skin. Both areas showed a dual series of pinprick-sized holes. He looked as if he had two sets of Frankenstein-sized stitches—one on his left cheek, one on his forehead.

"I'm going to clean and bandage your injuries, Tony," Jackie said, already reaching into her backpack.

Cuddy gave Tony a reassuring pat on his shoulder then rose to his feet, both mentally and physically exhausted. Again, he looked around for the elusive Brian. Maybe he'd fallen down a manhole. *Oh, to actually be that lucky.*

Kyle stood with him, forcing out a breath through puffed cheeks. "That was pretty awesome . . . saving us twice in the last hour. Cool little brother."

Cuddy shrugged it off. "All in a day's work," Cuddy said with a half-smile.

"We should get going. There're a lot of items on that list still."

chapter 11

Seven years ago . . . Woodbury, Tennessee

The oppressive little log cabin seemed to close in around Cuddy. His eyes were drawn to what the old man was clutching in his right hand. Still lurking in the semi-dark hallway, Slatch seemed to be quietly considering something.

"Whatcha' got there, Slatch?" Cuddy inquired. Slatch then moved forward. Exiting the hallway, he entered the larger room. Sure enough, what he was gripping was some sort of book.

Momma had a book that looked nearly identical, only its cover was red and this one was green. She called it a photo album. Slatch sat next to Cuddy on the couch. Moving his *spit-can* out of the way, he positioned the book on the coffee table in front of them. Smelling strongly of sour body odor and fresh-cut field grass, Slatch wore a dingy Band-Aid wrapped around his left pinkie. His old hands were dry and cracked from a lifetime of working on the farm.

"I want to show you how your pa looked," Slatch said, with a glance in Cuddy's direction. "He was about your age . . . maybe twelve . . . or maybe a tad older than that." He opened the cover of the big green album then quickly flipped through six or seven pages. Cuddy leaned over the book, wanting to tell Slatch to slow down. That he didn't mind looking at some of the other photos that might be of Slatch's ma, or even his grandma. All the photos were black and white and most were faded and scratched—the corners dog-eared.

Slatch then made an involuntary snort. With the pages spread open, he pointed and tapped at a photograph in the upper left corner. Swallowing hard before speaking, he said, "That's your pa right there, sitting up on a buckboard."

Cuddy studied the image. Sure enough, the boy looked to be about his own age. He also had blond hair, though not trimmed in a bowl-cut like Cuddy's. The boy wore short trousers, exposing his thin ankles. They were held up by long straps. "What are those?"

"Suspenders."

Cuddy, glancing at the other photographs on the page, recognized some of the locations. "Hey . . . that's our farm!"

Slatch leaned in and studied the photo. "Yeah . . . your dad grew up right there."

"And that's you standing next to him, huh?" Both boys were holding up plump chickens. "You were best friends?"

The question seemed to catch Slatch off-guard. Suddenly, as his eyes filled with tears, he replied—first clearing the phlegm from his throat, "That we were . . . Slatch and Brody; back then, we were inseparable."

Cuddy didn't know what that long word meant, but the way the old man said it, it had to be a good thing. "Why aren't you friends now?"

"How do you know we're not?"

"Because you're only showing me photographs taken a hundred years ago."

Slatch's expression dulled. "I made a mistake. Unforgivable, I guess . . ."

Cuddy caught sight of a photograph—a little girl in pigtails wearing a Sunday-kind of dress people went to church in. "Hey . . . isn't that my Ma . . ."

The book was suddenly banged closed, almost snagging Cuddy's hand in the process.

Standing, Slatch said, "We were all friends back then. But that's enough looking at pictures for now." He tossed the photo album on the seat of the old recliner, then said, "Best I get you home now, kid. Imagine Dotty will be worried sick 'bout you."

"Can you take me to see my pa, Slatch?"

He hesitated; his tongue looked to be probing around the inside of his mouth—as if searching for something—maybe a tobacco seed. Then, a smile crept across his lips and the corners of his eyes crinkled. "That might not be such a bad idea, young man. And it just might get the old coot to utter more than two words to me." He crossed the room and stood before an old clock on the wall. The kind of clock that looked like a small house and where, every so often, a tiny bird would pop out a small door and make a racket.

"We'd have to leave now . . . it's not too long a drive. Maybe an hour each way." Slatch rubbed the white bristles on his chin then, staring at Cuddy, asked, "You really want to see your pa?"

Cuddy nodded enthusiastically, although at that particular moment he couldn't remember the name of the old man he was talking to or why he was seated in his house.

Slatch clicked the switch off on the warming plate in the kitchen and the amber light went dark. "We should be able to make it back before dark . . . but best we be going, boy."

chapter 12

"Captain!"

Cuddy and Kyle spun in the direction of the AI-orb's voice. Bob, though out of view, was somewhere nearby within the building's rubble.

"Coming," Cuddy said, pulling Tony to his feet, as Jackie steadied him—ensuring he was capable of now walking.

"I'm fine. My face feels a little funny . . . but I'm okay, I think."

Together, they circumnavigated around a ten-foot-high mound of fallen rubble. Bob had indeed found Brian. All eyes gazed up at the metal girder suspended above their heads. Bob said, "I found him here like this."

"What are you doing, Brian?" Jackie asked.

"What's it look like I'm doing?" Brian curtly replied.

Only then, did Cuddy realize the girder hanging above them now, was no longer suspended by the lone metal cable he'd noticed earlier. The girder was held up in the air by one thing only—Brian's mental focus. End over end, the thousand-pound-plus expanse of metal rotated on its axis fifty feet above their heads like a giant propeller.

"That's dangerous," Cuddy said. "It could fall . . . hurt someone. Stop showing off, Brian, and start being part of the team."

"Oh . . . it already fell. Came within a foot of my head, but I stopped it. Total reflex action. Can you believe that? I didn't even have to think . . . I simply responded with my TK. Obviously, my powers have evolved." Brian let his eyes flash to Cuddy, then over to Jackie, then back up at the girder again.

"I'm serious. We sure could have used a medical doctor's help back there with Tony. Those insects—"

"I fucking hate bugs," Brian retorted, matter-of-factly, cutting Jackie off mid-sentence. With his hands placed up before him—palms facing out—he took in a lungful of air. Then, following an exaggerated shoving-off motion, the girder silently rocketed away with incredible speed. They all watched until it was a mere pinprick in the distant sky, then it was gone.

Cuddy was more interested in Brian's fixed, wide-eyed expression than his latest feat of telekinesis. *Was Brian walking a tightrope between sanity and insanity*, he wondered. Was he dangerous to the mission; to this team?

"What's next? Oh . . . that's right, Tow's shit list, Brian scoffed, seeming to be his normal, obnoxious self again. For the first time, Brian took in Tony's face. "Mother of Christ . . . and I thought I was the ugly one around here."

* * *

Twenty-five miles northeast of the Tripette City Records Conservatory, in a more industrial section of the city, Cuddy set the *Evermore* down in an open field. He mentally reviewed the one item they hoped to find in the adjacent, still intact, three-story-high warehouse.

Stepping off the ramp, together they quietly moved as a group across the field. Cuddy took in their surroundings. Like the rest of the city, like the rest of the planet— where constant aerial bombardments had evidently taken place—he could still visualize what had once been a beautiful, futuristic city—one constructed with clean, sophisticated architecture. Perhaps Earth, in a hundred or 200 years, would progress, advance, to something equally as modern and compelling as this world must have been before the war. Perhaps, though, the Howsh would reap the same kind of destruction there . . . *maybe they already had*? Cuddy couldn't think about that right now, he had a job to do. A monumental task, if left uncompleted, could result in hundreds . . . thousands dying of the shingles epidemic.

Three large, roll-up-type doors were at the back of the building. Not too different from those found in the rear of similar buildings on Earth, where trucks would back into loading bays to either pick-up, or drop-off, deliveries. The door on the left began to roll up first, then the door in the middle, then that on the right.

"Take your pick . . . any door . . . any door you like," Brian said in a sing-song whimsical voice.

"Now you're just getting cocky," Jackie responded.

"Where, specifically, is this wellness chamber located in here?" Kyle asked, keenly aware of their mission.

Bob hovered past them, going within the building's dark interior while communicating telepathically to Cuddy en route. *I will check on the power situation.*

"According to what's listed on the *Transitine* sheet . . . it's here . . . I have the location," Brian said.

They entered the cool, wide-open space. Again, certain similarities to Earth were apparent. It was basically a simple warehouse, containing row upon row of towering shelves. When the overhead lights suddenly came on, the space seemed to extend in size by a magnitude of ten.

A distantly motor-like sound engaged. Several moments passed before Cuddy spotted a vehicle approaching, a hovercraft of some kind—one piloted by Bob. Slowing, it came to a halt, hovering several feet off the floor in front of them, a forklift-type vehicle. In addition, it possessed two metal prongs, protruding in front, along with a set of large securing clamps set behind them—they looked like bug pinchers.

Cuddy stepped up onto a small metal platform, next to Bob at the controls, getting a firm grip with one hand. "Hold tight here, we'll be back in a few minutes," he told the others. He gestured forward with his chin and Bob goosed the throttle—speeding the craft up and away into the bowels of the warehouse.

The tightly packed shelves flew past them. Passing by the myriad high-tech equipment, Cuddy had no clue what all the various contraptions were used for. As they approached the farthest end of the warehouse, Cuddy became aware that the building's structure hadn't gone completely unscathed. Howsh bombing had taken out the front right section. The sharply sloping ceiling had caved-in, toppling shelves in the process. Since much of the overhead lighting was also destroyed, it was difficult to see much of anything.

The vehicle slowed, then descend nearer to the floor.

We are looking for row 694; shelf 55; item 12,453, Bob telepathically communicated to Cuddy.

Cuddy could now make out the green, glowing, symbolic designations beneath every shelf item. As they approached the last, still-standing shelving units, Cuddy worried that what they were looking for might be buried under thousands of pounds of collapsed shelving, and warehouse roofing.

"Here we go," Bob said. The AI-orb spun the hovering forklift vehicle around to face directly into the last upright shelves then rose up about ten feet. When the vehicle's two forward headlights abruptly came on, Cuddy saw what they'd come to retrieve. It was *big!* So large, in fact, he seriously doubted it would fit within the *Evermore*'s sub-deck hold. Tow would have taken that into account. *Wouldn't he?*

Although it was under the same layer of dust that coated everything else in the warehouse, its metallic surface still reflected the forklift's bright headlight beams. Cuddy estimated the *thing* to be about the size of a medium-sized RV . . . like the abandoned 1973 Winnebago half-buried in a field back home. Not quite as long perhaps, but certainly as wide.

Bob used its articulating clawed arms to activate the front

forks, moving them forward to disappear into what looked like a containment pallet beneath the unit. Then the large fork pincers came alive, grabbing ahold of item 12,453 and pulling it free from its storage location. Bob backed away from the towering shelving unit. Suddenly, *movement.*

Startled, Cuddy yelled, "Bob . . . stop!"

Huddled behind where the wellness chamber unit had been positioned only a moment before sat a small Pashier being. Only this was no collection of disconnected bones—or dried-out decomposed flesh—but a living, breathing, alien child . . .

chapter 13

The child's movements were frenetic, quickly looking both left then right, *perhaps weighing her best escape route.* Every muscle on her lithe body was taut—her expression terror-stricken. A good few inches shy of four foot, she had bright-blue eyes and small delicate features. Like all other Pashier, she was hairless and wore no clothing.

"I think she's going to bolt," Cuddy murmured. He spoke to her telepathically—hopefully relaying his earnest, harmless intent. *Don't run. It's okay . . . I can help you . . . I promise. We are not the Howsh.* She didn't acknowledge his words. If possible, she looked now more frightened now.

My name is Cuddy Perkins. One month ago, I met a Pashier being . . . his name was Tow. His spacecraft landed on my home planet, Earth. I was a little scared when I first met him, too. But we . . . me and my friends . . . now find heritage pods for him then transport them far away to safety. We're only here to help.

Recognition flashed in her eyes—if only momentarily—perhaps putting her escape strategy on hold.

We have no weapons. We simply came here for that big piece of equipment . . . not for you.

Finally, she communicated back to him. *Am I . . . the last of my kind? The lone survivor?*

No! Thousands of others, Pashier just like you, now live on another planet.

Primara? She asked. Her eyes conveying a glimmer of optimism; of hope.

That's right! Cuddy figured every Pashier, from a young age on up, probably knew about that mythical refuge world. Still, he could tell the child was smart.

Pashier is where we just came from, he informed her.

Instinctively, Cuddy knew they were at an important juncture. He was sure pressuring her wouldn't garner positive results. Only frighten her more—push her away.

What is your name?

It took a while for her to answer. *Haffan . . . my name is Haffan.*

Good to meet you, Haffan. Okay, we're going to leave now. We have much to do before we head back to Primara. I wish the very best for you. Good luck.

Bob initiated the forklift's backing-out process. Cuddy kept his eyes on the young alien. A new expression of fear was registered on her face.

Hesitantly, Haffan reached out a hand. *You're going to leave me here?"*

Cuddy gave Bob the signal to stop. *Are you hungry?*

Gazing up at Cuddy, innocent pleading in her eyes, Bob

readjusted the controls and the forklift moved closer to the shelf space that Haffan stood upon.

Um . . . there's limited room on this thing, but I can scooch over a bit. Cuddy held out a hand, *Come on, hop on over.*

She jumped across the gap with zero hesitation. Apparently, once the young Pashier decided to trust him, she was all in. Cuddy verbally spoke aloud to her for the first time. "Can I ask . . . how old are you, Haffan?"

She looked up at him with a quizzical expression, as if the tone of his actual voice didn't match what she'd expected to hear. "I am thirty-five."

That took Cuddy by surprise.

Bob informed him, "Note, Pashier years are not the same as years on Earth. In human years . . . Haffan would be seven years old.

"You're just a little kid," Cuddy said, more to himself than her, speaking in English instead of her native language.

What's a kid?

He looked at her with a sideways glance, "You understood my words?"

She screwed up her face and shook her head. *No. You* tele-speak *and talk at the same time. It's really annoying.*

Once Bob put the vehicle into forward gear, they rapidly moved toward the front of the warehouse.

"No way, do I really do that! *I mean . . . do I do that?* Cuddy asked, making sure he didn't actually speak the words and use telepathy at the same time.

For the first time, the Pashier child smiled.

How in the world did she survive alone here? Cuddy wondered. The irony that she was the same as he'd been, when he fell from that hayloft years ago, struck him.

Now studying the child, her small hand still grasped in his—her Pashier *glow* was almost non-existent. *How* had she survived the elements? Had she somehow found food and water here? What about the Dirth? How had she survived?

"Where are we going?" she asked, in her native tongue.

"We're heading back to the rest of the team . . . to my friends," Cuddy replied in her native Pashier language. At this point, since his heritage pod transformation, languages came easy to Cuddy. "We'll take you to the ship first, then see what we can rustle up for you to eat. How does that sound?"

She shrugged a surprisingly Earth-like gesture. "Ever had a grilled-cheese and bacon sandwich?" he asked, this time conveying a mental image of the food.

She nodded with an all-knowing expression. "All the time. Grilled cheek is one of my favorites."

"It's called grilled cheese, not grilled *cheeks.*"

"I know that. You heard me wrong."

Bob slowed, descending to the concrete-like floor where light poured in through the three open bay doors.

"Where are your friends?" Haffan asked, her words faint and most of her weight pressed against Cuddy's leg. Heavy-lidded, she seemed to be fading fast. In one swift motion, he stepped from the forklift, taking her into his arms. Haffan's eyes were closed—sound asleep.

Cuddy spotted Tony, a quarter of the way down an adjacent

row of shelving. He was putting something into a bright-orange tote bag.

"Who have you got there?" a voice asked from behind.

Cuddy turned, seeing Kyle and Jackie heading his way. He didn't want to think about where they'd been—what they'd been doing.

"This is Haffan . . . a survivor."

"A miracle is what she is," Jackie exclaimed astonished. "Oh my God, she's just a child . . . a baby."

"I'm thirty-five," a faint voice proclaimed.

Jackie stepped forward, reaching her hand toward the young Pashier. Haffan, squirming, turned away—burying her face into Cuddy's chest—Jackie's well-intentioned gesture, rebuffed.

Cuddy noticed the hurt look on Jackie's face, which she quickly hid behind a forced smile.

Kyle said, "What are you going to do with it?"

"It?" Jackie asked.

"Okay . . . her. What are you going to do with her?" Kyle clarified.

"She's coming with us. We'll take her back to Primara . . . right after the mission," Cuddy told them.

"I want my grilled cheeks." Both Kyle and Jackie, puzzled, looked to Cuddy.

"She means grilled cheese," Bob explained.

Without turning around, Cuddy said, "Put everything back where it was." He then turned to face Tony, now approaching them.

Tony's guilty expression said it all. "Nobody's left here . . . who's around to miss this stuff?" His attention then locked onto the child.

"Does that stuff belong to you?" Cuddy asked.

"Oh, come on! Are you serious?"

"Just put it back, Tony. It's not worth getting into an argument about," Jackie said.

Tony let out a groan. Then, allowing the strap to slide off his shoulder, the tote dropped to the floor with a loud thud. Whatever was inside was heavy. He used the side of his boot to slide the tote, and its contents, back in the direction he'd just come from. "So, what's with the curtain-climber?" he asked.

"This is Haffan," Cuddy said, clearly still irritated Tony hadn't fully done what he'd asked.

* * *

Gathered together in the kitchen, Cuddy and Haffan sat at the suspended glass table, while Jackie, Kyle and Tony stood around them and watched her eat. The AI orb did the honors—programmed the food replicator, then delivered the hot grilled-cheese sandwich, with two strips of perfectly cooked bacon peeking out the sides.

As she ate, Haffan muttered little sounds of bliss. She'd eaten all but the sandwich's outer crust. Forcing the last bite into an already overstuffed mouth, she asked, "Is this everyone?"

The others were still just in the beginning stages of learning the Pashier language—they looked to Cuddy for clarification. Until that very moment, Cuddy hadn't thought about Brian, who once again had drifted off from the team to do his own thing. "No, there is one more of us. His name is—"

Brian's voice resounded behind Tony's shoulder: "My name is Brian."

Haffan stared at the latest arrival into the kitchen with wide-eyes. Cuddy felt her breathing constrict. Brian, by no means as awful looking as before, was still odd-looking. His features seemed to have settled into a perpetual snarl.

Brian brushed past Tony and, without hesitation, sat on the bench seat next to her and held out his right hand and spoke in her native tongue. "Nice to meet you, Haffan." She stared at his extended hand like it was a bug.

Brian, using his other hand, took ahold of hers and showed her how to shake hands. "That's how Earthlings greet each other, kiddo . . . its called *shaking hands*." Letting go of her hand, he looked down at the assortment of crust and crumbs left on her plate. "Bob . . . how 'bout you make me one of those too?" He then looked at Haffan with a raised brow. He said, "I'm getting a clear message . . . she wants another one . . . and extra bacon, huh?"

Haffan, trying to hide her smile, tried to match Brian's snarl. It wasn't working. *But who would have thought*, Cuddy pondered,*Brian could almost be human sometimes.*

Jackie, arms crossed over her chest, watched them in silence. Cuddy knew that expression. The way she chewed the inside of her cheek when she felt unsettled. She let out a breath then said, "Well I have work to do."

Haffan watched her leave the kitchen, then looked at Cuddy with a new expression—he couldn't quite read.

chapter 14

Seven years earlier . . . Woodbury, Tennessee

Even in the shade of the low overhanging porch it was still stifling hot out.

"You know, there really are some bad people out and about; people who'll take advantage of someone who lacks good sense. The problem is . . . Cuddy trusts people. He doesn't see that side . . . the dark side . . . of anyone."

At twelve, Jackie was aware of such things, though she didn't like to think about them. Mamma Perkins was beyond mad. She was beside herself and Kyle was in big trouble.

Twice they'd gone out to look for him and twice they'd returned, hoping Cuddy had found his own way back home. In the distance, Jackie could see Rufus running back and forth along the fence line. Every so often, he stopped to stare out into the grassy fields beyond—ears twitching—his attention pulled this way and that at the slightest sound.

"How could you?" Momma demanded, not waiting for an answer as she paced the rickety front porch for the hundredth time. She then stopped, just long enough to glare at the youngsters sitting together on the top step. "What did I say to you right before you left?"

"To watch out for Cuddy," Kyle admitted, one notch above a whisper.

"So, what the hell happened?"

Jackie had never heard Momma swear before and felt uncomfortable, to the point she wondered if she should leave. The only problem was she'd have to ask Momma to use the phone to call her dad—right now didn't seem like a good time to ask Momma for anything. So she just sat quietly next to Kyle, doing her best to shrink down into the wood-planked steps.

Kyle glanced at Jackie, and then up to Momma. "He was so slow . . . kept getting distracted. One minute we were running through the field, you know . . . just goofing and laughing and then . . . I don't know . . . Cuddy was gone."

Jackie nodded. She'd been vaguely aware he'd fallen behind them once again. A few times they slowed—calling out for him to hurry and catch up. But then, suddenly he was gone—nowhere in sight.

The screen door slammed shut. A moment later, they heard Momma on the phone. Jackie heard the concern in her voice as she spoke to somebody on the other end of the line.

"Sorry, Kyle. I should have been watching out for him too," Jackie said.

"Why are you sorry? He's my brother, not yours."

"Because I've always been the one to watch out for him," she replied, with more indignation in her voice than she intended. *But it was true.* Maybe because she'd always felt responsible—at least partially—for what had happened to Cuddy five years earlier. *Was that day much different from today?* Hadn't she and Kyle gotten so involved with each other that Cuddy got pushed aside—*pushed right off the hayloft*? She'd had to live with the certainty that she'd also been responsible for nearly killing her best childhood friend. Had contributed to his brain injury, being mentally handicapped the rest of his life?

They sat in silence for what seemed like an hour. Momma continued to pace, while Rufus continued his vigil at the fence.

Now seeing the sheriff's cruiser slowing, then pull into the driveway only accentuated the seriousness of the situation. The police weren't notified unless a possible crime had taken place. Jackie wondered if Momma could *be right. Did some back-woods perv get ahold of Cuddy and was doing bad things to him right now*? She felt sick to her stomach as she looked across the field—past the worried dog. Would they find his buried bones fifty years from now and never know whom they belonged to?

Jackie flinched at the sound of the police car door slamming. Sheriff Bone, tall and imposing, placed his cap atop his bald dome and headed their way. Momma came out of the house, wringing her hands on a floral-patterned dish towel.

"Dotty . . . kids . . ." he greeted them, touching the brim of his cap.

"Two hours, Dale! Tell me . . . was there some other Woodbury emergency that took priority over a missing child?"

The sheriff didn't reply, obviously not about to be goaded into an argument with Momma. Instead, he turned toward the open field, seeming preoccupied with the dog. Finally, he said, "Dotty . . . let's take a walk."

His words froze Momma where she stood. Why didn't the sheriff want the kids to hear what he had to say? Right then, Jackie knew things had gone from bad to worse. Cuddy had been found—*lying in a ditch, or tied to a tree, or floating face down in Gilby Creek.* Or maybe some other God-awful thing had happened, brain injury or not, to the best friend she'd ever have. Jackie found it difficult to swallow.

chapter 15

Cuddy was dreaming of Woodbury. Of a simpler time when Rufus was still a puppy and the kitchen floor was covered with open, spread around newspapers. Both he and the three-week-old yellow lab were playing beneath the kitchen table as Momma moved back and forth between the stove, the refrigerator, the sink, then back to the stove. The air was filled with rich smells—of vanilla and cookie dough—while in the background, the constant droning of an old Sunbeam Mixmaster whirled away atop the kitchen counter.

Haffan screamed, waking up Cuddy. Disoriented, he looked about the *Evermore's* dimly-lit portside sleeping compartment. Rolling out of his berth, he made his way to the young alien, who was tossing and turning in her bunk. Her lips were moving—either speaking or yelling something as she slept. Cuddy wondered if she was reliving some terrible past event in a dream. Perhaps re-witnessing the loss of her parents or a sibling. She hadn't spoken of such disturbing things yet. Perhaps she never would.

He gently rocked her shoulder. Whispering, he said, "Haffan . . . wake up. You're having a nightmare."

Haffan's eyes immediately opened and she blinked several times in rapid succession. Her Pashier glow seemed to have improved some. Her face, small and heart-shaped, stayed immobile for several moments before she turned toward Cuddy.

"You know where you are?" he asked.

She nodded her head.

"Bad dream?"

Another nod.

"You want to get up for a while?"

Haffan, pushing forward onto her elbows, peered about the compartment. "Everyone is asleep?"

Cuddy looked around and found Jackie's berth empty, although the others were sound asleep in their bunks. He said, "Not everyone. Come on, you're probably hungry."

As she pulled back the covers and swung her legs over the side, Cuddy noticed several prominent cuts on her feet. There were additional, though less severe, cuts on her legs. Again, he was reminded of what tough times she must have endured. Clearly, exposure to the elements was prominent among them. He'd talk to Bob about configuring the wellness chamber for her later on today.

On the way to the kitchen, they found Jackie curled up on a couch in the main cabin. As they entered she didn't look up from the book she was reading, continuing to twist ringlets of hair around her twirling finger.

Haffan watched Jackie with interest, assessing her. She glanced at Cuddy then back at Jackie.

She is mad at you.

I know . . . but I'm not sure why.

Still holding Cuddy's hand, Haffan stared hard at Jackie. Only then did Jackie let her eyes roam over the top of the book. Suddenly, the book slammed shut while still in her grasp, making a loud *clap* sound.

Jackie jumped. "Why did you do that?" Her forehead creased, she leveled an annoyed glare at the alien child.

Haffan offered a perplexed, *I have no idea what you're talking about*, expression.

Up to that point, Cuddy hadn't personally witnessed any TK abilities coming from the child. Watching both females stare intently at one another, he found the situation slightly funny.

Haffan said, "Cuddy . . . will you ask her if she wants a grilled cheek sandwich? With bacon?"

"I understood you just fine. And its cheese . . . not cheeks."

Haffan, pursing her lips, waited, then said, "You should eat. You may not have another chance for a while. Not with the coming attack."

Jackie and Cuddy glanced at each other, his alarmed face hardening. "What are you talking about? What attack?" he asked.

Haffan shrugged a shoulder. "I saw it in my dream; was seeing it when you woke me up."

Jackie, putting down her book, moved closer. Kneeling

down to Haffan's level, she asked, "How do you know it was real? That it's really going to happen? Maybe it was just a dream, sweetie."

"That's a stupid question! I know the difference. There are dreams and there are *glimpses* . . . not the same thing."

Cuddy had heard the word used before—*glimpse* was a Pashier term for a particular kind of psychic experience.

"Just like I knew you would come to row 694; shelf 55; item 12,453 in that warehouse. Why else would you think I was there?"

Cuddy had only thought they were extremely lucky—finding the young alien in that exact place at that exact time. Now things were making better sense. He reappraised the young Pashier. She was smart. A lot smarter than any seven-year-old he'd ever come across.

"So tell us about this attack . . . is it the Howsh?" Jackie asked.

Haffan nodded. "I don't know exactly *what* happens . . . only that it *will* happen . . . soon."

Cuddy noticed the AI-orb, quickly making its way through the cabin and headed for the bridge. "Can you stay with her for a while?" Cuddy asked Jackie, already turning to hurry after Bob.

Cuddy reached the bridge in time to witness two Howsh spacecraft approaching on the viewscape display. *How had they found them?*

In the near-total darkness outside, the decimated buildings within the Tripette City landscape were nearly impossible to discern. Then he saw a light coming from the warehouse next door—a single beacon of light shining into the darkness. Of course! Someone turning on the building's power generator would naturally show up on Howsh sensors just as prominently as if a bonfire was lit, or a flare set off. *Stupid!*

"How much time do we have?" Cuddy asked the orb.

"No time . . . they are close, and charging weapons."

chapter 16

Cuddy watched as the two scout ships engaged their landing thrusters—the night's darkness momentarily breached as the brightly-lit plumes revealed the enemy ships' downward descent.

The AI-orb managed to cut the *Evermore*'s power just prior to the scout ships' arrival. With her energy signatures now masked, the *Evermore* would be as inconsequential to the Howsh as all the dilapidated buildings surrounding them. Cuddy hoped their attention would strictly be focused on the lit-up warehouse—probably wondering why the generators were powered on.

"Amazing they can't see us, sitting out in the open like this," Cuddy said. He spoke in a hushed voice, not wanting to jinx their good fortune. Knowing, that come dawn in two hour's time, their ship would stand out like a bright moon against a backdrop of inky black space.

"Apparently, they cannot," Bob agreed.

"One thing's for certain . . . we can't stick around here, hoping our presence won't be noticed eventually."

Jackie entered the bridge, with Haffan close behind. "What's up?" she asked, peering out the portside window. Tucking a long lock of hair behind her ear, she exclaimed, "Crap . . . they're like . . . right there! Don't they see us?"

Cuddy shook his head. "Bob's got us pretty well hidden . . . at least from an energy signature standpoint." Feeling a presence near him, Cuddy turned and found Haffan standing close by his side, her concentration also centered on the two scout ships outside.

Is this part of the attack, Haffan . . . the one you had a glimpse of?

Haffan, continuing to stare out the window, wobbled her head. *Maybe . . . but in my glimpse there were three ships.*

The AI-orb, now on the move, apparently wasn't averse to eavesdropping on other telepathic conversations.

"Talk to me, Bob!" Cuddy said, shifting his attention back to the viewscape display, where nothing showed. Bob made an adjustment to the zoom-level settings and then, sure enough, another Howsh vessel came into view. "Warship . . . Marauder-Class."

Two small scout ships on the ground were one thing, but a powerful Marauder-Class warship was something else entirely. *They were in big trouble. No way that advanced vessel hadn't spotted them.*

Jackie, standing tall, faced him directly. Cuddy was surprised by the intensity of her stare. "I understand you want to live the Pashier way . . . the whole *pacifist* thing. But we have to put up a defense. We need to do *something* to save ourselves,

Cuddy." Her eyes settled on Haffan for a moment. "You do realize that it's not just us anymore."

For weeks, Cuddy had somehow found a way to avoid killing any Howsh. Even now, he felt self-treachery for even considering the use of lethal alternatives.

"Bob, wake up Brian. Bring him to the bridge . . . drag him here if you have to."

It would be far faster if you contacted him telepathically, he reminded himself. Cuddy never communicated with Brian that way—not something you'd want to do with someone you didn't like. Perhaps due to the level of intimacy involved—allowing another person into your psyche. Okay, fine! *Brian . . . wake up . . . you're needed on the bridge. Hurry!*

About ready to send Bob, Brian staggered onto the bridge. "This better be important." Yawning, he unconsciously scratched at his crotch.

Cuddy said, "Three Howsh ships . . . two already on the ground. One, a whole lot bigger, is inbound."

Brian looked out the window, then at the viewscape display. "What do you want me to do?"

"Fend off that incoming Marauder to start."

Jackie, gesturing with a wave of her hand, said, "Send it to the other side of the galaxy . . . where it can't return for a long, long, time."

"No problem, sweet cheeks . . . I can do that." Brian stared at the icon representation of the Marauder on the display then closed his eyes for several seconds. When he opened them, making a casual hand gesture in the air almost identical to

Jackie's, he said, "That should do it. If there's nothing else . . . I need my forty winks."

No one spoke. All eyes were locked on the viewscape display, watching as the Howsh Marauder warship continued to make steady progress toward them.

"That's impossible!" Brian shouted.

"Try again," Jackie urged. "Concentrate!"

"Don't tell me to concentrate . . ." Avoiding her intense glare, Brian stared at the viewscape through narrowed eyes. Using both hands this time, he made an abrupt shoving-motion into the air.

If the consequences of the situation weren't so dire, Cuddy would have reveled in Brian's humiliation. But the apparent lack of some effect from his TK attempts was getting serious.

"Bob, how is this possible?" Cuddy asked.

Before Bob could answer, Jackie asked, "Is it Brian? Has he lost his . . ."

"Bite me. My TK is just fine, Jackie!" Brian responded defensively.

Bob, hovering higher in the air, rotated toward Brian. After a series of clicks and a few beeps, the AI-orb said, "Corresponding high-energy spikes indicate Brian is indeed correct. His TK is exactly as it should be. My presumption is that the Marauder ship has passive induction shielding. I suspect new experimental technology has been retrofitted onto the ship . . . perhaps developed specifically to fend-off the type of telekinesis Brian just attempted.

"In other words, we're up the creek," Tony said. No one responded.

Cuddy went through their options in his mind. Lifting-off was now out of the question—they'd be blown to kingdom come and back by the fast-approaching Marauder. Maybe attempt a speedy break along the surface then high-tail it into space once they were outside the city?

"Howsh!"

Cuddy looked to the view outside to the pair of scout ships. Both craft had lowered their gangways and two teams of five armed Howsh raiders were double-timing it toward the *Evermore*. Nighttime had given way to dawn. *If we can see them, then the raiders most assuredly can see us,* he thought.

"Move!" Cuddy yelled, bulldozing Tony out of the way. As he rushed to the forward console, he shouted out commands: "Bob . . . light up the propulsion system. Brian, do something about those approaching fur-balls." No sooner had those words left Cuddy's mouth, when plasma fire erupted from multiple directions outside.

Cuddy took the nav controls in his left hand while initializing the lift thrusters with his right.

"Shields are holding at ninety-three percent," the AI-orb said.

"Just small-arms fire. It's the incoming Marauder I'm worried about," Cuddy said, guessing it was about thirty seconds out.

Suddenly, the *Evermore* was slammed ferociously on the

side then struck again and again. Bridge lights indiscriminately flashed on and off and a claxon alarm began to screech somewhere above them.

"Bastards! One of the scout ships has repositioned... they're firing their big guns," Kyle said.

"Shields down to twenty percent," Bob updated.

Flashes of red filled the *Evermore*'s bridge. Ten feet off the ground, the big Emersion drive coughed once, twice, then died and they dropped back down to the surface like a load of bricks. The crash was enough to throw them all to the deck. Cuddy wrestled to his feet, tasting blood—he'd bitten his tongue. He looked for and found the viewscape display. The Howsh Marauder was almost upon them.

Brian, attempting to stand, had a wide gash on his forehead. He staggered then fell limply back to the deck.

Fortunately, it appeared Brian had some success with the Howsh raiders earlier, as half of them were now gone. Cuddy was fairly sure they were discovering what it was like to walk in space without a spacesuit.

"Shields are completely down, Captain Perkins."

Cuddy felt something wrap around his leg. *Haffan*. She was hugging him—gazing up at him with panic in her eyes. Placing a comforting hand on her back, he looked around for Jackie, who suddenly appeared at his side. Her terrified expression was a close match to the young alien's.

Outside, the Howsh raiders were continuously firing their energy weapons. A magnificent flash, emitted from the second scout ship—was quickly followed by a plume of dirt and rock exploding mere feet in front of the *Evermore*. A miraculous, fortuitous, miss.

"Look! The other scout ship has repositioned to also fire on us . . . we're toast," Kyle yelled.

But Cuddy wasn't listening to Kyle, or to the shrill claxon above them, or to Haffan's relentless screaming. He was trying to concentrate; attempting to call up his TK power. With Brian down for the count—it was strictly up to Cuddy. That, or they would all be dead within seconds.

The Howsh Marauder suddenly dropped down into view. Easily four or five times the size of the *Evermore*—the enormous craft began firing its big plasma cannons almost immediately. With each thunderous-concussive blast, the deck beneath them shook. But, strangely enough, it wasn't the *Evermore* taking on fire. . . .

chapter 17

The Howsh Marauder spacecraft fired twice more, though at this point it was overkill. Both scout ships were already toast—eviscerated as angry flames roared, and black smoke billowed high into the air.

None of the crew spoke; none daring to hope the attacking vessel would stop its definitive assault. But apparently it had. Cuddy tracked the progress of the Marauder, now moving away from the flames. Soon, clouds of dust rose as the Howsh vessel engaged its landing thrusters.

"She's landing," Kyle said, stating the obvious. Fearful, no one commented.

Within moments, a lift platform descended beneath one of the craft's wings. Standing upon it, a lone figure came into view—partially obscured by all the flames and smoke.

Whoever it was, Cuddy noticed, was tall, as the figure stepped off the platform. Hooded, wearing a long robe, in his right hand he walked with a staff nearly as lengthy as himself. Skirting the two smoldering ships, he eventually came to a stop directly in front of the *Evermore*.

"It's the grim reaper! Coming to take the rest of us . . ."

Jackie slapped Tony's shoulder. "That's not a bit funny."

Bob rose then descended amid a chattering of beeps and clicks, obviously agitated.

"Talk to me, Bob . . . who is that, since you obviously know?" Cuddy asked.

"That is a dead Howsh," the AI-orb replied. Not one to volunteer such dramatic or shocking opinions, Cuddy was somewhat surprised by Bob's comment.

Brian, at some point, had risen from the deck. Blood still trickled down one side of his face, oozing from the wound on his forehead. "Who the hell is that?" he asked.

"That is Lorgue Supreme Eminence Calph," Bob informed them all. "Although it has long been speculated he died a number of years ago."

Cuddy was all too familiar with the once-supreme military commander of the Howsh. Not that many weeks ago, the AI-orb pretended to be the very same being—a ruse that enabled the *Evermore* to receive safe passage across space and, ultimately, to Primara. But from all news accounts, Calph was supposed to be long gone.

"I read about him," Brian said, with some admiration in his voice. "He's the same dude who used to gut his misbehaving junior officers with the swipe of a claw. Gut them right where they stood and they never saw it coming. Then . . . at the height of his military career, he just vanished . . . same say he went into hiding. Had had enough of the Howsh Imperial High Counsel. But no one knows for sure. He'd be an old codger by now, I guess."

"Why is he here? Why would he destroy his own kind like that?" Jackie asked, staring up at Cuddy. "What do you think he wants?"

Me.

Cuddy looked down at Haffan—her arms still tightly wrapped around his upper leg.

He's come for me... I can feel it, Haffan conveyed telepathically.

Cuddy, pulling her arms away from around his thigh, lowered down next to her. "No one's going to let that happen." He gave her arm a little squeeze and stood. "I'm going out there... see what he wants."

"Are you out of your mind?" Kyle barked. "No way... that Gandalf-looking mother-fucker will shred you where you stand."

"If he wanted us dead, we'd already be dead," Cuddy said. Glancing then at Brian, he added, "But if he does... do me a favor. Send him straight into orbit."

Brian smirked at that. "Gladly."

* * *

Cuddy stepped off the gangway and made his way to the *Evermore's* bow. The Howsh military leader, still standing where he was last viewed, stood tall, his staff held at his side. Several paces behind him now stood a rail-thin robot. Cuddy heard it communicating in low digitized-sounding tones to Calph.

Cuddy and Calph's eyes met—neither wavering from the other. Cuddy halted two paces in front of the hooded figure. Now, on seeing him close up, Lorgue Supreme Eminence Calph was a beastie-looking creature. His long fur was gray and scraggly; much of it matted into tangled clumps. A foul musky odor wafted over to Cuddy. But what completely captivated him were the Calph's eyes—so cold and penetrating. *Perhaps this guy truly is the grim reaper,* he mused.

"My name is Cuddy Perkins... I'm the captain of the *Evermore.*

Cuddy heard the robot speak again—it seemed as if it was passing along added information. The language was not that of the Howsh nor Pashier. "You can call me Calph. Now bring out the sprout."

"Sprout?"

"The child Pashier. Don't play games with me, human..." his voice suddenly faltered. Leaning forward, his eyes now narrowed, he continued, "Not human... at least not entirely. Mutant?"

"For lack of a better word... I suppose I am."

And so... you understand then, what I am saying to you now, mutant?

Cuddy was momentarily caught *off-guard* by the Howsh's use of telepathy. At one time, thousands of years ago in their ancient past, all Howsh shared the same capability. Back when the two cultures were reversed—when the Howsh were the beneficent and enlightened species, and the Pashier little more than savage killers. A secret long buried within the vaults of *Calirah*—on the nearby planet of Darriall—for over 8,000 years. Why were the planets reversed? What happened to the Howsh that they can't telepath anymore?

Pashier ancestors, both recent and old, wanting that fact to never become public knowledge, buried the information. Cuddy's near-perfect memory flashed to a video Tow had made when he was traversing space alone—trying to evade his Howsh pursuers. Made out of something resembling old animal hides, the video showed ancient-looking scrolls. Each scroll was highly detailed, with beautiful diagrams illustrating how the ancient Howsh once appeared. Magnificent beings, with luxurious, shimmering, long hair—like the silky long manes and tails on well-groomed show horses. On one of the scrolls, Cuddy recalled seeing six Howsh, stooped—lowered to one knee—gazing skyward, their arms raised in reverence. Each one was glowing. Another scroll showed a lone, glowing Howsh standing on the shore of a large body of water. With his arms raised high, a giant boulder levitated above the water. Three Pashier savages, concealed in the rocks behind him, held raised spears. Their murderous intent clear . . .

Cuddy knew hundreds of scrolls had been unearthed in the vaults of *Calirah*. Pashier elders would not divulge what had been discovered there, so only a few knew the truth—that the Howsh were once great and wondrous beings: benevolent and highly spiritual. They introduced, instructed, primitive Pashier tribes in the ancient rituals of mind and spirit.

Returning to the present, Cuddy raised his chin. *Yes... I understand you perfectly. And I hope you understand... that you are not getting anywhere near Haffan. Best you return to your ship now... be airborne and gone while you still can.*

Irritation flashed in the old Howsh's eyes, then was quickly replaced with something else. Surprise... *perhaps incredulity*?

Cuddy heard the robot communicating again. As it stepped closer to Calph, Cuddy watched the way it moved—like an elderly man with a hesitant gate. The thin leg appendages looked as if they could snap under its own insignificant weight any moment. The robot's face was more of an artificial projection than having actual features, such as eyes, nose and a mouth.

"I'm not here to harm the one you call Haffan," Calph said. "On the contrary, she is immensely important. Far more than you could possibly know."

The Howsh had spoken vocally, in near-perfect English. Cuddy, taken aback by the alien's surprising ability to throw one curve ball after another, replied, "Let me ask you a question. Why destroy your own ships... your own kind?" Cuddy let his eyes drift toward the smoky remnants of the still-glowing ships' superstructures.

"Feculence of the cosmos... any association I once had, other than genetic, with the Howsh has long since passed."

"Then you side with the Pashier?"

Calph sneered at that. "You arrive at childish binary conclusions. This or that... good or bad... Howsh or Pashier. You, yourself, a freakish hybrid of human and Pashier genome, exemplify my point. Rise above all that, Earthling, and you may one day elevate into something more than . . . the present, poor excuse of organic protoplasm standing before me."

Cuddy, unsure how to respond to that, said nothing.

"I do not wish to destroy you and your cohorts. Your ship has no weapons; you come before me unarmed. I am not sure if that is a sign of bravery or stupidity. Hand-over Haffan. She will not be harmed."

"I'd die before I let that happen," Cuddy responded back flatly. The Calph appraised him wearily. "I am sure you would," he said. "Commendable."

Cuddy shrugged. He didn't need or want the alien's approval.

"There is one other choice," Calph offered.

"I'm listening."

"Come with me. Come with me . . . and help fulfill the prophesy."

"Prophesy?"

For the first time, Cuddy saw the old Howsh smile. "The Prophesy of Harkstrong . . ."

chapter 18

Seven years earlier . . .

Once they'd left the cabin—drove away in his American Motors Rambler a half- mile along a winding, two-track lane—Slatch made a right turn onto the main road. He glanced over at the boy, sitting quietly next to him on the bench seat. Slatch recognized so much of the youngster's father in his eyes.

Everything about the boy was awkward; Cuddy's bowl-cut bangs needed to be trimmed. He wondered if that was Dotty's way of telling everyone the boy met that he was a retard. Slatch knew that word wasn't used anymore. Wasn't . . . *what did they call that?* Oh yeah, politically correct. There were a slew of tell-tale signs that this eleven/ twelve-year-old kid wasn't playing with a full deck—like the magic-marker arrow on only one sneaker; the t-shirt worn inside out and put on backwards, and that ridiculous, home-cut hair.

"Where are we going?" the kid asked.

"We talked about that already . . . twice now."

The boy nervously fiddled with his sock. "Momma says I'm not supposed to go anywhere without telling her first. Does she know where I'm going?"

"Sure, she does . . . you're going to meet your pa." Slatch rolled down his window and spit tobacco juice into the wind. He felt the boy's eyes on him as he wrangled a can of chew out of his pocket. Thumbing open the lid, he secured a pinch of the stuff deep along his lower gums.

"Every boy needs his pa. Things a pa can teach you ain't the same as what your ma teaches you. It's called balance. You understand what I'm *saying*?"

"I guess. Um . . . what's your name again?"

"Slatch."

"I don't remember much about my pa. Will he know who I am?"

"Of course, he will. Word has it, he's stopped with the boozing. Got his temper under control."

Cuddy looked back at Slatch with uncomprehending eyes. "Why doesn't he live with us anymore? I don't remember much . . . but I know he doesn't live with me and Ma and Kyle. Oh . . . and Rufus." Cuddy looked into the backseat with sudden alarm. "Where's Rufus?"

"Dog's fine. I'm sure he's home with your ma. Why don't you quiet down for a spell? We got a ways to go and I need to think."

* * *

Jackie replaced the receiver back onto the ancient-looking wall-mounted telephone. Her father would arrive to pick her up in about twenty minutes. She turned and stared out the kitchen window. Another cruiser had just joined the mix of police vehicles out front. Sheriff Bone, standing center stage, was making exaggerated hand movements, like a general directing his troops on where to make the next attack. Only this was no military action—it was a full-out search for a missing kid. A special-needs boy she'd left alone in the middle of a field. This was all her fault. Sure, Kyle said it was his doing—since Cuddy was his brother, but she knew different. Cuddy was her best friend. How could she have been so . . .

"Is he coming?" Kyle asked from the hallway.

Jackie nodded. "On his way."

The screen door's hinges screeched, followed by a loud *clap,* as the door slammed shut. Momma Perkins strode into the kitchen, her face flushed, inhaling long, deliberate, gulps of air.

"What's happening now, Momma?" Kyle asked.

Joining them at the window, she replied, "They've sent a patrol car around to all the neighboring farms. All six of them."

"He wasn't there?" Jackie asked.

Momma shook her head—still wringing an old dishtowel in her hands. "Well . . . no one was home at one farm. The old McFarland place . . . Slatch's farm." Momma's brow furrowed—as if something new had occurred to her. She looked from Jackie to Kyle, then asked, "You see anyone working the fields when you were out there?"

"Sheriff already asked me that," Kyle said.

Jackie considered the question. *No one had asked her.* "There was puffs of smoke."

"What do you mean *puffs of smoke*?" Momma asked.

"It was pretty far off. Only reason I noticed was because I heard a distant sound . . . could have been a truck."

"Or a tractor?"

"Yeah . . . but I didn't see it. And I know the McFarland farm. I'm not supposed to go anywhere near that place. Not sure why. Weird. My dad just reminded me again the other day." Jackie watched Momma's face suddenly lose all color.

chapter 19

Cuddy used telepathy to reach out to Bob. *Stay with the ship and watch over Haffan. Instruct the others to join me out here.* Surprised, he heard the Howsh grunt under his breath. *How is it my telepathic communications are so easily eavesdropped into, even by aliens?* Cuddy mused.

Jackie was the first one to join Cuddy's side. From her expression, she was appraising the alien with a mixture of distaste and fascination. Her eyes narrowed as she took in the robot, standing several paces behind Calph.

Kyle and Tony arrived next. Both, standing somewhat taller than normally, were undoubtedly trying to look bigger and tougher than they actually were. Last to arrive was Brian, acting bored and disinterested, though Cuddy had learned a long time ago they were simply defense mechanisms. Distrust, also an inflated ego, influenced much of Brian's outer actions.

Cuddy said, "This is Lorgue Supreme Eminence Calph. Apparently, he's come here for Haffan."

"That's not going to happen," Jackie said with alarm.

"Why'd he torch his own ships?" Tony asked. "Not that I'm complaining or nothing."

"It seems he no longer associates with the Howsh . . . or any single race, creed, or doctrine." For Calph's benefit, Cuddy pointed to the others. "This is Jackie, those two are Kyle and Tony . . . that one over there is Brian."

"And this is Spilor . . . my assistant," Calph said, without so much as a gesture toward the spindly-looking robot behind him.

Jackie's nostrils flared wide. Clearly, she'd just gotten a good whiff of Calph's stink. She asked him, "So, what do you want with Haffan? How did you even know she was here . . . here with us?"

"It does not matter how or why I do the things I do. What you should be more concerned with is your own survival."

Brian gestured toward the Marauder ship. "He has a point. I say we give him the brat and be done with it. Not our circus . . . not our monkeys."

Jackie waved off his ridiculous comment. "Again, what do you need her for?"

"Her involvement with the quest was foreseen 8,000 years ago. Without her, it all stops here, Calph said. "Ten years of my life in seclusion. Wasted . . . all for nothing."

"What quest?" Cuddy prompted. "Is this related to that Prophesy of Harkstrong - thing you spoke of earlier?"

"Correct. She must accompany me to *Calirah*—to the vaults there, on the nearby planet of Darriall."

"What are you after?" Kyle asked.

"It is where ancient scrolls were unearthed decades ago by Pashier elders . . . the hidden history of both Pashier and Howsh. That . . . also writings referencing Harkstrong, but only in vague . . . nonspecific passages."

"Why do you care, Dude? Eight thousand years ago is a long time. Maybe time to move on. Namaste and all that . . ."

Calph assessed Tony a few beats before replying. The alien looked tired, in no mood to be answering all their questions. "That, human, is a good question. Why should I care? Do not think I haven't asked myself that same question a thousand times across a thousand light years of space. The Howsh are intent on nothing short of full extinction of the Pashier race. On the other hand, the Pashier are content to excuse their own past crimes; to let them go unaccounted for. The destiny of the two races are woven together . . . neither cognizant of the fact that their own survival depends on the continuance of the other. It is so written."

Kyle said, "Well . . . we need to get back. Have an important delivery to make. Time is ticking and as interesting as your quest appears . . ." he let his words trail off.

Cuddy was reminded that Kyle's singular driving purpose was to lessen his own guilt in bringing the chicken pox disease to Primara. But he was right. The Pashier were in dire need of the wellness chamber, sitting within the hold on the *Evermore*'s lower deck.

"As I've stated . . . you are all free to go. My interests lie with the alien child. Bring me Haffan and you can be on your way," Calph said.

It hit Cuddy in that exact moment that his own future was, somehow, inexplicitly tied to this strange alien being. Perhaps something tied to telepathy or perhaps the last prophetic words spoken to him by Tow: *Soon I will travel to the other side of Rah. There I will better assist you and my people. . . .*

Cuddy said, "Give me your word . . . on your honor . . . that nothing will happen to Haffan."

"Wait. You can't be considering handing her over to him!" Jackie said.

"I do . . . I give you my word . . . she will be safe."

"No!" Jackie said, defiantly.

Cuddy turned to Jackie. "I will go with them. The rest of you return to Primara."

"Sounds good to me," Brian said.

Jackie pursed her lips, attempting to grasp the quickly unraveling situation. "Are you sure about this, Cuddy? Following such an extreme course is necessary?"

"If feels right."

Calph said, "As we speak, the imminent demise of Primara is underway. That vessel," he gestured toward his ship, "the Marauder . . . belongs to Lorgue Prime Eminence Norsh."

"We know perfectly well who Norsh is," Kyle said.

"That is his warship. A prototype, outfitted with new technology, having advanced capabilities . . . ones that even shield against telekinesis." Calph looked at Brian. "As powerful as you are, human, your powers are useless against that kind of passive induction shielding."

Brian merely shrugged in response.

"How did you acquire the ship?" Cuddy asked.

"I stole it."

No one said anything for several moments.

"The world you call Primara . . . the Pashier Promised Land . . . will be attacked soon. An entire fleet of Marauders is being retrofitted with the very same technology. Your Earth may, soon, be next. Perhaps not immediately, but the Howsh are well aware of the ancient writings. The reference to an azure and emerald planet make Earth the obvious one."

"Why would Earth be of any interest to the Howsh?" Jackie asked.

Her query seemed to amuse Calph. "It isn't so much Earth . . . as it is *you humans*. A secular band of young humans, you are chronicled about in the ancient writings. *A band* of *redeemers,* is the more accurate phrasing . . . a small band of redeemers, dwelling on the third world beyond the yellow star . . . an azure and emerald planetoid. It is so written that the band of redeemers will deliver upon the soil of Primara a heritage pod and new Pashier life will thence reemerge."

"So, we're like famous?" Tony asked. "What else do those ancient writings say about us?"

"More than I can share with you at this time. Let me just say this . . . as the destinies of the Howsh and the Pashier are closely intertwined, so too are yours. But the final fate of the Pashier, as well as the Howsh, is not set in stone. Nor is yours. The decisions you make today . . . here and now . . . may very well have immense repercussions later on. I have been careful to let such decision-making be yours and yours alone."

"What's your angle in all this?" Brian asked. "What do you get out of meddling in everyone else's business?"

"As I said, we're talking about the fate of two intertwined civilizations. I simply am a warrior turned scholar. Their ancient past was inscribed onto animal hide scrolls. Or chiseled into stone tablets. So too is their future. The Howsh and Pashier civilizations may have come to their respective ends . . . a crossroads is now upon us . . . one where billions of lives lie in the balance. How could I not become involved with such an endeavor? What could possibly hold more importance for me . . . for anyone?"

"How long before Primara is attacked?" Cuddy asked.

"It could be days . . . possibly weeks," Calph said.

"And this quest of yours. How exactly does it help? Stop an attack?" Cuddy asked.

"By the dissemination of knowledge, human. I want you to listen to me carefully . . . because this is important."

"I'm listening . . ." Cuddy said seeing the seriousness on Calph's face.

"As it presently stands, few Howsh know of their forefathers' true natural capabilities; that Howsh life forces too can re-cycle over many lifetimes, via heritage pods. Like the Shain Ritual of Awakening, of the Pashier. What you do not know, could not know, is the simple truth . . . that the Howsh are dying out. Becoming extinct. They are unaware, as a species, of the need to re-cycle their life forces—the only solution to their impending demise as a people. They need to return to their old ways."

They let that sink in.

"You say certain Howsh higher-ups . . . elders . . . know about this," Jackie said. "That they've read the ancient writings too, and know about their commonality with the Pashier, right? I would think they would see it as a good thing; a way to save their species and live on forever having incredible telepathic and telekinetic powers. Why keep it a secret from the masses?"

"The answer is simple," Calph replied. "Hatred."

"Hatred?"

"The Howsh elders . . . those who comprise the Howsh High Council . . . rule with an unforgiving power. They are a deeply religious . . . sectarian, bunch. They have followed a doctrine of hate for millennia. Where their differences with the Pashier have been an ongoing, timeless, drumbeat, the mere future prospect of developing a closer bond with their interminable enemy . . . well . . . that cannot be allowed."

"That's bogus," Tony said.

The others looked to Cuddy, who noted in all their glances that they would probably follow his lead. Even Brian. "I'll instruct Bob to pilot the *Evermore* back to Primara and deliver them the wellness chamber. Those here who wish to return to Primara with the orb, that's fine."

"Nah . . . I'm with you, kemosabe," Tony said, and Brian, rolling his eyes, said, "Fine. I'll come along," just as Kyle said, "Me too."

Jackie smiled. "Well, there's no way I'm letting Haffan go off with this guy without me. So, I guess we're all going . . . together."

chapter 20

Moving up the gangway, Cuddy, holding onto Haffan's hand, entered what he surmised was some kind of airlock compartment, something the *Evermore* didn't have.

The others were already onboard—*somewhere.* It had taken close to thirty minutes for the team to assemble whatever belongings they deemed essential from the *Evermore* and transfer them over to the Marauder ship. Continuing into the main lower deck, Cuddy was surprised to see a flurry of activity ahead. For some oddball reason, he'd assumed Lorgue Supreme Eminence Calph was traveling alone on the big warship. Just him and the odd robot—but now, in retrospect, he knew that to be improbable. Piloting the *Evermore*, less than one quarter of its size, would have been no easy feat for Cuddy. A spaceship this large and complex would require a sizable crew.

Cuddy heard a power saw in use—also hammering and clanging—sounds of new construction going on. Over the racket, Haffan yelled, "What are they doing in here? It's so loud!"

A partially constructed bulkhead, taking shape ahead, had a slew of various types of cabling hanging down like bundles of spaghetti. Cuddy spotted Calph across the wide expanse of the lower deck, assisting two Howsh with a large piece of equipment. Still partially wrapped in its protective shipping material, they were jockeying it into position. Surprised and angered by what he saw, Cuddy strode up to the Howsh Lorgue Supreme Eminence.

"What have you done? This wellness chamber is needed by the Pashier. Lives depend on it reaching Primara within the next few days!" And then, in an instant, Cuddy realized that particular piece of equipment was somewhat different from the one strapped down within the sub-deck hold of the *Evermore*. Most definitely a wellness chamber, although somewhat larger than the one they'd found.

"Sorry . . . I just assumed . . ." Cuddy's voice faltered.

But Calph's attention was still focused on getting the chamber positioned into the exact right place. "Push . . . scoot it up against the bulkhead." The two Howsh did as instructed and the big chamber slid into position. "Get the cabling harness configured and test it, then retest it before closing up that access panel."

Both subordinates, giving him a half bow in response, said nothing. For the first time, Calph looked over and acknowledged Cuddy, then stared down at Haffan. Cuddy tried to read the Eminence's expression. *Was it concern?* No . . . more like *reverence.*

As the Howsh knelt down to her level, Haffan screwed up

her face and said, "You reek like a dead animal," and placed a palm over her mouth and nose.

Calph's grin was somewhat unsettling—almost as if the Howsh's physicality was not configured for that kind of facial expression. "After today, there will be operational washing rooms in place. And I promise you, Haffan, I will be the first one to take advantage of them." Glancing up at Cuddy, he said, "I told you this was a prototype ship. As you can see, we're in the process of building necessary accouterments in it now. Come . . . I will show you to your cabins."

Cabins? Cuddy thought. There were none onboard the *Evermore,* only communal sleeping berths.

They followed Calph through more construction zones. So far, Cuddy counted five crewmembers besides Calph. Stepping onto an open platform, he waved Cuddy and Haffan to join him. The platform began to move—ascending upward. Cuddy briefly caught a glimpse of two other deck levels in the same disarray, construction-wise, at the lower level. He thought he spotted the robot, Spilor—a ghostly figure—only a blur of movement lurking within the construction area. He felt unsure about what he'd seen.

The lift slowed and came to a stop on level four. Cuddy wondered, *how many more levels exist above this one, if any?*

Following closely behind Calph, as he moved quickly along a softly lit passageway, no signs of construction work was evident here. Calph stopped and gestured to the end of the passageway—an oblong cul-de-sac, of sorts. "We completed our alterations on this section of the ship first . . . in anticipation of your arrival."

Eight hatchways currently stood wide open. Jackie appeared from one, off to their right. "Hey, I have you both situated on either side of my quarters. This definitely is a step up from the *Evermore*! Nice having my own head here."

"I will leave you to get situated. You can come find me later . . . on the lower deck . . ." With that, Calph headed off. Jackie waited a few beats before remarking, "In anticipation of your arrival? So he really did know that we'd all be coming along . . . even before we'd agreed to do so."

"Yeah. I don't know . . . I found that a strange thing for him to say too." Cuddy shrugged.

"Are we going to live here now?" Haffan asked.

Jackie held out a hand. "Come on, let's go find where everyone will be bunking."

Haffan didn't hesitate, quickly exchanging Cuddy's hand for Jackie's. Cuddy followed them through the hatchway—into a compact, nicely laid-out quarters that held a bed, a small desk, and a small vertical closet. An adjoining hatchway led to a head.

"Your quarters and mine, Cuddy, are pretty much identical to this one," Jackie said. "There's even a shower, which I'm looking forward to using as soon as possible."

Cuddy, gazing out a circular porthole window, could just make out the *Evermore* in the distance. All cabins faced forward—situated along the ship's bow.

"I'll be staying in here all alone?" Haffan asked, her forehead creased with concern.

"No worries; we're right next door . . . on either side of you," Cuddy said.

Whereas everyone had brought along several satchels each—filled with clothes and an odd accumulation of *stuff*—it occurred to Cuddy the child had brought nothing with her. She didn't wear clothes and, being homeless, had nothing now to unpack, which only underscored the alien child's state of vulnerability.

The three turned toward the entrance hatch, hearing raised voices. Kyle, Tony, and Brian were in the corridor, in the midst of a loud argument.

"What's wrong... what's all the commotion about?" Cuddy asked.

Kyle and Tony glared at Brian, who responded, "Hey, Cuddy's no longer the captain. We're on a whole other ship so I take orders from only one person now... me!" Brian stared at the others defiantly.

Kyle said, "He stole something... when down on the first level."

"What did you take?" Cuddy asked. "We've been here less than ten minutes and you're already causing a problem?"

"Hey... I'm watching out for us. We don't know anything about these aliens. What their true motives are for us."

"What did you take?" Cuddy asked again.

Finally, Brian lifted his shirt—just high enough to expose some item tucked into the waistband of his jeans.

"Is that..."

"A weapon," Jackie blurted before Brian could answer. "Where did you get that?"

"It was just lying there . . . next to a bunch of tools on the deck. I'm keeping it."

"Do you even know how to use it?" Kyle asked.

"No clue, but I'll figure it out. I'm smart that way."

"You gonna let him get away with that?" Jackie asked Cuddy.

"Brian's right, I'm not captain of this ship. He wants to start stealing from these guys . . . he can face the repercussions when they come." To be truthful, Cuddy wasn't completely sure what Brian stole was a terrible idea. Though he probably shouldn't have, knowing they had some kind of protection on hand might not be such a bad thing.

"Where are you going?" Jackie said to Cuddy.

"To talk with Calph. Bob just informed me the *Evermore* is ready to head out. I want to get a better idea what will be happening to us before our sole, only alternative means of transportation leaves the planet."

chapter 21

Cuddy retraced his steps and headed back down the corridor, then stepped onto the lift platform. It took him a moment to decipher the controls, before sending the contraption downward.

The AI orb, back on the *Evermore*, telepathically spoke to him. *Shall I return once the wellness chamber is successfully delivered to Primara?*

Cuddy, thinking he detected concern in the AI-orb's question, quickly discounted it. An AI-orb, no matter how intelligent, was incapable of having feelings.

No... wait there for further instructions. I know we are heading to Darriall, but after that... I have no idea.

Understood. Is there a message for Tow, Captain Perkins?

Cuddy wanted to say *yes, of course*, he had a message for Tow, but what could he possibly say in a succinct, perfectly wrapped-up, short sentence, or two? Especially since he didn't know why he was there—about to place the lives of his fellow crew in jeopardy, and the alien child as well. Even, perhaps, an entire race of people he'd come to care so much about.

Just tell Tow we're doing all we can to save Primara. We're heading into uncharted waters . . . he'll understand the reference.

The lift settled onto level 1—back to construction racket noise and the robot Calph called Spilor.

Goodbye. Have a safe voyage home, Cuddy conveyed telepathically to Bob. He thought he heard the sound of the *Evermore's* lift thrusters engaging outside, underneath the construction noise.

The robot approached him in its knee-jerky-stepping stride. Its projected-on face, like a mask conveniently worn, looked both serious and beyond creepy. Cuddy wondered if Calph too shared a similar perception of the robot, or if he'd simply, over time, become too used to its strange appearance.

"I'm looking for the Eminence Calph."

"Then you have come to the wrong level," Spilor replied flatly.

"What level can I find him on?"

"Come, I will direct you to him," the robot said, stepping onto the lift alongside Cuddy, and setting the controls for Level 3. As they rose, subtle flashes of light caught Cuddy's attention. Glancing to his right, he noticed Spilor cycling through a variety of facial expressions—as if unsure what the appropriate emotional response should be in any given moment. The robot finally settled on the serious—almost angry-looking—mask projection it had worn mere moments before. *Weird.*

The lift slowed and came to a halt. Spilor stepped off and

headed directly forward. Cuddy following, took in the new surroundings. Like Level 1, construction was taking place and more Howsh crewmembers were hard at work. Cuddy caught their sideways glances turn in his direction as he walked past.

"What exactly is being built on this level?" Cuddy asked to the back of the robot's head and narrow shoulders.

"Back over there are the officers' quarters . . . and right there is the officer's lounge."

"What's that?" Cuddy asked, gesturing with his chin, before realizing the robot would have no idea what he was referring to. Surprised, Cuddy heard Spilor reply, "That is the Tacticians Espy Table . . . or simply the Espy."

As they approached the large table-like affair, Cuddy better assessed the thing. Rectangular in shape, it seemed higher, about twice the size of a standard pool table. Something crewmembers would stand around, he figured. Spilor, perhaps sensing his interest, reached out a spider-like arm appendage. Touching the edge of the table, it powered up and came alive. Cuddy leaned over the surface, watching it take shape, and realized it was far more than just the average 3D display. Reaching down, he touched a miniature building and actually experienced *full-tactile* realism. Then, on waving his hand over what remained of two tiny, smoldering scout ships, he felt the sensation of heat rising up to touch his fingers. *Very cool*, he thought. Spilor moved a finger-like digit along the table edge and more of the surroundings lying outside Tripette City came into view. "Incredible realism and detail."

"We steal only the best."

Cuddy, turning to see where the voice came from, watched as Calph approached from the direction of the bow. His robes rustled as he moved, and his tall staff was grasped securely in his right fist. "Come . . . let me show you the rest of the *Farlight's* bridge."

"*Farlight*?"

"Roughly translated . . . so what do you think of the moniker I chose for her?"

"Works for me," Cuddy said.

"Leave us," Calph snapped, directing an unrelenting gaze toward the robot.

No wonder his mechanical cohort has such a lousy disposition, Cuddy thought, not sad to see the robot move away.

Turning, Calph raised his staff, using it to point out various things of interest around them. Cuddy noted there were no seats anywhere—no place to sit down.

"Like with the Epsy, the crew is expected to stand when on the *Farlight's* bridge."

Much of the horseshoe-shaped space was further along in construction than the rest of the ship. A curved observation window dominated the front of the compartment. On both sides were separate bridge stations—four to a side—though Cuddy doubted they were typically manned at the same time. One thing was sure: everything possessed the very latest technology. "How much of this is Howsh tech?" Cuddy asked.

"None of it. Ripped out nearly all the Howsh prototype bridge components in existence when we acquired the vessel. Some is Pashier, some is Gulk, some is Womak. Now, over there... forward and to the starboard side... we have the Communications Station. Next, we have the Tactical and Weaponry Station, and across... over there on the port-side bulkhead—is the Engineering Station. Forward is the Navigation Station. I will explain the other stations at a more appropriate time."

Cuddy didn't think a more appropriate time would ever be necessary. *He wasn't along to crew for the Howsh officer.* Calph then moved to the center of the bridge. A semi-circular red railing sectioned-off the area where a bridge commander, or captain, usually stood, when directing his bridge crew personnel. Turning around, the Espy table was right there—easily viewable by both a commanding officer and his junior officers. To Cuddy, it seemed a smart, well-thought-out, layout. A far cry from the tight little bridge on the *Evermore*, though it was a bridge he already missed.

Cuddy found the old Howsh commander staring at him. "What is it you wish to speak to me about, Cuddy Perkins?"

"You mentioned the fate of the Pashier was not set in stone, but isn't it? You knew exactly where to find the Pashier child, Haffan. Where to find the *Evermore,* and the rest of us, here in Tripette City."

Calph nodded, gesturing with his staff to their surroundings. "Don't confuse advanced navigation and tracking technology with what the ancient writings provide. After ten years, one becomes somewhat proficient at deciphering the meanings of things. The clues are there, if one knows how, where, to look for them. But I have gone as far as I can, and that is why you are here. More important, that is why the child is here."

"So I want to see these ancient writings . . . these tablets . . . for myself," Cuddy said. "See how you determined so much from something . . . so . . . completely detached from our present reality. How can 8000-year-old writings provide that kind of detail?"

"Perfectly understandable questioning. You still do not know if you can trust me; if our priorities are in alignment. You are having second thoughts."

Cuddy shrugged. "If what you told us is true, that the fate of an entire people . . . their world, yours too . . . hangs in the balance of the ongoing quest you are on, that we are all on . . ."

Calph cut in. "Then it is time now we leave this ruined world. Time we venture to the vaults of *Calirah*—onto the nearby planet of Darriall. There you will see, for yourself, why young Haffan is the key to understanding the Prophecy of Harkstrong."

chapter 22

V*ordiff* was certainly in a class by itself, meant to exemplify Howsh superiority. To whom, though, Norsh didn't know. He stood among other oglers on the floor level, staring up at the ongoing proceedings waiting for them to finish up. The newly constructed Howsh *Vordiff* Council Hall loomed both high and somewhat daunting before them. Against a distant backdrop—one as black as obsidian and meant to represent deep space—the entire hall appeared to hover like a great, cleaved-in-half world, totally unique unto itself. Norsh took in the rotunda's exposed, curved, inner architecture—admiring the unique mathematical simplicity of design and engineering finesse. Tiered layers of individual, semi-circular, alcove seating areas—hundreds of them—were hierarchical; specifically assigned to council members by rank.

Facing toward a central dais, no fewer than a thousand Howsh listened to some council member windbag pontificate on the importance of propagating Howsh decency and morality across the galaxy. An endless diatribe Lorgue Prime Eminence Norsh had heard many times before.

Norsh had been summoned to attend unexpectedly, by Council Member Leshand. Leshand too was an Elder, though not many council members were similarly entitled. Elders held the real power; positions inherited—mostly passed down—from fathers and from grandfathers who were Elders. One did not decline a summoning, not if he cared to maintain his standing among the fleet, so Norsh traveled thirty-eight light years to attend the newly constructed Howsh center of government—*Vordiff* and *Vordiff Hall*—where he now stood. Norsh pondered what Leshand wanted from him—*some special favor*. For all the power the Howsh dignitaries carried, they were not above feeling nervous of late. Only a few Howsh in attendance were still unaware of the ancient, secret scriptures found in buried caverns on Darriall; scriptures chronicling how the Howsh long ago were conquered. Conquered, then enslaved, by the savage Pashier. Still humiliated by that prospect, their rage turned to bitter hatred, which only intensified over the years. The Pashier were demonized. Their recycling of life, via their heritage pods, and their extra- ordinary mental powers were proof enough of their hellish influence. But the scriptures, mostly inscribed on rock tablets, told of Pashier and Howsh both capable of using esoteric powers during various eras throughout their entangled histories. That kind of information could never be shared with the Howsh masses. Even discussing the secret Darriall scriptures could quickly lead to an expedient execution.

The problem was there were hidden dissenters among the attending council members—a handful of Elders ready for change. Ready to bury the proverbial hatchet and unite with the abhorred Pashier. Council Member Leshand, Norsh suspected, was one such individual.

Meeting adjourned, it took close to an hour for the hall to empty out. Norsh took in the recently vacated *Vordiff Hall,* marveling how beautiful it was without countless furry dignitaries clamoring around within its fine walls.

"Ah . . . there you are, Lorgue Prime Eminence Norsh."

"Sire," Norsh greeted back, not hearing the dignitary Elder come up behind him. Like all Elders, he wore a draping of scarlet ivy leaves—angled across one shoulder, then positioned on the opposite hip. The Howsh Elder looked ancient to Norsh. His long matted body fur, that long ago had turned silver, was almost pure white in color. Norsh briefly wondered how the old coot ever managed to climb the hundreds of stairs, leading up to the hall rotunda where his seating alcove was located.

"Thank you for coming. Walk with me, will you, Eminence Norsh?"

"Of course, sire." Noting that the Elder was quite stooped and walking very slowly, Norsh offered him an extended elbow for support, which Leshand accepted. Feeling a surprisingly strong grip on his arm, Norsh was reminded how much he detested the old, misleadingly innocuous, council member. That it was he, plus several others, who had continuously blocked his orders—orders allowing him to destroy Primara once and for all; and bring the Pashier one step closer to complete eradication.

Norsh was selected to command a new fleet of Marauder spacecraft, the most advanced warships in the quadrant. A high-visibility position, it would ratchet him up from Lorgue *Prime* Eminence to the highest rank—Lorgue *Supreme* Eminence. Not since Lorgue Supreme Eminence Calph, had anyone attained to that lofty position—nor wielded as much power. But now the title was well within reach. This powerful council member could make that decision possible for him. Norsh tuned back into what Leshand was saying.

"... perhaps, with the exception of the Womak, the Gulk are an interesting adversary, with surprising military capabilities. An enemy of highly strategic importance whom you must contend with ... immediately."

"Yes, sire. But the Gulk are on the far side of the quadrant; eighty-seven light years away, to be exact. First, with your permission, I would like to complete my current mission ... the full destruction of Primara, and the eradication of any more hidden heritage pods."

"That topic is not open for discussion, Lorgue *Prime* Eminence Norsh. The council members have already made the appropriate determination."

Norsh doubted the Gulk were any more a threat today than they were ten years ago when that race of green humanoid vermin were first discovered, lurking around the far side of the sector. Now, with war imminent, the issue of Pashier extermination had conveniently been put on hold.

"It comes down to limited resources. Examine who would do us the most immediate harm. The Pashier have no weapons;

no intention to expand beyond their world, while the Gulk... a known militaristic aggressor... are seeking further spatial conquests. The Pashier can wait."

Norsh expected nothing less from Leshand, who seemed oblivious to what the real threats were within the galaxy. Still, he was his superior and Norsh could only push things so far. "Sire... I am at your command. Once I intersect with the fleet, in three days' time, we will make haste to deal with the Gulk. Although I don't fully agree with the decision, of course I will follow both your, and the council's, directive in that regard."

"That is good. I would like to promote you, Lorgue Prime Eminence Norsh. It is long overdue. You have proven your loyalty. Not forgetting also your relentless hatred of the Pashier, which many of the council members find appealing."

Yes, but not you, Norsh thought.

"As you know... I have substantial influence over my colleagues."

"Yes, sire. You are highly-regarded among your peers."

"One other thing you need to be informed about... concerns your brother."

"My brother?" Norsh repeated. He only had one brother. Two years his junior, Lorgue Sub Eminence Langer, like himself, was on the fast track within the fleet. To say the two were highly competitive, both having fleet advancement ambitions, would be a gross understatement. But Norsh did have a measure of affection for his brother—as long as he did not interfere with his own aspirations.

"He has been informed of his position in an upcoming,

highly important, mission. He will report directly to you. He will be commanding a small crew onboard the *Dubon*, a fine smaller ship. Keep me well informed regarding his progress. Make contact with him immediately; have him set a course for Darriall. Once there, his mission is to enter the vaults of *Calirah*."

Norsh hesitated. "Yes, sire. And . . . what is he assigned to do there?"

"Await the arrival of the young Pashier sprout . . . the chosen one."

Norsh, acquainted enough with the secret scriptures, nearly rolled his eyes. He was well aware of the *mythical* young being the Elder referred to, although he personally regarded that inscription as nothing more than fable. Only scratchings on stone tablets, thousands of years old. It became clear suddenly that Leshand had lost his wits . . . *lost his fucking mind.* In spite of what he was hearing, Norsh tried to keep his expression neutral. "Sire, you are . . . certain . . . that this *sprout*, this Pashier child, will . . ."

"Do not patronize me with that tone of voice, Norsh. I know exactly how crazy this sounds. But with that said, there is much you still do not know. Too many ancient writings, prophesies, are exhibiting . . . certain truths . . . here in our present time."

"Are you certain my brother is best suited for this—"

Cutting Norsh off, Council Member Leshand said, "Apparently, Lorgue Sub Eminence Langer has something no one else possesses."

"And what is that, sire?"

"A clandestine connection, like non-other. Young Lorgue Sub Eminence Langer has assured the council that this *illusory* contact of his will bring the chosen one to us . . . like those ancient writings foretold."

"Who is this—?"

"Your brother refuses to divulge that information. But if there is even a small chance his assessment is true . . . we cannot ignore it."

Norsh was instantly relieved he hadn't been assigned to lead this ridiculous mission. All of a sudden, his mission to fight the Gulk no longer sounded quite so terrible. Still, he wondered what his brother was up to. He would have to press Langer for answers when he spoke to him next.

"What is it you would like him to do . . . when he finds her?"

"Convince the young sprout to locate, then open the vault, containing the ancient writings . . . those which refer to the Prophesy of Harkstrong. We must gain possession of this heralded prophecy. And then, upon completion, he is to eliminate anyone who is with her and bring her to me. Then he is to kill his crew . . . all those who would speak of the mission, the sprout, and the existence of the ancient scrolls."

chapter 23

Heading back up to Level 4, Cuddy contemplated two questions, then three. First, how was it that a Howsh, like Calph, possessed telepathic powers? Second, did he also have telekinetic powers—the psychic ability to mentally move some physical mass? And third, how did he come by those capabilities—was it similar to what happened to Brian and him? The automatic result of time spent within a wellness chamber?

The answers would have to wait. In the meantime, he needed to take extra care to protect Haffan, since she was the one the alien Calph was most interested in. Although Cuddy didn't think he meant her any harm, he wasn't confident enough to take any undue risks.

Where did you go?

Cuddy was halfway along the corridor when he mentally heard Haffan speak to him. Standing in front of her open cabin door, arms tightly crossed over her chest, she looked small—a petulant child impatiently waiting to confront him.

Cuddy hadn't come right back up after meeting with

Calph. Instead, he'd taken the lift—first down to Level 2, then to Level 1, wandering throughout their construction areas for several hours. He'd peered inside many compartments, examining various, newly installed equipment that he assumed was pilfered from some other ship, or even some other world.

Approaching Haffan, speaking aloud, he said, "Well . . . I talked to Lorgue Supreme Eminence Calph for a while. He showed me the bridge. Where they steer the ship from."

"I know what a ship's bridge is, stupid human," she retorted angrily.

"After that, I took a walk . . . checked out the rest of the ship."

"Didn't you think that I'd like to see the rest of the ship too?" she asked, indignation in her voice

"Okay . . . we can go for a walk later on. Maybe Jackie will come along and—"

Abruptly, Haffan spun on her heels, disappearing back into the cabin. The hatch door slid shut soundlessly. Cuddy stared at it, unsure how one should talk to children—Pashier or otherwise. Uncertain he wasn't just a grown-up child himself.

The other hatchways, with the exception of his own, were all closed. He thought about knocking on Jackie's, but decided against it. It was late and she was probably asleep. Entering his own quarters, he gasped, startled to find someone waiting inside for him.

"How is this even possible?" Cuddy asked, not entirely sure it wasn't some kind of trick or illusion. "How can you be here?"

Tow offered back a warm smile. "I am not here, Cuddy, not

really. I actually am . . ." Tow looked around the confines of the compartment. "On the other side of Rah."

It had already occurred to Cuddy that Tow's appearance was more ghost-like than physical, as he could still see the bulkhead, and the porthole window, behind his nearly transparent form.

"So, is this a telepathic communication?' Cuddy asked.

"Something like that," Tow replied.

"I didn't think you were going to leave for Rah yet. You said it would be days, possibly a week—"

Tow cut him off. "I could no longer wait, Cuddy; too many events now converging. It is where I will be of the most help to you and my people."

"Are you . . . like dead? Is that what the other side of Rah means . . . ?"

"You have asked me that before. The answer is no. And your human concept of death is utterly ridiculous. I will be here for a long while, and there are certain rules I must follow. Definitive structures one must always adhere to."

Cuddy's attention was suddenly drawn to a blurry movement near Tow's legs. Twice, something flitted past him, then disappeared just as quickly at the edge of the visualization.

"I am so sorry, Cuddy. I did not realize Rufus had followed me into the heritage pod." This time the yellow lab stopped short; sitting down, he leaned his big body against Tow's legs. Then, suddenly noticing Cuddy, he barked loudly several times as his short tail gyrated back and forth.

Conflicting emotions caught Cuddy off-guard—throat

constricting, his vision blurred with moisture. *God, there was so much he missed about his old life—that so much simpler life.* "Will Rufus be allowed to come back?" Cuddy asked, afraid to hear the answer.

"I honestly do not know as there are so many rules. Again, I am very sorry. But what I can tell you, he obviously is ridiculously happy to see you."

Yes, his dog did seem quite happy, Cuddy acknowledged, then wondered if Rufus would prefer, if given the choice, to be back on the farm. So much more there, for a dog to do. Or maybe not . . .

"My time here with you is short. There is much I must tell you so you must listen and hold off questions . . ."

"Okay," Cuddy said, nodding in compliance.

Rufus, lying on his side, immediately began to lick his testicles. Apparently things weren't so different on the other side of Rah.

"Pay attention, Cuddy. Soon, you will be landing."

Cuddy considered his comment. Strange, he wasn't aware the *Farlight* had even taken off, yet Tow somehow knew he was on the Howsh ship. Knew about them accompanying Lorgue Supreme Eminence Calph. He *really* wanted to know how Tow could possibly know these things.

"Darriall is a small planetoid; a neighbor to both Mahli and the Howsh home world of Rahin. Darriall is a 100%-automated library world. Once operated by sentient species, it all too often was a point of contention . . . of disagreements . . . between the Howsh and Pashier. So it was mutually agreed upon long ago that Darriall would remain neutral. But the only way to achieve that was to make it computer-operated and fully automated with robots as custodians."

Cuddy watched Rufus rise to his feet and walk out of view and briefly wondered if he would ever see his dog again.

"But the Darriall library fell into disuse," Tow continued. "Now, it has become more of a mausoleum than anything else; its power source, the robot attendants, are using ancient technology. Not that they are rusted, but clearly in a state of disrepair from lack of maintenance . . . and neglect."

"Perhaps Spilor will be able to repair them," Cuddy volunteered.

"Speaking of robots, there are security bots, protectors, around to prevent looting and the unauthorized removal of materials. Something you should be aware of. The actual Vault of Calirah is part of the tech library on Darriall. When I was last there, we found destroyed automatons lying around, which had been left there. We assumed it was due to an earlier Howsh raid, though I am not completely certain of that."

"Wait! I need to check what you want me to do. Should I be helping the Howsh . . . this Calph guy?"

"For now, yes. I do not believe he has ulterior motives, although the future is not set in stone by any means. That is why you must find the Prophesy of Harkstrong."

"And Haffan, somehow, is the key to that?" Cuddy asked.

"That is right," Tow said.

Tow's ghostly form was beginning to fade. Cuddy was having a hard time seeing him.

"The Prophesy of Harkstrong . . . is it a physical thing? Is it there, on Darriall?"

"Questions I do not have the answers for. You have progressed in time, beyond what is prophesized in the ancient writings. What is inscribed on the scrolls and tablets . . . Only you can avert catastrophe, Cuddy. You and the Pashier child."

"Tow . . . I can no longer see you."

"I must go now, Cuddy."

"Will I see you again?"

"Yes . . . eventually."

"Please, Tow, take good care of Rufus."

Alone in his cabin, Cuddy felt the weight of Tow's words. Sitting on the bed, he looked toward its end where, in his former *other*life, Rufus would be curled into a ball fast asleep. Cuddy let gravity and exhaustion pull his head onto the pillow. Within seconds, he was fast asleep.

chapter 24

Cuddy, blinking awake from a deep sleep, heard someone pounding on his hatch door. Glancing about his surroundings, remembering where he was, he rolled out of bed and went to the hatch. He waved a hand over the auto-latch mechanism and, as the hatch slid to one side, found Jackie and Haffan standing out there. Haffan scooted in past him as Jackie handed him a steaming cup of *something*. Bringing it up to his nose, he grunted approval. "Where'd you get the coffee?"

Jackie nodded. "I brought some with me."

Cuddy only recently had acquired a taste for the strong bitter brew. Of late, he found it tough to get going in the morning without drinking a cup. Surprised, he recognized the mug as one he'd used on the *Evermore*. Jackie, obviously, had put more thought into packing for the trip than he had.

"Who were you talking to last night in here?"

Cuddy spun around to stare at Haffan. "Talking to?" Before she could respond, he said, "What are you wearing?"

Haffan's eyes darted to Jackie—past Cuddy's shoulder.

"It's one of mine . . . just an old T-shirt," Jackie said. "Haffan kept asking me why she was the only one without clothes on."

Cuddy looked down at Haffan, now wearing Jackie's orange and blue Denver Broncos jersey—Number 18. One that fit Jackie nicely, but on Haffan was baggy, hanging down to her knees. He knew the Broncos were Jackie's favorite football team and she often slept in that jersey. Staring at the alien child, he frowned. Pashier did not wear clothes. Was this a mistake . . . were they already influencing her culture?

"Let it go, Cuddy, it's only a shirt. Not a big deal." Jackie went into the head and he heard running water. Coming out, she said, "Showers running. We're going to look for the galley."

About to tell them where to find it on Level 2, he decided to let them have the fun of exploring the ship, just as he'd done the night before. Grabbing his duffle bag, he hurried into the head to, hopefully, a hot shower.

* * *

Stepping off the lift on Level 2, Cuddy's senses were immediately accosted by nearby sounds of loud voices and laughter. Wonderful aromas too—hot pancakes, sizzling bacon, and other scents he didn't recognize but found equally tantalizing. When he entered the dining area—just outside of the galley kitchen—no less than twenty were seated around a large metal table. Several others were standing around the periphery—holding mugs, in either hands or claws, whatever the case might be. Four humans, one Pashier child, and seventeen Howsh aliens were passing plates of food around, conversing over and around each other, like it was some large family Sunday brunch get-together.

Kyle and Tony both gave him a quick nod then went back to eating and gabbing. Brian, sitting at the far end of the table didn't acknowledge Cuddy's arrival. Talking to one of only two female Howsh crewmembers, she laughed at something he said. Howsh females were anatomically bear-like. Like the Pashier, they typically didn't wear clothes or uniforms. As she scooted her chair back, she revealed a series of six full and round teats—three per side—down her furry abdomen. Cuddy felt his cheeks flush and averted his eyes.

He spotted Calph in the nearby open kitchen, standing in front of a stovetop grill. Wearing a long white apron, one claw held a formidable-sized spatula. Jackie got up from the table and, moving to Calph's side, took the spatula from him. "You've almost got it right. We'll let them cook just a tad longer. She waited a few seconds then used the spatula to pry up, and peek beneath, one of the still-cooking pancakes. "Perfect!" She flipped the pancake over and, sure enough, it was a delightful golden-brown in color. Glancing over at Cuddy, she said, "Grab a plate, sleepy head. Bacon and *jamma-rounds* are on the counter."

"Jamma-rounds?"

Lorgue Supreme Eminence Calph replied, "What you humans call breakfast. The Howsh refer to it . . . roughly translated . . . as morning-gorge. Jamma-rounds are served at every morning-gorge." He gestured with the spatula he retrieved from Jackie. "Take several . . . I made them myself."

Cuddy was handed an empty plate by an alien standing

nearby. One of the largest Howsh he'd ever laid eyes on, he was easily eight feet tall. "Thanks," he said, eying the bacon strips and Jamma-rounds, which looked like some kind of gooey-eggy concoction. No sooner did he start filling his plate, when Jackie grabbed it away. Handing it to Calph, he slapped three still-sizzling pancakes onto it.

"Syrup's on the table," Jackie said. "You can take my seat . . . I'm through eating."

Cuddy eyed the open space, then wedged his body between a Howsh crewmember he remembered seeing the day before and Haffan. With a mouth full of food, she asked, "Who were you talking to in your cabin last night?"

Cuddy remembered her asking him the same question earlier that morning, before Jackie scooted her from his quarters. "I was speaking with Tow."

From across the table, he got Kyle and Tony's attention.

"Does Tow look like me?" Haffan asked.

"Uh huh. He is Pashier, like you. He asked about you and told me to look out for you. Said you were very important." Cuddy took his first bite of the jamma-rounds.

Haffan watched him chew. Cuddy noticed Jackie and Calph watching him eat too.

"It's *kinda* like quiche," he said. Jackie made it for them several times back on the *Evermore*. If he was honest with himself, he liked these jamma-rounds a whole lot better. "Wow . . . this is really good!"

Cuddy caught Calph's triumphant expression then heard him utter a few self-satisfied growls.

Jackie, now behind him, leaned her weight into him. Her lips brushed his ear as she whispered, "Should we be talking about Tow, you know, around the Howsh? They are the enemy . . ."

Cuddy didn't answer her right away. The longer she pressed into him, the better. He breathed in the fragrance of her strawberry shampoo, while pretending to need extra time to chew his food, and then whispered back, "Tow thinks they're okay . . . but yeah, I'll watch what I say."

She gave a squeeze to his shoulder before pushing herself away.

"When will I get to meet Tow? Where will I live when I get to Primara? With you and Jackie? Haffan asked.

Tony rolled his eyes in Cuddy's direction. "Non-stop . . . kid never comes up for air."

"That's not nice," she responded.

Cuddy studied Haffan. "You know . . . you speak near-perfect English, Haffan. Probably better than I do."

She nodded as though it were no big deal. "I can speak Howsh pretty well too," and then spoke the alien language with apparent ease. Cuddy already knew the Pashier were exceptionally intelligent, far more intelligent than humans. Since she'd only been onboard the Howsh ship a few waking hours, it seemed impossible she could be so language gifted. Her smart-ass smile reminded him he'd be smart not to underestimate the Pashier seven-year-old.

Talk around the table quieted when the tall robot awkwardly crept into the dining area. Spilor wore a somewhat inappropriate facial projection this time—jovial, but teetering more on the side of creepy than happy. The robot momentarily glanced in Cuddy's direction and then at Haffan, who didn't return his smile. As Spilor made his way past them into the kitchen area, she said, "I like Bob better."

Kyle said, "That could be a character from a scary movie . . ."

Calph now stood at the head of the table. Somewhere along the line, he'd removed the apron and once again looked like the ship's commander. "We are approaching Darriall . . . I must take my place on the bridge."

"Thank you for morning-gorge . . . and your delicious jamma-rounds," Jackie said.

Others' appreciation too erupted from around the table. Calph responded by giving a slight bow of his large head, as Spilor handed him his staff. Before turning away, he looked at Cuddy, and said, "When you are done, Cuddy Perkins, would you please join me on the bridge? Please bring the young sprout . . ."

"We'll be there directly," Cuddy said.

"I'm coming too," Jackie said.

"So am I," Brian said, from the far end of the table. The female Howsh, no longer sitting by his side, was seated on his lap. For the second time that morning, Cuddy's face flushed red.

chapter 25

By the time they arrived, Darriall dominated the dark cosmos from the bridge. Cuddy wasn't sure what he expected the planet to look like, but it sure wasn't what he was now viewing. Bright pumpkin orange, its north and south poles were nearly as black as the deep space surrounding it, giving the planet—at least upon first glance—a strange fractured look. Like some giant being had taken massive bites out of the top and bottom.

Lorgue Supreme Eminence Calph, standing by the red railing at the center of the compartment, partially turned around as they approached. Cuddy and the others made their way onto the bridge, including Kyle and Tony, who didn't want to be excluded should something important occur. Cuddy noticed three Howsh crewmembers, situated in perimeter stations, giving no obvious indication their arrival was even noticed.

Calph seemed somewhat amused, noticing Cuddy's teammates, then gestured with the top of his staff at the Jack O'

Lantern world out the forward window. "We have arrived at Darriall," he said. "Before we proceed farther, there are precautions which need to be discussed. This is an automated world. Not much in the way of indigenous life, still there are security bots in various states of disrepair."

"Lorgue Supreme Eminence Calph, I've already gone over much of that with my team," Cuddy said.

"You've been to Darriall prior to this trip?" Calph asked, appearing confused.

"No . . . but I've been recently briefed."

Calph slowly nodded to himself. "That makes sense . . . you've been in contact with the Pashier Master."

Cuddy hadn't heard Tow referred to as a master before, but the truth was, the term certainly fit. Who else, among the Pashier, had done the same things he had; even traveled to the other side of Rah . . . *whatever that was.*

"The important thing is to get in and out as quickly, and as efficiently, as possible. Normally, I would not support a team this size to undertake such a mission, but each of you has a definite purpose . . . individually singled out, in the ancient writings, in one form or another."

"No shit!" Tony exclaimed. "Someone's written something about me?"

"That doesn't mean it was anything good," Brian retorted.

Looking out the forward window, Haffan walked toward the front of the bridge. With her back to everyone, she softly spoke, "I've had dreams about this place."

"Dreams . . . or your inner *nudges*?" Jackie asked.

Haffan turned around, seeming to mull over her question. "Both," she replied, gazing directly at the grisly-looking Lorgue Supreme Eminence Calph. Raising an arm, she pointed at him, then said, "You . . . you will kill someone today."

Cuddy exchanged a quick glance with his brother.

Kyle said, "Considering what was just said . . . about no one living down there, do you mean one of us? How accurate are your . . . *nudges* . . . anyway?"

Haffan didn't answer, momentarily looking lost in thought.

At some point, Spilor, on joining Calph's side, spoke to him in low tones. Cuddy could hear most of what the robot said. Apparently, another vessel was just detected in the area.

Calph turned to a Howsh crewmember, sitting at the tactical station.

The tactical officer said, "Long-range sensors have matched the vessel's unique characteristics . . . it is the *Dubon,* Supreme Eminence."

Considering what Spilor just said to Calph, Cuddy briefly wondered how the robot could possibly know that.

"That is Lorgue Sub Eminence Langer's ship. I shouldn't be surprised, although that certainly will complicate matters. How much time do we have before the *Dubon* arrives at Darriall?"

The tactical officer gave Calph the approximate time. Cuddy mentally converted the Howsh timeframe—*two and a half hours.*

* * *

Calph led the way out of the ship's airlock and into bright

daylight, where a strong wind billowed his long robe and whipped tufts of matted white fur. Using his staff purposefully, he took long strides toward the closest building.

All in all, there were eleven, counting Spilor, including a defensive team of three well-armed Howsh. One was the ginormous, eight-foot-tall Howsh Cuddy met earlier that morning, named Marzon.

The *Farlight* was presently docked on one of five empty circular landing pads within the cloverleaf-shaped formation, in the city of Calirah. Ten other elevated, cloverleaf-landing configurations, within the sprawling complex, were unoccupied; an indication this once was a bustling center of activity, but now was like an airport, minus all departing or arriving traffic. Studying the area, it became apparent the transportation hub's best days were far in the past.

Cuddy walked alongside Haffan, in the middle of the others. As usual, Haffan held tightly to his hand, staying close by his side.

"Why is it so windy here?" Haffan yelled into the gusts swirling and encircling them.

Jackie, walking on the child's other side, said, "We'll be inside shortly."

Cuddy looked back and saw the trailing behind, waif-like Spilor struggling to remain upright on both robotic feet. Come another big blast of wind and the robot might very well be swept over the edge of the superstructure. Since no one else had seemed to notice, Cuddy found he didn't care that much either. He suddenly was aware Brian was communicating with him—telepathically.

Don't answer me back, Cuddy . . . you don't know how to keep your damn thoughts private . . .

Cuddy did not t answer, for—as annoying as Brian's request was—it was true.

Look up, man.

Cuddy did as told. There were about thirty sentry bots rapidly descending down upon them from above. They looked similar to Bob, but these bots were larger. Each was armed with weaponry—multiple barrels extended out from metallic, octagonal-shaped structuring.

It might be up to us to fend them off . . . I have zero confidence that our armed fur-ball friends can protect us.

Hearing the high-pitch sound of multiple motors, Haffan looked up. With eyes large as saucers, she pointed upward.

They'd all reached the front of a multi-story, all-glass building that offered no indication how to get inside. No entrance door was visible as the security bots dropped into a semi-circle, surrounding them, and hovered there. Nervously, the three-armed Howsh raised their weapons.

Calph raised his staff in the air, perhaps attempting to bring attention to himself. Stepping up to the closest bot, he announced, "We mean you no harm. We are simple researchers . . . our only desire is to view the records."

Cuddy didn't like the security bots' presence around them one tiny bit. Calph should have anticipated them. Now, looking down the barrels of their multiple energy weapons, the seriousness of their situation was brought to hand. Brian was right to warn him, and he mentally agreed it was perhaps time they put their TK abilities to use then and there. Cuddy gazed down at Haffan and attempted to give her a reassuring smile.

"I don't think they believe you," Tony told Calph.

Calph made an angry-looking grimace.

A distorted, scratchy-sounding voice blared from the bot hovering closest to Calph. "Access to the records on Calirah is no longer permitted. Vandalism. Destruction. Theft. Return to your vessel, immediately!"

"I assure you, our arrival has been anticipated," Calph said. "I am Lorgue Supreme Eminence Calph. Check your database. Check who has clearance to proceed."

That seemed to make some sort of impact as a series of small panels slid opened along the underside of the close security bot. Four wire-thin articulating arms appeared—each sporting a three-digit claw. The claw moved with a jerky motion, remarkably similar to the way Spilor moved. And now Spilor was at Calph's side, raising-up two spidery-thin appendages. The security bot's four claws moved, then repositioned, as if to make contact with Spilor's somewhat hand-like appendages. Cuddy, watching, thought maybe they'd engage in some kind of robotic fist-bump, but Spilor would have none of that. Almost angrily, the robot flicked away the security bot's claws—as if slapping away a child's bothersome hands—and proceeded to insert both mechanical hands inside one of the open panels on the security bot.

"There's something just *wrong* about that," Tony said.

Cuddy watched Spilor cycle through a series of varied facial projections, before settling on one that looked contemplative.

With a virtual eyebrow raised, the robot continued doing *something* up inside the innards of the security bot.

Cuddy felt a tug on his hand.

Haffan asked, "What's happening? Are we just going to stand around all day?"

"What exactly is going on here, Eminence Calph?" Cuddy asked.

"An attempt to neutralize this bot, and the other security bots. Configuration adjustments. You may have noticed a . . . similarity . . . between the two robotic technologies. This is Spilor's home world . . . once was a supervisor here, similar to what you would call a librarian. If anyone, anything, can alter the programming of this bot, and the other bots—"

Calph's words were cut short by a sudden movement when Spilor apparently touched something sensitive inside the bot. The security bot jerked hard, first one way, then another, and Spilor was momentarily pulled off both spindly feet and lifted into the air. The bot frantically tried to free itself from Spilor's arms, still inside it. As frenzied wrenching motions continued, Spilor was flung this way and that like a limp rag doll. Cuddy, feeling sick to his stomach, raised a hand—*enough was enough.*

"No! Do not intervene, human," Calph ordered, staring at Cuddy then at Brian. Continuing, he added, "The other bots have not intervened yet. Spilor still may be able to—"

"Do something! Help Spilor!" Jackie yelled.

As much as Cuddy didn't care for Spilor, he couldn't idly stand by and watch any longer. Using TK, he mentally grabbed ahold of the still-gyrating security bot and could feel the unbridled power of the thing. The more it tried to wrench itself free, the more irritated Cuddy became. *Just stop . . . let the robot go,* Cuddy demanded, as the security bot began to twist. Spilor's spindly legs spun around and around. *Enough!* With one definitive TK execution, Cuddy ripped the bot's metal body into two separate halves. Spilor, along with more than a few bot spare parts, fell—scattering on the ground.

Then, the first security bot of many began to fire off its energy weapons . . .

chapter 26

The first to go down was one of the three-armed Howsh. Cuddy was momentarily startled by the explosive effect of the energy blast—how flammable his Howsh fur apparently was. Immediately, Cuddy used his TK ability to mentally bat several security bots into the sky, sending them as far off as he could.

He then reached out telepathically to Brian. *Are you helping out at all?*

No answer.

Calph, using his staff, along with seemingly excellent telekinesis proficiency, watched as three bots exploded—*Bam! Bam! Bam!* The concussive blasts successfully wiped out two other nearby bots in the process.

An energy bolt struck Cuddy in the upper arm. Intensely hot, somehow it left little more than a scorch mark on his shirt. Apparently, the lack of maintenance on the old bots carried over to and affected their weaponry.

Cuddy positioned himself in front of Haffan and Jackie,

now crouched on the ground. Several new energy strikes struck his body—although two were inconsequential, the one hitting his abdomen was more serious.

Marzon, using his energy rifle, wasn't having much luck targeting. The bots were fast—almost intuitive—in avoiding all incoming fire from Marzon, and the other armed Howsh.

Two of the bots that Cuddy sent high up into the sky were now descending. *Damn!* Trying to fend off the attacks, coming from every direction, he snuck a glance at Brian. Down on the ground, he lay motionless. Tony and Kyle were nowhere in sight.

Lorgue Supreme Eminence Calph was tiring. His earlier persistence in using his staff was now far more tempered. Cuddy, unsure how the old Howsh leader was faring, knew the ongoing battle was obviously taking a toll on him. Although the right sleeve of Calph's robe was on fire, he fought on—seeming to give it no notice.

Fewer than ten security bots remained aloft. Continuing to dart into position, they'd fire off a volley of energy bolts then spin away. Somewhere along the way, Cuddy had figured out how to deflect much of their incoming fire. But, like Calph, he too was tiring. Checking on Haffan and Jackie, he found them both still crouched on the ground—only now, Jackie was holding one of the fallen Howsh's rifles. He hoped she would quickly figure out how to use it. Kyle and Tony were still MIA, though Brian appeared to be coming around.

"We could use your help, Brian," Cuddy yelled, just as two searing energy bolts struck him, hitting his upper thighs. He dropped to his knees, hoping the pain would quickly dissipate like it had before . . .

"Got it!" Jackie, now up on her feet, was triumphant. Firing the energy rifle, she'd taken out one of the security bots. What little remained of it crashed down onto the deck several feet before Cuddy. Eight bots were still on the attack. Marzon too was down for the count. They were clearly losing the battle.

A series of metallic clicks sounded behind Cuddy. One of the large glass panels was sliding upward. Seeming impossible, Tony, Kyle, and Spilor were yelling; beckoning everyone to hurry inside.

Cuddy scooped up Haffan in one arm as he managed to climb to his feet. With his free arm, he got a good grasp on Calph then noticed much of his robe had turned to burnt cinders or ash.

Jackie, standing at the open glass panel, fired her weapon non-stop. "Get inside!" she barked.

Staggering, mostly due to his thigh injuries, Cuddy still managed to heft the weight of both the Pashier child and the old Howsh, and made it safely inside. Kyle, now beside him, helped him lower to the floor, while Tony, back outside, was trying to drag Marzon's bulk. Like trying to move a mountain, Brian appeared at Tony's side and helped him. *Oh . . . now Brian helps out . . .*

The glass panel ever so slowly began to close. The last few security bots ceased firing the moment everyone was safely inside the building. Although that didn't seem to make much sense to Cuddy, he wasn't about to argue with their good fortune.

While Spilor attended to Calph, the old Howsh glared at Cuddy, then said, "I told you not to take action. Now two Howsh are dead and there are injuries. It did not have to go down that way."

Cuddy, glancing at Jackie, had seen the same expression on her face before. *Oh no . . .*

"Hey . . . someone needed to do something!" With fists on hips, she took a step toward Calph. "If you hadn't noticed, your robot was being demolished. Maybe if you grew a pair, things could have turned out better. But if it weren't for Cuddy, and that robot you evidently were willing to sacrifice, we'd all be dead. You need to get something clear in your head. We're not built to be spectators . . . I think you'll find that a common trait among this group of humans."

Calph stared up at her for several moments when a bemused smile crossed his lips. "I suppose you are right. I apologize." Then he narrowed his eyes, "Are your injuries serious?"

Haffan answered for him. "He'll be just fine. He's tough."

"And you, young sprout . . . were you struck by any weapon fire?"

"Nope."

"Good, then we need to keep going." Spilor helped him rise to his feet. Limping over to Brian and Tony, he knelt next to Marzon. From where Cuddy rested, he could see a pretty nasty-looking scorch mark alongside the big Howsh's neck.

Standing, Calph asked, "Any of you have medical training?"

"I do," Jackie said. Slipping the pack from her shoulders, she took Brian's place by Marzon's side.

Cuddy telepathically asked Brian, *What happened to you? I thought you were going to help fend off the bots?*

Brian gave Cuddy a sideways glance before responding: *At that point it was just the robot being roughed up a bit. I wasn't about to risk life and limb over a damn robot... especially one none of us likes. And then the bot exploded and I was hit in the head... with something.*

Helping Marzon to his feet, he teetered a bit and then nodded. "I am fine. Where is my weapon?"

Jackie retrieved it from where she'd placed it against a nearby wall. "Here you go. It's a nice gun."

He stared at her with something akin to admiration. "Thank you."

Spilor said, "We have less than an hour before the *Dubon* enters orbit." The robot's already strange gate was now further encumbered with a decided limp.

Cuddy hoped their destination wasn't far. All three— Calph, Spilor, and himself— were only barely ambulatory.

Jackie asked, "Hey... how did you guys get that glass panel opened? You know, you saved our lives."

Tony said, "It was Spilor. We saw the robot crawling along the other side of the building and figured we should do something too, instead of just standing around unarmed and getting shot at. We helped Spilor up and he led us to an alcove. We watched him open a small access panel and, like he did with that security bot, put his arms right inside it... and soon a door opened. Once we were inside, the robot knew where to go to open up the big glass panel."

"So where to now?" Brian turned to Calph.

"We follow Spilor . . . the robot knows the way to the Vaults of *Calirah.*"

chapter 27

Seven years earlier . . .

Cuddy sat quietly as the old Rambler ambled down one country road after another. Slatch was a channel changer—his fingers spinning the tuning dial, sometimes to the left, sometimes to the right—nearly non-stop. Although he seemed to prefer country music, he'd listen to a Beatle's song, or some other band Cuddy couldn't remember the name of.

"Are we almost there, Slatch?"

"You just asked me that, boy."

"What did you say when I asked you?"

"I told you soon . . . we just need to get up on I-24 going west. From there, it's a straight shot up to Music City." Noting Cuddy's confused expression, Slatch added, "Nashville . . . where your pa lives."

"Oh yeah . . . he's going to be excited to see me. I'm going to tell him about all the things he's missed. Like all but two of the chickens are dead. I think we used to have a lot more of them. And Momma sometimes works in town, putting books back on the shelves in the Library. And that the A&W closed down, due to not enough people coming around."

Slatch held up a palm." You can tell him all that stuff when you see him."

But Cuddy was already distracted, noticing the rear seat was empty. "Where's Rufus? I don't go anywhere without Rufus!"

The dog is fine . . . back at the farm. Hey, does your ma ever talk about things . . . like when she and your pa were young? She ever mention me?"

"No, why would she?"

"Because we were friends . . . the three of us. Oh, forget it. Never mind."

As country music continued to play on the radio, Slatch repeatedly opened and closed his window, spitting out then fiddling with the dial some more.

The car started making a strange noise. Slatch raised his chin and stared out the front windshield, peering down the car's hood, like he was trying to communicate directly with the old engine beneath it. "Ah shit!" Slatch murmured.

"What's that whistling?"

Slatch didn't answer. Instead, he turned the volume up on the radio. Glancing over at Cuddy, he pointed to the dial, "Johnny Cash. Folsom Prison Blues . . . I bet your pa knows this song . . . knows it real well."

Cuddy listened to the catchy melody—a song about a train rollin' along and a guy sitting in jail. "Is my pa a criminal?"

"Nah . . . forget I said anything. I'm sure he's on the straight-and-narrow these past few years."

"I have to pee."

"Can't you hold it for another fifteen or twenty minutes?"

"I think I've already held it that long."

"There's no place to stop . . . no bathrooms handy."

"A tree will do me just fine. Pull up over there. Maybe then you can check under the hood too."

"I don't need to check under there. I know what that sound is . . . it comes and goes."

"If you say so. I still need to pee. Come on . . . pull over, I'll be quick."

Grudgingly, Slatch slowly turned the steering wheel and the old Rambler moved off the main highway onto a dirt and gravel side road. Cuddy threw open the door and ran down a sloping hill toward a crop of tall pines some thirty yards away. Selecting the first big tree he came to, he relieved his bladder within seconds. In the distance, he heard the constant hiss of cars speeding along the highway. Then *wrrrrr*. Whatever was going on beneath the hood of the Rambler sounded a whole lot worse. Zipping up, Cuddy turned to head back, then suddenly stopped short. Another car was pulled in behind the Rambler. *A cop*. Flashing red lights on the patrol car's light bar gave Cuddy pause. *Was Slatch in trouble? Was there a problem with the noisy engine?* He weighed whether to join Slatch and the policeman or just stay put. He didn't think peeing on a tree was any big crime but wasn't completely sure about that either. He decided to wait a spell. As the seconds ticked by, Cuddy's short-term memory began to evaporate. Confused, he looked about his surroundings—the tall trees, the wet puddle at the trunk of a nearby pine, the sounds of fast-moving cars in the near-distance. Spotting the mud-colored Rambler, Cuddy recollected he'd been in that car before. As he tried to remember, he silently cursed. Just like he'd done a thousand times in the past. Irritated at his inability to recall what'd he'd been doing only ten-minutes before. *Well, standing here in the trees ain't gonna' do me no good at all,* he mused.

Cuddy walked toward the highway then suddenly cringed, hearing the same awful screeching noise. Up ahead, on the embankment, a police car was backing up. Throwing rocks and dirt into the air, its tires spinning, the cruiser sped away. Cuddy reached the Rambler and saw the old farmer—his head buried beneath the car's open hood. Slatch looked up when he saw Cuddy. "Best we be going, boy. Seems you're the center of a big commotion. And before you ask . . . I'm Slatch. You're on your way to see your pa in Nashville and your stupid dog is back home on the farm. Now get in the car!"

chapter 28

Present day . . .

As the old Howsh limped along up ahead, Cuddy enviously eyed Calph's sturdy staff. With each step forward, his own legs throbbed from the two energy bolts that struck him earlier. But observing the still out of it Marzon, who'd taken a direct shot to the head—or even Spilor, violently thrashed about at the hands of an out-of-control security bot—Cuddy reckoned he had little to complain about. He supposed things could be a whole lot worse for him physically.

Not knowing what to expect, once inside the structure, he found an abundance of bright light coming in from the outside. Glass panels surrounded them, and overgrown plants, shrubbery—even out of control tall trees—gave the place a lush greenhouse feel.

According to Spilor, currently gimping along at Cuddy's side, *Calirah* was a cross between a museum and a Hall of

Records. Before the war, although the site was open to the public, Howsh and Pashier visitors were never present on the grounds at the same time. Even the few regular employees working there, whether Howsh or Pashier, weren't scheduled to work on the same days. And even though the Pashier had been exterminated, on the nearby planet of Mahli, few Howsh officials ever visited Calirah. It wasn't uncommon to be accosted there. Over the years, deaths had racked up into the hundreds at the hands of the protective security bots. It was assumed that one of the last acts of the Pashier, prior to their near total demise, was to program certain safeguards into the security bots—ones that would help keep *Calirah* safe from plunder.

Spilor, gesturing toward another empty walk-up counter, said, "I remember . . . years ago . . . hundreds would come here every day. Both species were highly academic. Education was paramount. And as you'll soon see, *experiential* education was what brought so many parents and their young offspring to *Calirah.*"

"I don't remember ever coming here," Haffan said, walking beside Jackie, a few paces behind them.

Cuddy was aware that she'd been listening to their conversation. The Pashier child didn't miss much—was always absorbing. Again—an interesting contrast to what he was like at the same age.

"You weren't born yet, when this place was open to everyone," Jackie said.

"If I were . . . could I have found out more about my relatives?" Haffan asked.

It then occurred to Cuddy that Haffan hadn't yet spoken of her parents, or any family members, prior to her being left all alone back on Mahli. He wondered if it was because it was simply too painful to go there, or due to some other, still unexpressed, reason.

"And not just records pertaining to the Pashier . . . or the Howsh," Spilor said, now projecting outward a facial expression showing both interest and patience, "but other alien life forms also, with records pertaining to their own species. Even humans are chronicled here . . . as they relate to the Prophesy of Harkstrong."

Cuddy heard the sound of water dripping, emanating from a low, long planter to his right containing an automated drip-watering system. Wide, shiny-leaved, plants spilled over onto the walkway.

Calph stopped up ahead then turned to face the group, one sleeve of his robe burnt away. "We are about to leave the administration section of this structure. As we descend to the lower levels, security will undoubtedly tighten. Perhaps more bots, perhaps other security measures. Stay alert. We must find what we came for, then leave this place quickly." He turned and focused his attention back on Spilor.

Cuddy and the others approached an open vestibule section in the shape of a square. Four stairways, one at each corner, provided access down to the lower levels. Standing by a thick, glass-like banister, Cuddy noted what looked like a courtyard five levels below them, while the tops of no less than twenty immense trees almost touched the glass panel ceiling, thirty or forty feet above his head. *What happens when those trees outgrow this place?* He eyed the stairway—around and around it went. Hundreds—maybe thousands—of steps, leading upward.

Jackie, joining him, commented, "You'd think such an advanced society would have installed a few elevators. Right?" She glanced down at his legs. "I've been watching you. Your limping's gotten worse."

"Hurts just to watch you walk," Brian added, standing several yards away at the banister. "Hey, Spilor . . . how many levels down are we going?"

Looking annoyed at their being interrupted, Calph replied, "All the way to the ground level," then continued his conversation with Spilor in hushed tones.

"Go stand at the top of the stairs, man," Brian said.

"Me?" Cuddy asked.

"Yeah you . . . chop chop, before I change my mind."

Cuddy exchanged glances with both Jackie and Haffan, who smiled at Cuddy's mistrust of the situation. Walking to the stairway, he heard Brian coming up behind him.

"Keep your arms and legs inside the *ride* at all times . . ." Brian said, laughing at his own humor. Cuddy then felt his body being gently lifted several inches off the walkway. Unconsciously, he continued to walk—placing one suspended foot in front of the other. Moving out over the top steps down he went, keeping a good foot or so above the next descending step. Brian stayed close beside him, taking the steps two at a time. Looking over his shoulder, Cuddy noticed Jackie and Haffan close behind them. Soon, the others, including Spilor and Calph, were also following them down.

"If you get tired, you can always put me down . . ." Cuddy said, feeling somewhat guilty for the special treatment he was receiving. But the truth was, he would have had a near impossible time maneuvering down that many steps on his own. Kyle and Tony kept throwing verbal jabs at him, but Cuddy wasn't listening to them. Instead, he focused on the trees—on the surrounding architecture. A beautiful complex, it was a shame no one visited there anymore—that the ravages of war had, once again, ruined such a positive thing. Cuddy's musings turned back to what Brian was currently achieving—lifting, and propelling forward a man six-foot-five and two hundred-and-twenty pounds of dead weight. He wondered how Brian had perfected his TK abilities so much more effectively than he himself had. Wondered if he had squandered away similar abilities. Hadn't given them the time and attention necessary that Brian had. He remembered something Tow had once told him. "Your telekinesis gift must be exercised . . . strengthened. Your potential capabilities go far beyond that of any Pashier . . . even those of Brian."

"Brian spent more time within the wellness chamber . . . a lot more," Cuddy had reminded him.

"You radiate *source* power, Cuddy. So does Brian . . . but yours is on a whole other level. If you were interested, you could do . . . be more."

At the time, Cuddy didn't know how to interpret his comments. *Was it an insult? Had he just been told he was an underachiever*? If so, he hadn't cared at that moment. *Why didn't I?* They'd reached the second to last level, now descending the final flight of stairs. *Why hadn't I cared? Do I care now*? Yes, I think I do.

Cuddy felt himself lowered to the ground. Once back on his feet, the pain in his thighs quickly returned. Brian stepped off the last step—his face red from exertion as beads of sweat ran tracks down his cheeks.

"Thank you, Brian. I'll have to return the favor one day."

"You? I won't hold my breath. Best you leave the heavy lifting to those that . . . well . . . can."

Smiling broadly, both Jackie and Haffan seemed impressed by Brian's latest TK feat. He gave Jackie a quick wink and let Haffan give him a high five. Cuddy had never been particularly competitive; had little concept what that spirit was all about. But something had changed, because right then all he could think about was how to out-TK Brian.

"This way, humans . . . we must hurry," Calph said.

chapter 29

Lorgue Supreme Eminence Calph tapped his staff at a point near his feet. "As you can see . . . we are standing upon solid, uneven, rock. Understand, this whole complex is built directly upon sacred ground, where 8,000 years of combined history are chronicled . . . conserved within subterranean vaults."

"The Howsh, they're from Rahin . . ." Cuddy reasoned.

Calph waited for a question.

"And the Pashier's home is Mahli. So why is everything chronicled here? And why together?"

"I was wondering the same thing," Kyle said.

"Not always have our two species been at war. Certainly, a turbulent relationship did exist. But it has always been clear that both existences were linked . . . intertwined. When this complex was first built, it was hoped it would bring forth a new era of unification."

"Guess things didn't turn out that way," Kyle muttered.

"Just the opposite," Calph said. "Some secrets should have stayed buried, remained back on Rahin, or Mahli, and not brought here. Although buried, they were still accessible to certain individuals with not the best intentions."

Calph studied each one within the group. "Do not venture off on your own. We will proceed forward now, into the Virtual Exhibition Hall. Remember . . . time is not on our side." Calph proceeded them, leaving behind the open courtyard with its tall trees and overflowing planters. On entering into the Virtual Exhibition Hall, it took several moments for Cuddy's eyes to adjust to the darkness. He felt Haffan take his hand.

"Why is it so dark in here?" she asked.

Suddenly, a cone of light emanated downward from high above them as they proceeded forward into the hall. Within the illuminated, approximately ten-foot-diameter area, was a circle holding an intricately carved symbol. Other cones of light then shone down from above. Soon, there were over ten distinct cones of light, beaming down from high above. Ten or so circles holding uniquely engraved symbols within them. Although Calph and Spilor moved past the circles, and through the hall at a good clip, Jackie strayed off to the side—stepping into a nearby cone of light. She screamed, then immediately stifled a laugh, covering her mouth with her hands. Haffan ran into the circle and stood by her side. Her first reaction was nearly identical to Jackie's own.

Cuddy chose a different circle of light to step into. Startled, he didn't expect to see what he was viewing. As if instantly transported to a different time and place, he stood cliff-side on a different planet. Hovering bright on the horizon was another world. One so large, it felt like he could reach out and touch it—a world that would drop into an azure ocean void of waves and motion, like an ultra-calm lake. Cuddy spun around and found a field of tall violet grasses. A gentle breeze moved the willowy stalks in unison. Cuddy was certain he had never seen anything quite so beautiful. Not sure how he knew, yet nevertheless he did: This world was Rahin—home world of the Howsh. Spinning around, taking in the 360-degree view again, he stepped out of the lit circle and back into the darkness of the Virtual Exhibition Hall. He watched some of the others excitedly move from one circle over to another.

Jackie smiling, and out-of-breath, grabbed his hand and pulled him in the direction of a circle of light to his left. They moved into the cone of light together. This place was dark. Stars filled the heavens around them as they stood within a pasture. Silhouetted in starlight were grazing creatures. Rotund, the four-legged animals were closer in size to Earth's elephants than to cattle—their hides bore large scales the size of dinner plates. Each shimmered with an opalescent rainbow of colors.

"Can you believe how beautiful this place is?" Jackie asked.

Staring down, he melted into her eyes. "Truly beautiful," he said, and she caught his meaning.

"Come on . . . we should go find Haffan."

They emerged into a far more dangerous situation than one of slow grazing beasts. The overhead cones of light were being extinguished, one by one—the hall loomed ever darker with each passing second.

Kyle, standing next to them, glanced at Cuddy then gestured with his chin toward the periphery of the hall. Darkness was nearly absolute, except for tiny clusters of blinking lights. Numerous, odd-looking, shapes became outlined. "What are those things?" he asked.

"Crawly-bots."

Haffan spoke, but Cuddy didn't see her until he leaned over, looking past Kyle's other side.

"You know what those things are, Haffan?" Cuddy asked, amazed she could make anything out at all in the pervading dimness around them.

"Yeah, they used to be all over Tripette City. Bugs with guns . . . police droids."

Cuddy saw there were far too many of the creatures to count. Lurking in the darkness, they quickly surrounded them.

"Guess we should have kept up with Calph," Kyle said. "What now?"

"We slowly need to get out of here. Which way did Calph go?"

"Over this way," Tony said, a short distance away in the darkness.

"Keep talking to us, Tony," Cuddy said. "We're headed your way. Let's not make any sudden movements, everybody."

"Haffan?" Jackie asked.

"I'm here with Brian."

"Okay . . . take his hand, then head toward Tony."

Tony continued to speak, "Here I am . . . walk this way."

It took a couple of minutes before they all stood together at the far end of the hall.

"That's the way they went . . . out that corridor," Tony said.

"The same corridor that's congested with all those bug *things*?" Brian asked.

"Crawly-bots," Haffan corrected.

"Whatever."

Cuddy caught movement in the nearby darkness. Crab-like, the bot moved sideways on six spindly legs.

"The exit is completely blocked. Must be fifty of the things right there in front," Tony told them, the first to attempt to move toward the corridor.

"Let me by! Move, Kyle!" Brian ordered, pushing past Kyle then Tony. "Watch the sides and behind, Cuddy . . . let's move."

A scraping sound was heard, like multiple claws being pushed, or dragged across rock. Brian was using his TK power to plow the bots out of the way.

"Let's just hope there's not a repeat of what happened up above," Cuddy said. Then, glancing around, "Hey . . . anyone see Marzon?"

"He's gone . . . I think he made it out of here with Calph and Spilor," Tony said.

Making slow, but steady progress forward, they moved all together out of the hall. The crawly-bots still scurried around them, but primarily stayed back in the shadows.

The next hall was nearly as large as the first, though more illuminated and full of ancient artifacts. Each item was artistically spotlighted, maintaining its own hovering text description. Included were three full-sized Howsh warriors, running with spears; a mock village, made of stone blocks; and a large pond in the middle of the hall, depicting furry Howsh nomads aboard a big wooden boat made of reeds, or something similar. Apparently, this hall contained Howsh historical material. Although something wasn't ringing quite true about the Howsh depictions, Cuddy was too preoccupied mentally with crawly-bots to worry about it. Fortunately, the bots mostly remained where it was dark, back in the Virtual Exhibition Hall.

The next hall was dedicated to the Pashier. Like the previous hall, there were numerous full-sized, life-like, depictions of everyday life of the ancient aliens. There was even a full-sized heritage pod, situated toward the back of the room. Someone had painted a big X over the surface—graffiti, obviously.

Cuddy realized next that nearly all the Pashier lifelike depictions had been vandalized, one way or another. Heads lopped off models; models placed in inappropriate sexual positions; even a Howsh figure—brought in from the other hall. Standing upright, its foot was suspended over the head of a prone Pashier male. Cuddy heard Haffan's voice ahead, asking Jackie questions. Undoubtedly, she wanted to know why anyone would want to desecrate the scenes, like these had been.

The next hall held advanced technology. Model representations of space vehicles, against a backdrop of planets and stars, were both beautiful and impressive. Mahli and Rahin, as well as Darriall, were all depicted with incredible life-like realism.

Bringing up the rear, Cuddy kept up with the group. They moved through the planetary system, holding almost too much to take in. Spaceships of every size and shape—some planets—also several space stations, Cuddy was unaware even existed.

A scream broke the silence. If Cuddy wasn't mistaken, it came from Tony.

chapter 30

Tony, over the months, had become a close friend—like family. So hearing his screams evoked a strong protective response in Cuddy. *What in the world had happened?* His mind raced—throwing a few dire possibilities up for grabs. *Had the crawly-bots attacked up ahead? Had he suffered some kind of accident? Perhaps fallen?* He'd lagged behind, bringing up the rear, but now, his fists clenched, Cuddy came around the corner at a dead run, prepared to handle whatever emergency presented itself ahead.

But he wasn't prepared for what he discovered next—not even close.

Eight Howsh soldiers, each was holding a raised energy rifle—their muzzles pointed in his direction. Lorgue Sub Eminence Langer was there too. It took several beats for Cuddy to process the scene around him. It was uncanny. They looked almost identical. He'd seen the Howsh leader's brother once before, via the *Evermore's* viewscape display, but that was over a month ago.

Spilor was splayed out on the rocky ground. Both his spindly legs twitched like a sleeping dog in the midst of a dream.

Tony—suspended in the air by Langer by a fistful of hair—hung several feet off the ground, an arm's length out. No longer conscious, it was a small blessing, Cuddy figured, considering the amount of pain he must have already withstood. Kyle and Brian had their arms raised high. Jackie, with Haffan in her arms, wore an expression of either hate or contempt. Perhaps both.

Cuddy ignored the fact that Marzon too was pointing his weapon at him. It was hard to read the big Howsh's expression. But seeing Calph, now the end of his staff extended forward in Cuddy's direction, everything suddenly was brought home. The vessel supposedly pursuing them—the *Dubon*—had not been pursuing them after all. Their meeting, instead, was pre-arranged. Calph and Langer were not enemies, just the opposite. Cuddy's face suddenly felt flushed. He knew right then the reason he shouldn't be leading the group. He didn't have enough life experience to know when *not* to trust others. When not to place his life, and those he cared about, in the hands of someone with an ulterior motive. He had been duped—it was as simple as that.

"Do not, even for a moment, consider using your telekinetic powers, Cuddy Perkins, to protect your friends . . . your brother." Calph pivoted his staff toward Brian. "Same goes for you, Brian Horowitz. Every one of you is only a trigger-pull away from being terminated."

"What is this all about? Why go to all this trouble?" Cuddy asked.

Langer answered this time, still holding Tony; his arm unwavering under the weight. Suddenly he relaxed. Opening his clenched claw, Tony dropped hard to the ground. Langer then walked over to Jackie, towering over her, and stared down. Not at Jackie, but at Haffan.

"The sprout. She is the most important living creature in the galaxy. Everything revolves around her." Langer's eyes stayed locked on the child as he spoke. "Powerful, this one."

"She's only a child! What are you talking about . . . powerful? You don't know what you're talking about." Jackie fumed, turning herself and Haffan away from the imposing Howsh commander.

Bemused, Langer turned to Cuddy. "These vaults . . . are virtually impossible to breach. Even with our most advanced energy weaponry. And there are so many vaults. I do believe the elders may have anticipated this precise moment in time. Did everything they could to avert what I . . . we . . . are intending to accomplish here today."

For the first time, Cuddy looked past Langer and Calph, and all the armed soldiers, now standing within an enclosure made of solid rock. Reaching high over their heads, the area spanned—tunnel-like—deep into the planet's surface. If there was an actual end point to the tunnel, Cuddy couldn't make it out. And there were ginormous metal doors, not so different from those used by banks back on Earth to keep would-be thieves out. There were hundreds of such doors—the vaults of

Calirah. It occurred to Cuddy that somewhere within them were the ancient writings, giving the location of the Prophesy of Harkstrong.

Calph said, “I never hid the fact that the child would be our only key to opening the one vault that contains the ancient writings we seek.”

“You also said no one would be harmed. And that you were no longer aligned with the Howsh . . . obviously that too was a lie,” Cuddy scornfully responded.

“No, I told no lies. I am not in alignment with the Howsh. As I expressed, I detest politics. I simply failed to mention a certain partnership I have with my one-time protégé, Lorgue Sub Eminence Langer. I am not in favor of his use of violence, but then I no longer hold command over him like I once did.”

“Tell us the truth,” Brian interjected. “Why do you really need to find this . . . uh . . . Prophesy?”

Langer smiled at his question and, in that moment, looked truly evil. “Only by knowing the future, can one possibly alter it. The ancient elders precisely foresaw the current timespan. Prophesized about this moment in time, when events would begin to unravel for the Howsh—the beginning of the end, so to speak. Eight thousand years ago, the historic time we are now in was carved in stone—the inevitability of our species’ sudden demise.”

Brian questioned, “Wait . . . where’s the logic there? I think you’re missing the damn point. I mean . . . why does knowing what the prophecy foretells help you to change it? Isn’t a prophesy something that happens, like it or not, and you’re stuck with the outcome?” Then, visibly shrugging, he looked at Calph and asked,

"Tell me you're not basing all your actions on this guy's bullshit rationale."

Lorgue Sub Eminence Langer seethed, obviously not used to being second-guessed, especially by a lowly human. Through a clenched jaw, he said, "And that is why we need the sprout. Enough talk! We owe you no further explanation, human. Give her to me . . . now!"

"Go fuck yourself," Jackie said—her voice full of contempt. She tightened her hold around Haffan and took a step away from the towering Howsh.

With surprising speed, Langer reached a long powerful arm out and plucked the Pashier child from Jackie's grasp. It all happened so fast Cuddy had no time to react.

But Brian did. Cuddy instantly knew what Brian was about to do. Raising both hands the way he did; the set expression of total concentration on his face. The raw energy that emanated out from Brian's TK thrust was enough to shove Cuddy, along with the others, awkwardly off-balance. In that exact moment, Haffan was freed of Langer's clutches and, seemingly weightless in the charged air, headed back toward Jackie's still open arms.

But three others in the cavern were not caught off-guard by Brian's defiant actions. Three armed Howsh soldiers pulled their respective triggers nearly simultaneously. Brian was struck down by their combined weaponry fire—receiving two blasts in the chest, approximately in the heart area; and one in the head—smack in the middle of his forehead. Brian dropped to the jagged rock floor, but Cuddy knew he wouldn't feel the impact—wouldn't feel anything again. He was already dead.

chapter 31

As concerned as Cuddy was for Brian, his attention was focused on Haffan only. Haffan was alive. Haffan was in peril. Brian was neither of those things. Using his TK ability to draw the child to him, Cuddy whisked her through the air and into his own arms. It was a huge risk. One glance down at Brian's lifeless body told him that, but he'd reacted on impulse; on instinct.

"Stop!" Lorgue Supreme Eminence Calph's deep gravelly voice filled the cavern. Fury was evident in his tone—the way he struggled to breathe. He moved his staff back and forth between the soldiers, and said, "The next one to fire his weapon will die where he stands." Then, looking over to Langer, added, "Do not try my patience, Prime Eminence. Have you forgotten the terms of our arrangement? Or shall I take this action to mean you were disingenuous?"

"Hold your fire!" Langer ordered. With only mild conviction in his tone, he said, "I apologize, Supreme Eminence Calph. I will let you convince the human to release the child. Know, though . . . without her . . ."

Calph cut him off. "I am well aware of the situation."

Cuddy wondered what kind of arrangement the two Howsh leaders had made. As he held Haffan—her face buried into his shoulder—Calph scrutinized him. Kyle then moved in front of him, shielding Haffan with his own body. Jackie, transfixed, stared down at Brian's body and soon began to weep uncontrollably.

"Listen to me, Cuddy Perkins. There is no need for further violence here. I promised you the sprout would not be harmed. I mean to honor that promise. What we require of her is most simple. She will provide us access to the right vault. At that point, she will open the vault. Please, do not make this situation cost more lives here."

Through her sobs, Jackie asked, "What makes you think she can do what you ask? Why would she have any idea what you're even talking about?"

Cuddy felt Haffan stir in his arms. She lifted her head and stared over her shoulder at Calph. "I will do what he wants. Let me down."

All eyes went to the Pashier child.

"Haffan?" Jackie questioned.

She struggled against Cuddy's hold until he let her slide down so her feet could touch the ground. Although his attention should be fully on Haffan as she moved toward Calph, and the perilous situation at hand, something was nagging him . . . something important. . . . *something immensely important.* But all he could pull out from deep within was a bright red X. Over and over the symbol kept forming in his mind. And then he had it: *Oh my God!*

Cuddy turned to Kyle, then to Jackie. "Go with Haffan. She goes nowhere unless you all go too. Do you understand me?"

They nodded in unison though it was clear they didn't understand. "Why just us? Why don't you go with her too?"

But Cuddy was already on the move. In two long strides he reached Brian. Kneeling, he slid his arms beneath his body and lifted him up, cradling him in his outstretched arms. Glancing down, he saw that Tony was just now starting to come around.

Jackie asked, "Where are you going? He's already dead, Cuddy. Haffan's the one who needs you . . . ." Her words trailed off. It was as if a light bulb had gone on over her head. She got it. "Oh my God . . . Run, Cuddy, run!"

But Cuddy was already gone, midway through the Hall of Advanced Technology, and running for its opposite entrance. Though he knew the odds of what he was about to attempt were stacked against him, he still had to try.

He hurried past the stars and planets exhibits of the hall and sprinted into the Pashier Historical Hall. Glancing down at Brian's face, his open, lifeless eyes seemed to be staring up at him.

The hall was nearly dark. Only a few overhead lights remained on so it was difficult to see. Even so, Cuddy quickly snaked through the myriad of Pashier mannequins. He tried not to look too closely at how they were arranged. How the vandals had placed them in various sexual positions: a female Pashier model straddling a male; another male Pashier taking another male from behind. Then Cuddy tripped. Running, he hadn't noticed the female mannequin lying on the floor, her legs spread wide. He staggered, trying desperately not to drop Brian. One of Brian's legs came loose from his grip. Flopping and jerking about, it almost seemed the one appendage had miraculously come back to life on its own.

Regaining his balance, Cuddy noticed ahead what he'd come for. The bright red graffiti X, painted on the side of the heritage pod.

New doubts flooded his mind. Why did he think the pod was even viable? *Since the figures weren't real Pashier beings . . . only props . . . the heritage pod could, most likely was, also a prop!*

As Cuddy slowed down his running pace, it was as if his pent-up emotion somehow caught up with him. Eyes brimming, he tried to swallow but couldn't. As much as he sometimes—most times—hated Brian, he knew Brian had whole-heartedly been one of them. Had chosen to give up everything back on Earth to join them on this crazy Interstellar adventure. Part of the crew, he'd uncharacteristically given his life to protect the alien child. Had bravely demonstrated he wasn't the selfish, self-centered, jerk he often came across as.

Standing now before the ten-foot-high leafy, organic-looking, pod, Cuddy felt foolish. It obviously was a stupid prop, made from some kind of plastic, or some alien composite material. What on earth made him think this could somehow work? *Brian was gone . . . he would always be gone.*

He gazed down at the corpse in his arms. "I'm sorry this happened to you, Brian. Truly, I am. Letting out a long held-in breath, Cuddy gulped in a new one to replace it and noticed a musky, earthy smell in the air. A smell he'd encountered numerous times before. It occurred to him that no way could props smell like the real thing.

"You must hurry, Cuddy . . . I will assist you."

Cuddy spun around and stared. He'd never been more surprised, or happier, to see anyone in his life. "Tow?"

* * *

Jackie's sadness concerning Brian was replaced by other, equally powerful, emotions. Primarily, utter rage and hatred for Langer. This was all his doing: Brian's death, and the multiple energy weapons currently trained on them. And that the child was being forced into doing something she clearly did not want to do.

As they moved deeper into the cavern, there was a definite sameness to everything. Each big metal vault door looked identical to the one before it and the one after it. Taking Haffan's hand in hers, Jackie watched as the alien child swiveled her head, studying one rock wall after another. Expressionless, Haffan gave each vault door several moments of consideration.

A few paces behind them, Jackie felt Langer's eyes on them, his growing frustration. *Screw him.* Her thoughts next turned to Cuddy and what he was surely attempting to do at that same moment. She'd only made the connection when she saw him take Brian's limp body into his arms. She'd barely noticed the heritage pod; hadn't thought it was real. She already missed Brian; more than she thought possible. Such a difficult person, but all she could think about was having him back in her life. She fought back tears. There would be time to grieve later.

"That one!"

Haffan stopped—standing with her arm raised—her finger pointing. The vault door seemed no different than any of the others—one of hundreds looking exactly like it.

"What you seek is behind that door," Haffan said. Her voice flat, her facial expression was one of detachment.

Langer and Calph walked to the secured vault together. Jackie caught the growing anticipation, even excitement, on their faces.

"Now open it," Langer ordered.

Haffan pulled her hand loose from Jackie's and slowly approached the big metal door. It seemed she was seeing beyond the door to whatever lay within. Her lips began to move, though no sound left her mouth—repeating some kind of unspoken chant over and over.

Fleetingly, Jackie wondered if this was all a ruse on Haffan's part; a way to stall for time? If so, the young Pashier was an amazing actress. Then she heard it. The spinning of gears—sounds of internal mechanisms working. A definitive final clang signaled the vault door had indeed become unlocked.

chapter 32

Tow was there—but he also was not. He was coming to him from the other side of Rah the same kind of astral projection occurrence as before, when onboard the *Farlight*. Tow stood beside the heritage pod—his attention fully on Brian.

"Please tell me this pod is . . . viable, Tow," Cuddy said.

Tow acknowledged the bell-shaped pod indeed was. "Yes . . . there are life forces secured within it. But with that said, Cuddy . . . this heritage pod has withstood much trauma. Much stress."

"Will it open . . . accept Brian?"

Tow nodded. "You will first need to clear away all nearby objects."

Cuddy did as asked after setting Brian down first. He relocated four Pashier mannequins and several historical props—the most substantial was a mockup of an ancient Pashier dwelling. Cuddy, using TK, shoved items out of the way. Within seconds, there was a twenty-foot clearing all around the pod.

Tow stood nearby with his eyes closed. "Take my hand, Cuddy."

Cuddy, staring at Tow's wavering, partially transparent form, wondered how it was going to work. Moving close enough to take Tow's slightly raised hand in his own, Cuddy too closed his eyes and felt *something*. Not so much Tow's physical touch as more an essence—a tingling, coursing energy confined to the shape of his hand. Tow was already mid-process in speaking, communicating with the heritage pod at its highest level. Fear was evident. Both fear and mistrust. The heritage pod had endured much abuse at the hands of the Howsh vandals. Protecting Pashier life forms contained within it had been the pod's only purpose. Patiently, Tow communicated with the pod's true essence.

Cuddy's own impatience was quickly quelled by Tow's soothing, loving, communion with the pod.

It started with the slightest breath against his skin. A few hairs on his head were tousled. Then came an encircling breeze. Cuddy smiled and opened his eyes. A glittering fountain of light was emanating up from the top of the pod. Starting at the apex, leaves began to open and unfurl. The *Shain* ritual of the *rejoining* had begun. Already, a swirling galaxy of stars twinkled above and around them.

Cuddy knelt by Brian's side, once again sliding his arms beneath his body. Lifting him up, he took several steps backwards while some of the larger pod fronds unfurled onto the floor. Tow hadn't moved—didn't need to—since he wasn't really present. Not physically. His smile beckoned Cuddy to come forward—into the pod's *centripetal* space—where physical and spiritual elements merged.

Even though he'd experienced the same ritual in the past, Cuddy was no less captivated at being in this enchanted, magical, place—one not physical, as defined by space and time. A place the human language could not accurately define, or describe. The cool swirling winds increased—buffeting his clothes. Incredible light sparkled like a million diamonds all around him, and Cuddy was forced to close his eyes against the sheer intensity. Brian's body had become *feather light*—then no weight at all. Upon opening up his eyes, Cuddy saw Brian Horowitz standing—taking in all the magnificence around him. When he finally turned toward Cuddy, he was smiling, his form nearly as transparent as Tow's.

Brian gave Cuddy a cocky, casual, salute then winked. "Guess I'll see you when I see you . . . they want me to hurry."

With that, Brian waved goodbye at the now nearly invisible Tow. He walked tall, with confidence, toward a bright, undefined, epicenter somewhere in the distance. Another dimension that Cuddy instinctively knew he personally could not go to—*not now.Now* was not his time. When he turned back to face Tow, he was no longer there. Cuddy was filled with a sudden sadness, already missing his friend.

* * *

Jackie closely searched Haffan's face. Watched her while everyone's attention was solely focused on the slowly opening vault door. She watched the alien child—how her lower lip was held captive between her upper and lower teeth—how utterly distressed she seemed.

Excited, Calph and Langer, the two Howsh leaders, quickly strode into the vault, ignoring the rest of the group. Langer's soldiers maintained their vigil—their weapon muzzles still aimed at Jackie, Kyle, and the still-unsteady Tony.

Jackie draped an arm around Haffan, pulling her in close. "It's okay now . . . it's over."

Haffan gazed up at her, her eyes questioning, searching. Searching for something, perhaps absolution? "No . . . it has only just begun. I shouldn't have done that. It would be better if I'd let them kill us."

"Um . . . for the record," Tony said, "I'm good with the choice you made," as Kyle nodded in agreement.

"How did you do it?" Jackie asked. The tone of her question made it clear she wanted an honest answer.

Haffan didn't reply.

"Who are you? It's time you start leveling with us."

"Leveling?" Haffan repeated.

"Don't play dumb with me, Haffan."

Haffan's eyes flashed to Kyle and Tony, then back to Jackie. "You'll be mad at me. You'll hate me."

"That's ridiculous! Why would you even say such a thing?" Jackie asked.

"Because . . ."

Jackie waited for her to give a real answer as Haffan stared at the open vault door. "I think I am . . . what is called an *elder* . . . from a very long time ago. Actually, I do know that I am. I am a

Kartinal. I have memories reaching back eight thousand years. Memories usually forgotten ... undergoing so many *Shain* rituals. But I remember them all ... each one of my lives."

"So you do know what's inside that vault?" Kyle asked.

"Nothing good is inside that vault," Haffan replied, giving Kyle an exasperated expression normally out of place in such a young person. "You want to know why I haven't spoken of my parents, or talked about my home back on Mahli? It's because I don't have such things. At least, not for a very long time now."

"Well, you couldn't have just hatched out from a big egg ... you came from somewhere, Haffan, "Tony said.

"Actually, that's not so far from the truth. I exited from a small heritage pod. It opened and I, all alone, walked out of it. I'm remembering more and more now who and what I am. But I'm only a child. I know that. It's weird."

"What's in the vault, Haffan?" Jackie asked, again.

"Two things ... the true location of the Prophesy of Harkstrong."

"What's the other thing?" Kyle asked.

"A curse. One that I think I placed on the hide scrolls myself; those within the vault."

"What kind of curse?"

"Anyone who gazes upon the ancient writings ... the scrolls directly ... well, they are in for a really bad day. I'm trying to remember what the curse was about exactly."

"You don't remember? Didn't you just say it was your own curse?" Tony asked.

Haffan's brow furrowed, "Did I mention it happened eight thousand years ago?"

"So we shouldn't look at anything they bring out of the vault?" Jackie asked.

"No! Don't look! Though I think seeing it indirectly . . . like reflected off a mirror, would be okay."

"You think?" Tony asked.

"Give her a break. She already told you it was . . . thousands of years ago!" Jackie admonished Tony and Kyle, then thought of something else. "Can you remember how . . . um . . . powerful that curse is? I mean, will either of the two Howsh leaders walk out of there . . . any worse for wear?"

For some reason that evoked a somewhat mischievous smile. Haffan shrugged one shoulder, and replied, "What's the *human*, Earth phrase? Oh yeah . . . they're totally screwed. I do know that."

"Like hurt screwed, or dead screwed?" Tony asked.

Haffan thought about that. "Maybe both."

chapter 33

Cuddy returned, joining the others now standing deep within the rocky confines of the Vaults of Calirah. He was happy to see Tony back up and moving around, though his balance seemed a bit topsy-turvy. One of the armed soldiers, appraising him, spat a slick galk wad onto the rocky ground.

Watching Cuddy approach, Jackie's face reflected her growing apprehension. "Well?"

"It's all fine."

"Fine? What does that even mean? Was it an actual heritage pod, or not?"

"Yeah, it was . . . *is.* And Tow showed up to assist me." Cuddy let himself grin. "Brian walked right into the pod . . . to wherever it is their life forces go. Headed in like he owned the place."

"That sounds like him," Kyle said. "You know . . . you saved him. Totally saved his ass." Cuddy felt somewhat embarrassed by the comment, thinking that anyone else would have done the same.

"He's right, Cuddy. Sometimes you really do come through," Jackie said, fondness shining in her eyes.

"Brian owes you big time, man. If ever I see him again, I'll be sure to remind him," Tony said.

"You will!" They all turned to Haffan. "You will see him again . . . I'm just saying."

Cuddy, glancing first at the soldiers, holding onto weapons, stared at the now-open vault door. "How did that happen?"

"Haffan, it seems, is not who we thought she was. Perhaps a better way to say it, she's so much more than we ever thought she was." Jackie leaned over and then kissed the top of the alien child's head. An endearing gesture, making Cuddy appreciate Jackie even more—if that was possible.

"Saying Haffan is an old soul, is an understatement," Kyle said. "She's like six thousand years old."

Tony and Jackie corrected him, both saying: "Eight thousand," in unison.

Cuddy glanced down at Haffan, noticing her shamed expression of guilt. She stared at him. *Why she had concealed that fact,* he wondered.

"You know, you don't have to hide things from us. I thought you knew that," he said.

"I'm sorry."

Cuddy brought his attention back to the open vault. The child had not only found the one vault they sought—out of what? Hundreds of others? And she knew how to open it, as well. Undoubtedly, it seemed, strictly by unerring mental concentration. She was immensely powerful. Powers she'd convincingly hidden from the rest of them.

"She is a Kartinal, Cuddy. I think she came back to this particular time and place on purpose," Jackie said.

That made sense to him. He could tell the seven-year-old was equally tied to all current happenings. Jackie, with Haffan's help, proceeded to tell him the rest of it—including the bit about Haffan putting a curse on the ancient scrolls.

"So, how long have they been in there?" Cuddy asked. "Maybe I should go take a look—"

"No!" All three bellowed.

Cuddy, who was only kidding, got the reaction he wanted. Keeping his voice low, so the soldiers couldn't overhear him, he asked, "So how does this work? If Calph or Langer come strolling out of the vault, holding the . . . uh . . . what did you say they were . . . scrolls?"

"Uh huh. Animal hide scrolls. Nine of them," Haffan said.

"So, if they come strolling out with the scrolls, and we look at them, will we then be cursed too?"

Haffan thought about that. As her brow again characteristically furrowed, she began chewing on the inside of her cheek. Eventually, shaking her head, she replied, "No."

"No what?" Cuddy asked.

"Merely looking at the rolled-up scrolls isn't going to affect you. Only gazing upon the actual ancient writings does, even if you don't understand what the letters, words, mean. You will be affected by the curse nevertheless. And now I remember what the curse does to those—"

Her words trailed off as Calph, then Langer, chose that exact moment to emerge from the vault.

"Hurry, turn away!" Haffan yelled.

They did as told, even Marzon, who must have been listening in on their conversation. They spun in unison in the opposite direction, away from the vault door.

Cuddy hadn't actually caught more than a brief glimpse of the two Howsh leaders. He did note they were holding onto something—perhaps the rolled-up scrolls, divvied-up between them. "Shouldn't you look away too, Haffan?" he asked, seeing her still looking directly at the two.

"No. I'm the Kartinal that conjured it up. I am safe. Anyway, you can all look safely now. The scrolls are all rolled up. I counted them. Nine."

Cuddy decided to look sideways—peripherally, first—just in case. Langer and Calph were standing among their soldiers—both appeared exuberant, even jovial. Undoubtedly, they'd found what they'd come for: the location of the Prophesy of Harkstrong. Cuddy wondered if they, the Earthlings among the group, would still be needed.

Content upon finding the nine scrolls indeed rolled up, Cuddy, none the less, still averted his eyes. A hush had fallen over the group of Howsh. Both Langer and Calph were now standing perfectly still, each staring wide-eyed at the other. The soldiers too were staring, eyes going back and forth between the two leaders. Then Cuddy also noticed. He had to blink several times to ensure his eyes weren't playing tricks on him.

"And you came up with this curse all on your own?" Tony asked Haffan.

Cuddy didn't listen to Haffan's response, caught up with what he was seeing. *Heads*. Both Lorgue Supreme Eminence Calph and Lorgue Prime Sub Langer were sprouting tiny heads. Heads on their arms and on their legs. Even tiny heads sprouting out on their foreheads, cheeks, and the napes of their necks. *All over*. And they were growing—some heads already reaching full-size.

But that wasn't the worst of it. The many heads were all talking at once—some yelling—some wailing. The sound and sight was terrible. Far beyond anything Cuddy had ever witnessed. He tried shutting out the awful, mournful voices—but couldn't.

First, Langer teetered and toppled over backwards, then Calph went down. By now the heads, hundreds of them, were all begging for help. Cuddy could just barely make out Calph's original head—his face. Making eye contact, Calph mouthed the words, *Please kill me . . . please, Cuddy . . . kill me.*

But in the end, Cuddy wasn't obliged to make that difficult decision. From nearby came a startling eruption of weapon fire. First Calph's life, then Langer's life were terminated and—one by one—too many heads to count became still.

Cuddy turned to the Howsh holding the energy rifle, and said, "Thank you, Marzon. That must have been very difficult for you."

The big Howsh looked somber. Cuddy wasn't really sure

what Marzon and Calph's relationship had been, but it obviously went beyond officer and subordinate.

"Really . . . what in God's name made you come up with a curse that does . . . that?" Tony asked, peering over at Haffan.

Cuddy was well aware Tony was just being Tony, trying to break up the tension. But Haffan, still childlike, wasn't used to Tony's dark humor and looked horrified. Guilt and sadness began to fill her eyes. On the brink of tears, she ran to Cuddy. He opened his arms and swept her up, turning them away from the grotesque scene.

Real nice," Jackie said glaring at Tony.

As her tears flowed—to the point he could feel wetness on his shirt—Cuddy was unsure what to say to her—how to make things better. Giving her a few pats on her back, he thought about Tony's question and wondered the same thing. *How did anyonecome up with such an awful curse*?

"Here . . . give her to me," Jackie said, her hands raised. "You're not helping." Cuddy transferred Haffan to Jackie and watched as she softly, and soothingly, comforted the child.

Kyle, standing at Cuddy's side, asked, "What the hell do we do now? Go back to Primara? Go back to searching for heritage pods?"

Cuddy studied the jumble of animal hide scrolls strewn upon the ground. "According to Tow, the future of the Pashier, also the Howsh, hinges on us finding this Prophesy of Harkstrong. We need to find out what's written in those nine scrolls. Personally, I'd like to keep going with this. Finish what we started. But it needs to be a unanimous decision. I have a feeling things aren't going to get any easier."

"Or any less lethal, "Kyle added.

chapter 34

Seven years ago . . . approaching Nashville, Tennessee

Staring out the car window, the outside world flew past Cuddy in a blur of muted colors and undefined shapes. He liked the somewhat familiar song playing but didn't remember what it was called. Suddenly the radio started making an awful noise, like an alarm. A voice now speaking on the radio was so serious. An important announcement, he said. At the mention of something called an Amber Alert, Slatch stiffened upright in his seat. Judging by his response to the robotic-sounding voice, it was clear Slatch very much cared about what was being said. Cuddy listened as the voice spoke about a mentally impaired boy abducted in Woodbury.

Slatch quickly fumbled for the knob. Angry, he swore and the radio was switched off.

"That's where I'm from . . . and you too, Slatch. Woodbury."

"Ignore what he said."

"And I'm mentally imp . . . whatever that word was he said."

"I said to ignore it!" Slatch barked. "It'll all be worth it . . . when your pa gets to see you again. He'll be mightily happy . . . and he'll forgive me . . . no doubt about that."

"Forgive you for what?" Cuddy asked.

Slatch didn't say anything for several moments. "Nothing . . . go back to looking out the window. We'll be in Nashville in a few minutes."

"To see my pa . . . yeah . . . I still remember. Yup, he's going to be real happy to see me."

He watched as Slatch checked the rearview mirror for the hundredth time. *What's so important back there?* Cuddy wondered.

"There she is . . . you can see the skyline up ahead."

"Nashville!"

"That's right."

"What's in Nashville?"

"Your pa. But other than him . . . well . . . there's the Country Music Hall of Fame. There's something called the Parthenon. A copy of a famous building in Italy, or maybe Greece."

"Yeah?"

"And there's the Johnny Cash museum . . ."

"Okay. Does my pa live near there?"

"No. He lives in a place called the Lucky Apartments."

"That sounds like a nice place."

For some reason, the comment made Slatch chuckle. Rolling down his window, he spat out another gob of tobacco juice. Then up came the window and Slatch again twisted the knob on the radio. Stevie Wonder was singing about sunshine. A song Cuddy knew—had heard before falling off the hayloft. A song locked away in his memories and, thankfully, never to be forgotten. It was a great song. Cuddy pictured his pa. Maybe in that same moment also listening to the radio at the Lucky Apartments. Maybe he too liked Stevie Wonder and was tapping his toe in rhythm to the catchy melody.

Slatch pointed to a big green highway sign up ahead. "Here we go. This is our exit." He turned the Rambler's big steering wheel and descended an off-amp. The car curved around and around before the road straightened out. Slatch noticed Cuddy was showing signs of becoming mentally confused again. Starting to forget.

"We're on our way over to see your pa, boy. We're in Nashville . . . where he lives. You're dog's back at home. Oh, and my name is Slatch."

"I remember that. Well . . . some of that," Cuddy said, nevertheless glancing into the backseat in case Slatch was wrong about Rufus. "Why are you sweating so much?" Cuddy asked. "Maybe you should open a window."

Slatch gestured back, making a few fingers wave on the hand positioned at two o'clock on the steering wheel. "I'm fine. Humid here is all."

Cuddy hadn't known what to expect Nashville to look like—but this sure wasn't it. Most of the houses along the road were boarded up. A good number of them had yards strewn with old appliances, or wheel-less broken down cars, sitting up on cinder blocks. What once had been houses, long since burned to the ground, were now only charged chunks of timber. There was a definite sadness to the place.

"You must have made a wrong turn, or something, Slatch. My pa wouldn't live in a place like this. Maybe you should pull over and get some directions. There's a guy up ahead on the sidewalk, pushing a grocery cart . . . let's ask him where the Lucky Apartments are."

"I know where it is. Not far. We're on the right road."

"He might not be home. We might have come all this way and he's out. Like at the post office. Or washing his car, or something."

"Nah . . . he knows we're coming."

"How's that?"

"I called him before we left." Slatch fished a hand into a pocket on his overalls and came out with a cellphone. One of the older kind, you flipped open to use. Cuddy was curious why Slatch hadn't told him that before. But maybe he had and he just didn't remember. Still, something felt off.

The car slowed and pulled over to the curb. High up on rusted metal supports was a big sign with faded red lettering. Cuddy needed to crane his neck to see it all on account of its being so high. He had no doubt the sign read *The Lucky Apartments*. Beneath the sign was a dilapidated two-story building. The surrounding second-level walkway was missing part of an iron railing, which Cuddy thought was pretty unsafe. The lime-green doors each had a number on them . . . well, most of them did. Some only showed a faded impression where the number once fitted.

"My pa . . . he lives here?"

"This is it. Just remember, his home is his castle. Go on, hop on out."

Cuddy did as told and waited on the crumbling sidewalk. Getting a whiff of strong perfume, he turned to see a lady in a short skirt approaching from down the sidewalk.

Ruby-red lips smiled at him. "Hi sweetie . . . your shoe's untied."

Cuddy glanced down and noticed she was right. By the time he looked back up, her high heels were clicking and clattering up a concrete stairway—partially hidden by an overgrown shrub.

Cuddy wiped his sweaty palms on his trousers, all of a sudden feeling nervous. He wondered what he'd say to him when he finally saw his father. Not sure he'd recognize him, since it had been a lot of years. He wasn't sure how many.

Slatch, coming around the car's rear end, headed for the same stairs the lady had taken. "Come on, boy. Let's go meet the other Mr. Perkins."

Cuddy trailed after him, stumped. What did Slatch mean? *What other Mr. Perkins?*

By the time they reached the top of the stairs, Cuddy's confused second thoughts had evaporated. More than ever, he was truly excited about seeing his pa again. He'd have quite the story to tell Ma and Kyle. And Jackie! She'd want to hear all about it too.

Slatch, up ahead, held a slip of paper in his hand and would peer at it every once in a while, comparing the numbers on it to the doors he passed. Cuddy hurried—trying to catch up to where Slatch stood. It looked like Slatch had found the right door, though he sure looked concerned.

Excitement had built to the point Cuddy could hardly contain himself. Approaching Slatch, Cuddy saw the door hung partially open. *Pa had done that for them! Such a nice gesture*!

Slatch, looking back at him and in the process of raising a curtailing hand, was shaking his head. But Cuddy's physical and emotional momentum carried him past the old farmer straight past door 29 of the Lucky Apartments.

"Pa? . . . it's me, Cuddy." He waited a moment for his eyes to adjust to the dimness inside, finding the curtains were drawn. An old couch and one chair were in the sitting room. Paper plates—some with partially eaten meals—covered a coffee table. Busy cockroaches scurried from one plate to another. "Pa!"

"Cuddy, wait! Come back outside," Slatch said, lingering in the doorway. He seemed to be frightened.

Cuddy had noticed the strong odor when he first entered the room. It was gross—sweet and putrid. Giving a furtive glance into the nearby kitchenette, Cuddy figured Pa was pretty much a slob. More dirty plates. More bugs. "Pa! It's Cuddy! Hello . . . I've come to visit."

"Damn it, Cuddy, get back out here! Come on outside next to me," Slatch pleaded.

No way! They'd come all this way. *Leave now without at least saying hi?* Cuddy tentatively moved into a narrow hallway. Two doors—both closed. He chose the one on the right, knocked then entered. The curtains were wide open and Cuddy knew this was Pa's bedroom. An unmade bed, with dingy sheets and a threadbare blanket, covered a partially exposed mattress, lying on the floor. No other furniture, only several large black garbage bags strewn around. Cuddy noted a couple of the bags held rumpled clothing.

"Cuddy . . . you can't be in there. Please, come back outside."

The smell, if possible, had only gotten worse; even this far away from the kitchen. *Good God . . . what was that stench?*

Cuddy closed the bedroom door and, turning, knocked on the second door. He only heard the *drip drip drip* sound of water inside. *The bathroom.* "Pa? You okay in there?" Cuddy slowly opened the door, not immediately recognizing the man hanging from the pipe. He wore nice clothes—the kind people wore when they went to church. His face was discolored, purplish and bloated—a leather belt tightly cinched around his neck. A continuous dribble of water, flowing down from the showerhead, ran across his cheek and dripped off his chin. Cuddy stared into the one open eye that was cloudy and vacant. Of course, Cuddy knew the man was dead. He was highly forgetful but not stupid. And he also knew that the man hanging down from the brown leather belt was indeed his father.

Cuddy spoke up, just loud enough for the hanging man to hear, "Why did you do this to yourself, Pa? Didn't you want to see me again?"

Cuddy heard Slatch talking to someone outside on the walkway. Perhaps to someone on his cellphone, since he only heard Slatch's voice. He was apologizing over and over again.

Cuddy was okay, being alone with his pa. He knew this would be the only time—the last time—he'd be in his presence again. He knew too he would forget this moment. It might take ten minutes, or an hour, but forget it he would. So he waited near his father and thought about things, trying to make some sense of it all. He leaned there within the open threshold and stared at the dead man. He stayed there for a long time. Perhaps an hour—perhaps two. He listened to the dripping water and Slatch outside pacing and pleading for him to come back out. Cuddy ignored him. Instead, he told pa about the things he still could remember—about Rufus and Jackie and Kyle, too. And about the old ranch house falling into disrepair—about Ellie in the barn and that she didn't liked to be ridden by anyone except Jackie.

When he heard Momma's voice outside on the walkway, he wondered how long he'd been standing there. A distant siren was getting louder. Soon, her arms came around him and she gently guided him away—away from the small bathroom where his dead father hung from a shower pipe.

chapter 35

Vaults of Calirah — present day . . .

They each offered up their own two-cent's worth of advice. Giving the pros and cons of whether it was time to head back to Earth, go to Primara, or stay focused on their quest. In the end, Kyle, Tony, Jackie and Cuddy were in agreement. Young Haffan didn't voice an opinion either way. They decided they would finish their mission together. Using the nine scrolls, they'd follow, *somehow*, the clues set forth within those ancient writings. Whatever it took, they'd track down the Prophesy of Harkstrong and then hand it over to Tow.

Speaking in low tones, and huddled close together within the Calirah rock cavern, Cuddy almost forgot about the eight lingering Howsh soldiers. They hadn't left yet, busily preparing the deceased commanders for transport. The two disfigured bodies were now wrapped in large blankets, found within the museum halls. It struck Cuddy the whole contingent would need a ride—perhaps back to Tripette City on Mahli.

Hunched, and looking miserable, Marzon approached them. "I am ready."

Cuddy and Kyle exchanged a quick glance.

"Ready?" Kyle repeated.

"To be imprisoned, of course," Marzon said, staring at his feet.

Cuddy raised up a restraining hand to keep the others from saying anything. "And you think that is an appropriate punishment . . . for what you've done?"

He sniffed nervously. "I fired on . . . the human, your friend, Brian Horowitz. Then stood by while that other human was abused.

Tony nodded scornfully, in a way that said, *yeah . . . thanks for that, asshole.*

"No. Imprisonment will only be a precursor to what must come later. My execution."

"I see." Cuddy sighed, letting out a lengthy breath.

Marzon continued, "The brig . . . unfortunately, is not yet completed on *your* vessel. So I suggest manacles . . . chained within the *Farlight's* aft under-hold."

"My vessel?" Cuddy asked, bewildered.

Though Marzon's head remained lowered, for the first time his eyes glanced up at Cuddy. "Lorgue Supreme Eminence Calph, when you all came aboard, assigned each an officer position. Well . . . *not* the sprout. You were assigned as the Captain's first."

"First . . . as in second in command . . . the XO?"

"I thought you knew," Marzon said. "The vessel *Farlight* is a stolen Howsh prototype. The ship, and its crew, are now under your command, Captain Perkins."

Cuddy let that sink in. The *Farlight* was an amazing vessel. A true warship, with advanced capabilities he mostly was clueless about. Whereas the *Evermore* could practically be piloted singlehandedly, the *Farlight* required a full complement of specialized crew.

Kyle said, "We need to take command of that ship, Cuddy. I'm sure Bob's piloted the *Evermore* all the way back to Primara by now. I also assume we're not the only ones searching for the elusive Prophesy of Harkstrong-thing."

Cuddy, giving the eight, standing-up straight, soldiers a sideways glance, found some had weapons slung over a shoulder, while others held onto theirs in a casual—unthreatening—manner. But he figured whomever it was Langer once reported to, perhaps his brother Norsh, would not take defeat lying down.

"What about these soldiers. What about the *Dubon tial*?"

"They have not shared much information with me," Marzon replied. "I overheard something about this being a special mission, directed by Council Member Leshand. He desperately wanted the Prophesy of Harkstrong found. For what reason, I do not know. The Howsh soldiers around us are unsure about me. A former crewmember on a vessel that was stolen, I could be considered as much an enemy to them as they suspect you are. I presume they will return to their ship, along with the scrolls, and request further orders. Orders from the Howsh high council."

Cuddy nodded. "For now, your incarceration will have to wait, Marzon. You'll continue with your duties onboard the *Farlight*. Understood?"

The big Howsh suddenly seemed to grow in stature. With his head raised high, and his shoulders squared, he replied, "I would be honored, Captain Perkins."

Cuddy looked about the cavern. The Howsh soldiers were preparing to leave. Leave carrying the nine scrolls, which presented a problem. They needed to be faced now, or faced later. But he wasn't about to start killing—them or anyone else.

"Introduce me to them," Cuddy said.

Marzon hesitated a moment then nodded. Cuddy, watching him turn away, heading toward the assemblage of Howsh soldiers, turned to Haffan and spoke to her telepathically. *I know you can hear me.*

Without looking at him, she responded, *So . . . what if I can?*

Will you do me a favor?

What kind of favor?

In a moment, while I talk to those Howsh soldiers, can you use TK to secretly gather up the nine scrolls, the ones lying over there on the ground, then hide them, and yourself, around here somewhere?

Her eyes roved toward the rolled-up scrolls, mostly lying near the soldiers' feet. With a glint of mischief in her eyes, she silently affirmed, *Sure, I can do that.*

"What do we do about Spilor?" Jackie asked, unenthusiastically.

"I guess we take that bot back to the ship. Maybe the robot can somehow be revived."

"We'll check Spilor out," Kyle said. "Carry it, if we need to."

"There can't be that much heft to the thing," Tony added.

Cuddy, noting that Marzon was signaling to get his attention, gave Haffan a wink. She smiled at him conspiratorially.

As Cuddy approached the soldiers, he watched as they unslung their weapons—the muzzles pointing at his chest. At four paces out, one of the Howsh said, "Far enough, human."

Cuddy stopped, assessing the designated leader of the group. He looked identical to the other seven, with one distinction: Most of his left ear was pure white in color. Cuddy got right down to it. "I'm assuming that you will be taking the scrolls?"

"Those are our orders. We are prepared to fight for them, human."

"No fight necessary. Those aren't the ones we came for, anyway. They're worthless."

The only reaction from the one with the white ear was an almost indistinguishable flinching of his snout muscles, which Cuddy noticed. "There are no other scrolls in that vault," the Howsh said.

"Did you look up higher, overhead, at the storage locker in the rafters? Anyway . . . we'll bid you farewell now. Marzon, can you help me collect the other scrolls above the vault. With your height, you should be able to reach the locker. And let's make sure we get all twenty."

"Halt!" White ear raised his energy weapon. Over his shoulder, he barked off a series of orders and the seven soldiers hurried into the vault. "We will check to see if there is a higher-up locker. If so, and there are other scrolls there, then they will be coming with us."

Cuddy shrugged—appearing unconcerned. As the last of the seven Howsh disappeared into the vault, Cuddy, using TK, swung the big vault door closed. He heard its internal gears spin, the latching mechanism engage.

The white-eared Howsh ran for the door and frantically tried to open it. Enraged, he spun around, pointing his weapon at Cuddy. "Open the vault! Do so now or I will shoot!"

"You could do that . . . but then who will open the vault? You?"

The lone Howsh soldier glanced about the cavern then realized both Haffan and Jackie were gone. He also noticed all nine scrolls were gone—no longer strewn around on the ground.

"The way I see it, you have two choices here. One, you can shoot me, and the rest of us, and return to your ship . . . the *Dubon.* Of course, you'll then have to explain to the Howsh high council how you came to be duped. Not only losing all nine scrolls, but seven of their finest Howsh soldiers in the process."

White ear glared at Cuddy, hatred in his eyes, but waited to hear option two.

"Or you can lay down your weapon, trusting that your fellow soldiers will be released," Cuddy said.

"Released when?"

"As soon as we complete our business here. In fact, you can help to speed things along. The faster we get going, the sooner your soldiers will be freed."

"How do I know I can trust you?"

"You can, because I am honest," Cuddy said with conviction.

"And the scrolls?"

From across the caverns, Tony interjected, "Do you really need to ask, dude?"

White ear fumed silently, contemplating his options. Cuddy thought he could hear, just barely, yelling coming from behind the locked vault door.

As the Howsh soldier bent down and placed his energy rifle on the ground, he said, "This isn't over."

Marzon retrieved the weapon then pointed it at the enraged Howsh.

Cuddy yelled, "Jackie! Haffan! Come on out!"

Tony and Kyle somehow managed to get Spilor vertical. The robot, standing on its own; was now in the process of cycling through a myriad of projected facial expressions. Jackie, then Haffan, quickly reentered the cavern, each holding an armful of scrolls.

Tony asked, "What now, boss . . . back to the ship?"

"Still one more thing to do. There's a heritage pod needing transporting out of here."

chapter 36

For the fourth, nope, fifth time in the last hour, Cuddy stopped cold in his tracks. Fighting against the inner distraction, growing within him. *What is going on with me?*

The already embattled heritage pod, now ascending, was several feet off the floor. Using telekinesis, Cuddy maneuvered it around obstacles—including clusters of mannequins and mock dwellings—within both the Pashier and Howsh Historical Halls. Again, halfway up the stairs, he was confronted with strange thoughts. Remembrances he was unprepared for; unexpected scenes from the past. Apparently, there were longer-term effects from his sessions with Tow, many weeks ago within the wellness chamber. New effects he was having a difficult time processing. All those earlier years—starting with that fateful day, at age seven, when he fell from the hayloft, up until recently—that he thought were lost. Lost, like grains of sand in the wind. Not so.

"Hey, are you still with us?" Kyle asked.

Cuddy, brought back to the present, realized the pod was

listing to the right and about to careen into the banister railing. Righting it, he directed it back toward the middle of the stairs.

"What's wrong with you?" Kyle asked.

"Nothing," Cuddy replied, increasing his TK influences over the pod in order to speed things up a bit. Another two minutes and the pod crested the top of the stairs. He let it levitate there as he ascended the last few remaining steps.

The problem was, more and more older memories were coming to him in streams—both abstract sounds and visuals—arriving with little or no reference point. Since those memories weren't tied to any grounded recollections, there was a dissociative aspect to them. Like those unbidden memories belonged to someone else.

Cuddy, Tony, and Kyle gazed up at the dark-brown underside of the large heritage pod. Cuddy didn't recall ever seeing a heritage pod from that same perspective before. There was a cool symmetry about it—the way connecting fronds were all bundled together.

With another mental TK push, the heritage pod glided forward. Tony helped guide it—giving the pod a little nudge, first one way then the other—as they moved away from the open vestibule toward the building's entrance.

Tony, humor gleaming in his eyes, said, "It's kinda weird."

"What's that?" Kyle asked, walking alongside him.

"That Brian's in there. Or some part of him is . . . up in that pod."

Kyle, giving the pod a wistful look, smiled, but didn't reply.

In that moment, Cuddy was picturing Kyle, in a different

time and place. Younger perhaps by three or four years, Cuddy wasn't exactly sure. Another new memory was taking shape within his mind. The three of them, Kyle Jackie, and himself, were down at Tamper's Gorge, which looked more like a small pond than a gorge. Taking turns, they swung out over the murky water below straddling an old knotted rope. It was all about timing. Letting go of the rope at just the right moment to get the farthest distance out into the water. Memories were now coming back to him with amazing clarity—a bombardment of sensations—the feel of brisk water on his skin; the mossy smell off the surrounding trees; the pungent taste of filthy pond water in his mouth. Cuddy was the next one up to swing. Slippery at the water's edge, he lost his footing, which sent him sprawling into weeds along the shoreline. Only by chance did he glance back to see the others together—treading water—their faces mere inches apart. Their eyes held each other's gaze. In that moment, Cuddy realized the two loved each other—that his third-wheel presence there wasn't even noticed. Cuddy then wondered how many times he'd seen them together just like that. Witnessing their deep feelings for one another, only to forget about it, as he always did, minutes later.

In that moment, Cuddy felt betrayed. Betrayed by Kyle, but perhaps more so by Jackie. He wondered how long after the accident that he, *the pathetic retard brother*, lost Jackie to Kyle? Embarrassment warmed his cheeks as anger rose within him. He considered the possibility that the pair were still a couple today. *Oh god—had he been too oblivious to even notice?* He silently prayed that no more memories—memories of those forgotten years—would return to haunt him. *Drip drip drip* . . . another memory posed—just out of reach—water dripping off a pipe. Cuddy didn't want to think about that. Not now, perhaps never.

Jackie and Haffan were sitting on the floor by a wide span of glass panes, close to where they first entered the building some hours before. Both sat Indian style, speaking in low tones, the scrolls stacked next to them. What Cuddy normally would consider a tender scene, he now averted his eyes. He couldn't look at Jackie. Not like he once did, prior to his recent recollections.

"We still need to deal with those security bots outside . . . any ideas about that?"

Kyle asked Cuddy, now lowering the heritage pod until it rested on the floor. "Have you seen Spilor?" Cuddy asked.

"Um, I think Marzon took the robot . . . somewhere," Tony said. "Wait, it was to a maintenance depot here in this building. Spilor needed a new leg, or foot . . . maybe both. Guess there's robot spare parts available. I wasn't really listening."

"Here he comes," Kyle said.

Sure enough, the eight-foot-tall Howsh, armed again, along with the whisper-thin robot were approaching them from the opposite end of the building. Spilor was no longer limping, nor unsteady on his feet. A good sign—whatever caused the problem was now fixed.

Too impatient to wait for them to trek over, Cuddy yelled, "What do we do about the security drones? We need to get out of here . . . in one piece."

"If we make haste, we should be safe," Spilor said, projecting a fairly normal-looking facial expression. "I have initiated a mandatory maintenance recall." Studying the large pod, Spilor said, "Oh my, I will open additional glass panes," then moved across to an access panel on the wall. Within seconds, after-noon breezes billowed through the open glass panels.

"Are we leaving now?" Jackie asked, getting to her feet.

Haffan stood and looked at Cuddy, who had the oddest feeling they had just been talking about him. "Yes, Haffan. Can you open the vault door, again, from here?"

"Think so." Haffan stared back at the open vestibule and stairway and closed her eyes. Several moments later, she said, "It is done. The furry beasts are free."

"Then we really do need to hurry. Haffan, stay close to Marzon, okay?"

Haffan nodded. That Cuddy didn't make the same sugges-tion to Jackie probably wasn't lost on Jackie. But he was still mad and found he didn't really care how she felt.

Cuddy rallied his ability to concentrate and brought the heritage pod up off the ground. With Tony's help in guiding it, they maneuvered the pod through the opening into the late afternoon heat. Moving outside quickly in pairs—first Kyle and Tony; then Cuddy with the big elevated heritage pod; then Haffan and Marzon; then last, Spilor alongside Jackie, carrying an armful of ancient hide scrolls. In the distance, Cuddy saw the distinctive lines of the *Farlight*. The vessel was docked on one of five empty circular landing pads within the cloverleaf-shaped formation. It was a beautiful ship. It struck him for the first time—at least until someone took it away from him—that's *my* ship.

Both Tony and Kyle ahead were scanning the sky for security bots—s*o far so good*. Again, Spilor had come through. As Cuddy's intense concentration began to waiver, the pod dipped closer to the ground. He fought against new intruding memories, fighting for his attention. *What was it with the pipe? Drip drip drip.*

chapter 37

Halfway to the landing platform, he heard the same telltale buzzing noise he'd heard before—distant security bots were en route.

"Don't wait for me . . . get to the ship!" Cuddy yelled to the others, while mentally propelling the heritage pod to soar faster. So fast, he was now running along behind it just to keep up. Ahead he watched the group, now sprinting, reach the *Farlight*. Yelling over the ever-mounting noise, he shouted, "Oh, and Spilor . . . I take it there's a freight access lift somewhere on that ship, right?"

Spilor didn't answer, disappearing from sight at the top of the aft gangway. *Perhaps he thinks that was a rhetorical question*, Cuddy mused.

Several moments later, Marzon appeared. Descending the gangway, he clutched an even larger energy weapon than the one he carried before. As the enormous Howsh got his bearings, focusing in the direction of the sound he was hearing—the approaching security bots—he pointed his weapon toward the sky.

As Cuddy approached the ship, he eyed the gangway and reaffirmed the pod would be far too large to fit through that entrance. Then, hearing the high-pitched sounds of hydraulics, he watched as a section of the ship's belly began descending.

Marzon fired non-stop. The security bots, dodging and weaving, were fully upon them—all around—as Marzon returned fire. Cuddy ducked as their crisscrossing energy fire filled the air. One wayward bolt clipped the upper left side of the heritage pod, igniting several of the ancient fronds.

Cuddy noticed Spilor, now riding the freight lift down. Realizing it was arriving into deadly hellfire, the robot facially projected an expression of sheer terror—almost enough to make Cuddy laugh out loud. Tony and Kyle hastily clamored down the gangway, followed by no fewer than ten armed Howsh crewmembers. *Finally!*

The sky was ablaze with energy fire as the battle progressed in earnest. Three loud explosions followed in succession and three security bots were eviscerated. But for every bot going down, another Howsh crewmember fell, as well.

While propelling the burning pod forward toward the lift, Cuddy used a hand to make several TK swatting motions above his head, rocketing several attacking security bots high up into the upper atmosphere. But more kept coming. Far more than there were before. At this rate, their odds of survival weren't looking good. Still thirty feet away from the underbelly lift, Cuddy suddenly felt an incredibly hot searing pain on his upper back. *He'd been hit.* Knees buckling, down now on all fours, he fell the rest of the way to the ground then experienced a hard, face-planting hit against his left cheek. Incapable of standing, let alone walking, he did manage to send the pod roughly forward, toward the lift's direction. And then the pod, he realized, was under someone else's control.

I got this, Cuddy . . . Haffan communicated telepathically.

Cuddy didn't know just where, exactly, she was. Perhaps somewhere inside the ship; perhaps looking out a porthole window? His relief was short-lived as Kyle, the next to get hit, was struck by an energy bolt in the groin area. His brother screamed out in agony before he dropped to the ground, curling into a fetal position.

Cuddy glanced back the way they'd come and noted . . . *movement . . . off in the distance.* The Howsh, those recently released by Haffan from the vault, were emerging out the front of the building. Undoubtedly, upon seeing the distant, ongoing battle with the security bots, they kept low. Scurrying off in the direction of one of the other landing pad clusters, they headed toward their ship—the *Dubon.* Cuddy wondered how long it would be before that ship was airborne and joining in on the attack? He needed to get inside the *Farlight.*

Placing his hands beneath his chest, as if ready to do a pushup, he tried to raise himself up. Renewed pain in his back brought him to the verge of almost blacking out. Persevering through it, he slowly rose. Through blurry vision, he watched the heritage pod bobble as it was lowered onto the *Farlight's* freight lift. The fire was now out and smoldering smoke drifted slowly into the air. Two sets of strong hands suddenly gripped his shoulders and legs and he was lifted off the ground, just as two other Howsh crewmembers lifted up Kyle. The security bots' attack had not diminished in the slightest. Cuddy could see several more prone Howsh—also exhibiting scorch marks on their bodies from direct weapon fire. But they were moving some—like him, they were injured, not dead. Cuddy passed out as he was being carried into the ship.

* * *

He awoke with a start. He'd been slapped—not once, but twice. Groggily, he muttered, "Stop already! . . . I'm awake." He peered up to see who was slapping him. "Jackie?"

"You need to wake up . . . all the way up!"

"Why . . . what's—"

"Apparently, since you're now the captain of this ship, you have to let the ship's AI know that the rest of the crew can also pilot the ship in your absence."

"What do you mean? I don't under—"

"We're being attacked, Cuddy, by the *Dubon!* Say these words . . . Crew succession parameters resumed."

Cuddy tried to make some sense of what Jackie was saying. She looked so angry. Frantic, even. *Where am I?* he wondered. What was happening around him didn't make sense. Then he recognized the *Farlight's* bridge. He could see crewmembers' legs all around him—some human, some Howsh—as he lay on his side atop the deck.

"Damn it, Cuddy . . . repeat this now! Crew succession parameters resumed. Say it!"

He could hear distant weaponry fire that definitely was

not the small energy blasts from security drones. They were *big gun*sounds. Then he instantly remembered the *Dubon* and the Howsh running from the building. In a croak, he ordered, "Crew succession parameters resumed."

Immediately, the *Farlight* came alive. Through the decking, Cuddy felt the propulsion system begin to wind up. Overhearing bridge crewmembers, speaking rapidly in excited voices, he heard something about bringing up the shields—engaging weapons.

"We're going to have to put you back into a wellness chamber," Jackie said.

"I don't think so," he muttered, having already spent more time in a Pashier wellness chamber than was prudent. They weren't designed for *humans*. His mind flashed back to Brian, and the grotesque, distorted, effect it had on him. Too much time spent in a wellness chamber could play havoc on their genetics.

He blinked away the fog and Jackie's face came into focus. Showing deep concern in her eyes, he felt her fingers stroking the side of his head.

"Please, Cuddy, just do what I tell you to do for once, okay? Spilor insists the chamber on this ship is . . . like . . . the next generation. It no longer creates adverse effects. It only heals . . . that's it. Kyle is in the chamber now."

Cuddy thought about that. She had chosen Kyle over him to be the first one healed.

Apparently picking up on his train of thought, her eyes narrowed. "They needed you to enact that *crew succession* bullshit . . . you ass." She abruptly stood and headed for the exit. "I'll be back. Somebody get him into the wellness chamber as soon as his brother comes out. And move this ship as far away from this place . . . from *Dubon,* as possible."

chapter 38

Kyle was there, along with Spilor, when Cuddy emerged from the wellness chamber. He looked around, not seeing Jackie.

"How you feeling, bro?" Kyle asked.

Cuddy thought about it. "Good . . . pretty much pain-free. You? How's everything . . . um . . . down south?"

Kyle winced and replied, "Fine, now. Though it was pretty bad before."

"Any side effects?" Cuddy asked.

Spilor interjected, "This next generation chamber does not affect the Para hippo carpal gyros organ, which is located within the human brain, in the same way it did for both you and Brian on the *Evermore*. Kyle will have no adverse effects from this procedure."

"Yeah . . . I was kinda disappointed at hearing that," Kyle said. "Was looking forward to moving shit around with my mind and communicating telepathically."

Cuddy suddenly remembered what was going on prior to

losing consciousness. He tightly clenched his eyes shut then opened them up wide again. "The battle . . . what's happening with the Howsh? The *Dubon*?"

"Just before your lights went out, you resumed the crew succession parameters. Then Jackie took command of the bridge."

"Jackie?"

"Yeah . . . apparently, that's how Calph set things up. You were next in line as captain; Jackie, captain's first officer; then me as . . . well, I don't remember the title. Maybe the captain's second officer," Kyle said.

"And the *Dubon?*"

"We split . . . got the hell out of Dodge. We're now idling in deep space somewhere. I think Jackie's been waiting for you to come out of the chamber."

"Sounds like a smart move."

"Marzon wanted to fight it out, back on Darriall. Said the *Farlight* was more than capable of destroying the *Dubon*. Coming unglued, he then called her some kind of Howsh insult . . . that I think translated to *stubborn*."

Cuddy couldn't argue with Marzon's assessment, Jackie could be infuriatingly stubborn. But he suspected she'd done so for him. She knew he still wanted to respect the Pashier way—Tow's way—of pacifism. But even for Cuddy now, it was becoming more and more difficult to follow that peaceful path. Cuddy's human side was coming up hard against such merciless enemies, hell-bent on wiping out an entire neighboring species for reasons that were beyond petty.

Are you going to stand around there all day?

Cuddy didn't hesitate, instantly answering her telepathic message. *Hello to you, too, Haffan.*

I have something to show you, she communicated.

You're talking about the scrolls?

I'll tell you when I see you . . . how about that?

* * *

Cuddy found Haffan sitting on the deck within her cabin. Dark inside, the only illumination rose from her own Pashier glow—casting a bluish tint onto the scrolls spread out around her.

Cuddy hesitated at the hatchway. "Is it safe to come in here?"

"Hold on!" Haffan quickly rolled up several scrolls, then two she simply flipped over so the writings were face down on the deck. "It's safe now."

Cuddy entered the cabin, noting it was identical to his own. He sat down on the edge of her bed and gazed intently at her. Sometimes he forgot she was only seven years old. Small in size in human measurements for that age, she often emotionally acted her age—seeming like a petulant child. But at other times, like now, she seemed much older, more adult-like. Not only highly intelligent, but perceptive too. An *aspect* of her was 8000 years old. It made sense. He waited for her to speak.

"Jackie's mad at you again, huh?"

"I didn't come here to talk about that."

She looked around at the scrolls by her. "I've read every line, every phrase, every word, a hundred times."

"And you've discovered what?"

"That I don't remember as much as I thought I did. I know I was directly involved with the authoring of these writings, and I can pick out my contributions with little effort. I remember the curse I put on them. A safeguard, you would call it, to keep them out of the wrong hands." Haffan glanced up at him.

"The Prophesy of Harkstrong? These scrolls are supposed to lead us to it. Even the Howsh are aware of that."

"The Prophesy is mentioned throughout the writings. They even better explain what it is, but not where they are hidden—or meant to be hidden. When we wrote these writings, they were still back on Mahli."

Cuddy thought about that for a minute.

"Why are you looking at me like that?" she asked.

"You're a kid. A child," he said.

"So?"

"And you've been *rejoined* many times . . . from a heritage pod."

"That's right. I told you that."

"It's just that . . . when Tow emerged from the pod he was in, he looked pretty much the same age. How is it that you emerged out a child instead of an adult?"

Haffan tilted her head, as if trying to get her head around the peculiar question. "Because," she said, "you choose the age you want to emerge at."

"You chose to be a child?"

"What's wrong with that?"

"It's just that this is important . . . hugely important. The entire fate of the Pashier race may fall in your hands. And you—"

She finished his sentence for him, "Chose to come back as a kid, as you put it."

Cuddy nodded.

Haffan let out a breath. "This rejoining . . . this life . . . needed to really count."

"What does that mean?" Cuddy asked.

"Did you think the Pashier have an infinite supply of *rejoining* rituals?"

Cuddy shook his head. He had a feeling he knew where she was going, but he suddenly didn't want to know any more. Didn't want her to say the words he knew she was about to utter.

"Cuddy . . . this is my last life here. I'm sure you understand that I would want to live as long and full a life as possible." She stared at him—the face of a child, but with eyes that revealed the depths of a very old soul.

"I'm sorry . . . I don't know what to say, Haffan."

"I'm not asking you to say anything. And I don't want to talk about this anymore, if that's okay."

Cuddy put on a smile that didn't really fit what he was feeling inside. "How about we go over the scrolls one more time. Do it together. Maybe I can pick up on something that jogs your memory. It was eight thousand years ago . . . you're entitled to forget a few things."

"You already know you can't look at them."

"Yes, I know. Can you read them to me? Would the curse be averted in doing that?" he asked.

She thought about it. "That should work, Cuddy. Good idea!"

A soft knock heard outside the open hatch was Jackie, who looked down at the two sitting in the near darkness. "Hey."

"Hey there," Cuddy said.

"What's going on in here?"

"Haffan was about to read to me what's on the scrolls. Want to join us?"

Jackie hesitated, looking down the corridor. "I should be on the bridge."

"You're no longer responsible for the bridge," Haffan said. "He is." She gestured to Cuddy.

Cuddy said. "She's got a point." Sliding over, he made room for her on the bed. "I have a feeling that between the three of us, we'll figure this thing out."

"You think?" Jackie asked, studying the scrolls. "And we won't start growing heads all over our bodies."

Haffan, shrugging a shoulder, said, "It should be all right," as Jackie sat down next to Cuddy, though not looking directly at him.

chapter 39

It began with a history lesson—not the Pashier, nor the Howsh, but with humankind. Haffan said, "For us to have a clear understanding of the historical course of events, it may be beneficial . . . give perspective . . . to use your own civilization as a reference. For instance, do either of you know when human civilization first emerged on your planet?"

Jackie's brow knitted. "I don't know. I probably learned that in school, but . . ."

Haffan turned her eyes to Cuddy.

"Well . . . I don't know what you're looking for. Like, I can tell you the cradle of civilization is commonly thought to be the Fertile Crescent. Referring to Mesopotamia and Ancient Egypt. Other civilizations developed independently; in Asia, along large river valleys . . . like the Indus River. And then there are Indian subcontinent civilizations . . . and the Yellow River. Let's not forget too the Yangtze River in China . . ."

Jackie stared at Cuddy—an expression he couldn't quite read—as he continued. "But I think what you're looking for is the transition, from prehistoric times to when humans first began writing things down, like . . . for their offspring . . . for future generations. The time period between the Neolithic and the Bronze Age, during the 4th millennium BCE."

Jackie continued to stare at Cuddy, suddenly speechless.

"What is BCE?" Haffan asked.

"That's your question? You understood everything else that he said?" Jackie asked, incredulous.

"Before Common Era . . . pretty much means Before Christ," Cuddy said.

"So . . . written historical records started . . ."

"About two thousand years BCE. Let's say four thousand years ago . . . roughly."

"How the hell do you know all that?" Jackie asked. "I understand your brain was repaired in the *Evermore's* wellness chamber, but that doesn't explain how such historical information got . . . stored in your memory. I don't even know what Mesopotamia means. Is that a place, a people, or what?"

"I like to read. And pretty much everything I read seems to stick mentally," Cuddy told her. The whole issue of his memory suddenly brought back flashes from his past—memories thought to be lost forever. They pulled at his concentration—but he pushed them away—refused to acknowledge them.

"So you have total recall? Why haven't you mentioned it before?"

"I'm not sure it's anything like . . . total recall. That sounds so . . ."

"Obnoxious?" Jackie threw out.

"I just have a really good memory . . . let's put it that way."

On noting Jackie's annoyance with him, clearly evident by her expression, he didn't understand why. Just one of many aspects about her he didn't have a clue.

Cuddy turned his attention back to Haffan. By the bemused expression on her face, she seemed to enjoy his and Jackie's back-and-forth banter. He'd noticed her preoccupation with their bickering in past days too.

"Pashier, as well as Howsh civilizations, go back much farther. I can recall events as far back as twelve thousand years. Although it does get a bit murky going that far back."

"You're referring to personal experiences?" Jackie asked.

As Haffan nodded, Jackie then asked, "So how does that help us figure out the scrolls . . . the writings?"

Before Haffan could answer, the small compartment suddenly brightened—almost as if someone had turned on a light, although no one had. The brightness emanated from the being now standing before them.

"Tow!" Cuddy exclaimed, recognizing that his appearance there was an astral projection. He'd witnessed it twice before, and the third time was no less captivating! Tow looked at all three—acknowledging them with a slight nod of his head. Just as he was about to speak, Haffan reached a hand out, letting it pass into Tow's ethereal form. Tow, caught off guard, momentarily lost his train of thought. Haffan smiled mischievously, making Tow laugh. A laugh, both abrupt and unanticipated, that also was contagious. In that moment, Cuddy missed his alien friend's company more than ever.

Regaining his composure, Tow said, "Please . . . excuse my interruption. What you are doing . . . ," he gestured to the scrolls strewn around the compartment, "is immensely important."

"What is it Tow?" Jackie asked.

Cuddy noticed Tow's deep concern.

"I have made a terrible mistake."

"What kind of mistake?" Cuddy asked.

"More like an assumption, which turned into a mistake. One that affects your friend."

The three exchanged puzzled glances. Then turned to study the increasingly distraught Tow.

"So just say what it is you did . . . all this dancing around is annoying," Haffan said.

"Don't be rude," Jackie scolded.

"Sorry."

Cuddy inwardly agreed with Haffan. *Why didn't Tow just get to the point? Could it really be that bad?*

"Go on, Tow . . . I'm sure it's all fine," Jackie said.

"Well . . . it's Brian."

"Brian Horowitz? The one who . . ."

Tow cut Cuddy off: "I am so very sorry. Truly I am."

Haffan dramatically sighed.

"The heritage pod . . . the one I helped you transition him into . . . it wasn't Pashier."

"What does that mean? What other kind of heritage pod is there?"

Haffan answered Cuddy's question. "It was a Howsh heritage pod . . . wasn't it?"

"Wait! The Howsh also have heritage pods?" Jackie skeptically asked. "I thought they despised the Pashier for their ability to transcend death. They think it's . . . like a sacrilege . . . right?"

"No, you're forgetting Tow's video; the one where he explains ancient history, when the two cultures were reversed a millennia ago. At one time, the Howsh were advanced beings, possessing great mental capabilities, while the Pashier were savages. The common Howsh of today have no clue about any of that."

"That's right, I remember," Jackie said. "But I never once considered that they too used heritage pods. So . . . Brian, he's now stuck in a Howsh heritage pod? With Howsh life forces all around him?"

Tow slowly nodded.

"How did you find that out?" Cuddy asked.

"That part is truly a miracle. I never heard of it happening before . . ."

"Do you ever just answer a question?" Haffan asked.

"Stop being rude, Haffan!" Jackie chided, this time more sternly.

"A Howsh life form there . . . an elder of sorts . . . reached out across the empyrean expanse. There are areas of the expanse, *evidently* shared by both Howsh and Pashier. Today, there was a Shain ritual of the awakening on Primara. The information on Brian was passed on to me by an emerging Pashier."

"And you can't get to him? From where you're at?"

"No . . . I am not within the same realm, Cuddy."

Jackie asked, "So is Brian okay in that . . . ?"

"Empyrean expanse," Cuddy added. Jackie again rolled her eyes at his prompt recall.

"I'm afraid not. Brian is not welcome there," Tow said. They find his presence an unforgivable insult. Many would like to terminate his life-force . . . be done with him."

"And they can do that? Just kill him? I thought that expanse was like heaven . . ."

"It is . . . but not all life forces evolve at the same rate. I have been given only a glimmer of hope to save Brian."

"Whatever it takes. What do we have to do?" Jackie asked.

"Apparently there is a second Howsh world, a parallel Howsh civilization. Tiny, compared to the Howsh home planet of Rahin that you are familiar with. If you wish to save Brian, you must travel to Camilli-Rhine 5. With guarded reluctance, they will permit him to take part in their own version of a Shain ritual of awakening."

"That's great!" Cuddy exclaimed, but then noted no sign of pleasure exhibited on Tow's face.

"Be warned, if Brian emerges from the heritage pod during the ritual . . . and you are not there to retrieve him, he will be killed. It will be a prolonged and painful death."

Cuddy asked, "So we should put the search for the Prophesy of Harkstrong on hold for now?"

Jackie gave Cuddy a backhanded slap on his arm. "He's one of us! Of course, we'll put the search on hold, and anything else too. When does the ritual take place?"

"And just how do we get to Camilli-Rhine 5?" Cuddy added.

chapter 40

Soon after Tow's ethereal form faded from view, Cuddy stood, ready to leave Haffan's compartment. Scrolls with ancient writings would have to wait, since there was so much to do—a tight timetable to meet. Jackie said she wanted to stay a few more minutes; hang around with the young Pashier.

Taking the lift, en route to the *Farlight's* bridge, Cuddy was surprised at the increased level of excitement growing within him. The prospect of traveling to Camilli-Rhine 5 captivated his imagination. *What would that divergent breed of aliens be like? How were they different from their Howsh brethren? Were they, somehow, the key to finding the Prophesy of Harkstrong?* Cuddy could no longer ignore the recent confluence of events so rapidly taking place. At this point, it was more than simply saving the Pashier race, which certainly was huge in its own right. Where days earlier he felt adrift—like a small boat lost on an endless sea—he now was set on a defined course. His life had new purpose, other than searching for heritage pods flung across the galaxy.

Cuddy's thoughts turned to Brian, and the mess he'd walked into. He had mixed feelings about the oldest member of the team, who was selfish and arrogant. Also, Brian had the intimate relationship with Jackie that he himself hadn't fully experienced yet. Possessing such knowledge carried its own level of resentment. But Brian was part of the team and, strangely enough, Cuddy almost missed him being around. *Almost.*

Upon reaching the bridge, Cuddy found Spilor. The robot was standing still, unmoving, seemingly unaware of his presence. Out the forward window was only blackness and stationary twinkling stars. Glancing around the area, the bridge was quiet—only two Howsh crewmembers present. One sat at the Engineering station, and the other at Communications. Both gave him a sideways glance when he entered the compartment, as if too busy doing *something*. Cuddy felt their uneasiness, perhaps mistrust, of the whole situation—that an alien, *a human,* no less—was now acting-captain of their ship. But feelings of uneasiness were mutual. Cuddy knew that he'd personally have to do what he could to build some kind of relationship, rapport, with the Howsh crew, if at all possible.

Spilor's head suddenly spun in his direction—surprise exhibited on his projected face. "What is the situation with the *Farlight's* crew, Spilor?" Cuddy quietly asked.

"They are anxious. Unsure what you will do with them. Perhaps replace them with humans."

"What humans?"

Spilor did not answer.

"We have a new . . . important directive. Are you familiar with Camilli-Rhine 5?" Cuddy asked.

"I am not, Captain Perkins."

Cuddy then relayed the spatial coordinates that Tow had provided him. "I need the crew of the *Farlight* back at their posts. Look . . . in time I'll be able to speak with them individually. But now is not that time."

"I understand, Captain."

Within minutes, Howsh bridge crewmembers began to trickle into the compartment. They looked even less excited, seeing Cuddy standing at the red railing—at the center point of the bridge—than the other two. But Cuddy was encouraged, seeing Marzon's arrival, although his ambivalent expression made it clear that he, too, wasn't thrilled walking onto the human captain's bridge.

Joining them at the railing, Cuddy breathed in the giant Howsh's foul animal scent. Marzon caught the eyes of two late stragglers then gestured for them, with an upward motion of his jutting chin, that they needed to hurry and get to their posts.

Cuddy recalled how Lorgue Supreme Eminence Calph addressed Marzon when they were on the bridge together. "Get us underway, First. Take us into FTL . . . push the upper limits of the *Farlight's* propulsion system. I suspect we're in a race with the *Pintial*. A race we cannot lose."

Marzon, grunting in acknowledgment, moved off toward the Helm station. Cuddy watched as Marzon conversed with the officer posted there. Although he couldn't hear them, it was obvious a heated discussion had ensued. Marzon returned, fuming.

"Is there a problem?" Cuddy asked.

"No, Captain. No problem at all."

"Um . . . what do you want me to do?"

Cuddy turned to find Jackie now standing behind them. She looked about the bridge, "Seems you already have a full crew complement."

"How 'bout you spend a little bit of time at each station, Learn from the bridge crew . . . perhaps start with Tactical, okay?"

She eyed the Howsh, sitting solemnly at the post. He was particularly unkempt-looking, his mud-colored fur matted. Jackie did a lousy job hiding her displeasure at the idea, but she moved off, sitting down next to the tactical officer. He looked less than thrilled that he'd be sharing his post.

The forward window brightened, as the distant star field blurred into elongated streaks of light. They had jumped to Faster Than Light—FTL.

* * *

Cuddy, Kyle and Tony stood at the Espy Table, each playing with its various controls. Two red-giant sister stars, along with their encircling planets, took form before them—all in glorious 3D realism. Cuddy twirled the controls around—first one way then another—getting different perspectives on what he viewed.

It had been a four-day journey across space. They'd entered

the system less than an hour earlier. The sixth planet of the system, called the Kwo System, was Camilli-Rhine 5. One by one, the bridge crew found their way to the Espy. Cuddy could understand their interest in, what was up until today, a totally unheard of world. If their roles were reversed, and he was about to make contact with a sister world of Earth—a world with other humanoids—he too would be drawn to learn more. Only natural. Like learning about previously unknown family members.

Spilor moved to the opposite end of the table and stared at the planetary system. "Very little technological capability. The Camilli have not ventured into space. Do not possess advanced means of travel . . . not by land, nor by air."

"You're suggesting they're pretty much barbarians," Tony said.

Spilor said, "Barbarians that do not go to war with others. Barbarians that live in relative constant harmony . . . where there are no signs of poverty or deprivation."

Tony ignored Spilor's cheeky reply. "Well, they don't sound all that dangerous to me. What's the plan for getting down there . . . for rescuing Brian?"

Jackie headed their way, coming from her shared post at Tactical, located at the forward part of the bridge. She glanced toward Tony. "Maybe they're not that technologically advanced, but there are massive amounts of energy rising up from various points on that planet." Bumping Cuddy out of the way with her hip, she took up the Espy controls and zoomed-in on a particular area of the emerald-colored world. From that closer-in view, it was evident the planet was Class A. Lush with forests, expansive lakes, and flowing rivers, there were also five oceans—each pristine, in varying brilliant shades of azure. "Let me show you the specific site coordinates provided by Tow." All eyes were on the Espy and what appeared to be a view of a small community—from a 5,000 foot high-up vantage point.

"What did I just tell you? See, barbarians," Tony said, smirking. "What are those . . . huts? Some kind of shanty-shacks?"

To Cuddy, they certainly did look basic. No less than one hundred similarly sized and shaped structures, made of natural substances. Probably, clayed brick walls—with timber roofs—neat and orderly in their design.

"There," Kyle said, pointing to the farthest corner of the community. At the tree line was the familiar shape of a heritage pod. "Can you zoom in a bit more, Jackie?" he asked.

"I think this is as far as it goes. Looks like it could be a pod . . . if it's similar to a Pashier pod . . . no way to tell yet."

"So . . . you think they're expecting us?" Kyle asked.

"I don't know, but I think so," Cuddy replied. "Looks like some movement below." Squinting, he leaned over the Espy. "An assembly of sorts. We better get down there."

"Could be something akin to a Shain Ritual of Awakening?" Jackie said hopefully optimistic.

chapter 41

Seven years ago . . . Leaving Nashville, Tennessee

Cuddy wanted to say a proper goodbye to Slatch. You always say goodbye to your friends. *Why was Slatch so upset? Was it because Momma came and took him home?* She'd whisked him away in a hurry, just as lots of police cars and fire trucks arrived at the Lucky Apartments.

"Buckle your seat belt, Cuddy," Momma instructed, her left hand on the wheel and her right resting firmly on his left shoulder—as if he might float away if she removed it. "Let's think of something good. Something happy . . . how about that?"

Cuddy frowned at her. "I'm forgetful . . . not stupid, Momma." Taking her eyes off the road for an instant, she glanced at him.

"I can still remember Pa, hanging there, all blue in the shower."

Momma blinked several times in quick succession. Cuddy knew what that meant—she was fending off tears.

"Honey . . . there's no reason to remember that. No one should have to remember something like that. Perhaps it will be a blessing . . . soon . . . a few minutes from now—"

"I don't want to forget it!" Cuddy yelled, uncertain why he'd lashed out at her. Perhaps he knew, on some deeper level, that something important had just taken place. Something, whether good or bad, that should remain a part of his life. But he knew his faulty memory wouldn't allow him to hold on to it for long. *It wasn't fair*. No—he wouldn't let it fade away. Not this time. He'd keep talking about it, keep thinking about it—forever, if he had to. At least until he understood what happened to Pa. "Why did he do it, Momma?"

"Let's wait till we get back onto the highway. All these cross-streets, it's easy to get lost in big cities. I have a terrible sense of direction."

Drip . . . drip . . . drip as the water trickled off his chin. One of his eyes was open, glazed and unfocussed. "Pa was all dressed up. You saw that . . . right?"

Momma hesitated and then nodded. "Yes . . . that was nice of him." Her lower lip quivered. "I don't know why he did it, Cuddy. All I know is that he suffered. Always had. I knew your pa when I was your age . . . seems I've always known him."

"Why did he leave us, Momma? Was it because I'm a retard?"

Momma's eyes flared instantly with anger. "Don't you ever use that word . . . not ever! You know better."

"Well, was it?"

"Of course not! He just had issues. Swings of temperament, that didn't have a name when he was younger. Then, after the accident . . . oh, do we really need to talk about this now, Cuddy? Let's just wait. Talk later . . . I'm almost at the highway."

Cuddy briefly remembered Slatch saying something—something about when he was a kid in Woodbury. Frustrated, Cuddy made a fist and pounded his thigh. *What was it he asked me?* Ignoring the concern showing on Momma's face, he asked, "Did you know Slatch . . . like when you and Pa were kids?"

For the first time her hand left his shoulder, joining the one gripping the wheel. "We all grew up together. I grew up on the same farm . . . where we live now."

"Slatch was a neighbor?"

"Uh huh . . . so was your father. Both lived on adjoining farms."

Cuddy wasn't sure what *adjoining* meant. Something like being next-door neighbors, he figured. "I think Slatch wanted me to ask you if you remember him."

Momma tensed and began to chew the inside of her lip. "I don't want to talk about Slatch. And you are never . . . ever . . . to go near that . . . man . . . again."

"Slatch and Pa were best friends?"

Momma nodded twice and Cuddy clenched his eyes tight shut. *Please . . . I don't want to ever forget.* "Did Pa want to leave, or did you make him?"

"Cuddy... I understand that what you went through today was terrible. It's why I came and got you away from that place... that hotel... before the police came."

"Why did he leave us?"

"Where are you getting these questions from, Cuddy?"

"Momma!"

"I made him go. It wasn't you, or Kyle; have anything to do with the accident. He couldn't be around us anymore, Cuddy. That's all there was to it."

Cuddy sat quietly for several moments. Slowing, Momma made a hard right turn onto the highway on-ramp. Taking-in the passing scenery out the side window, he felt his head suddenly, like water filling up a bucket, fill with a thick haze. Tears filled his eyes as the sharp edges of the important things he badly wanted to remember began to turn blurry. Memories, once within an easy reach, began to float away. No matter how hard he tried to reach out and catch them—they turned to mist and were gone. *Drip, drip, drip...*

"Where are we going, Momma?"

She turned and looked hard at Cuddy. Poised to say something, she seemed to think better of it and just shook her head.

"Where's Rufus?" Cuddy peered in the back seat, then back out the window. "Did we go somewhere? To the store?"

Momma didn't answer him for a long while. He didn't understand the situation, why she looked the way she did. Like she was having a hard time breathing.

With her eyes brimming, Momma said, "Yes, sweetie... just picking up a few things at the store. Rufus is waiting for you at home. You two can go out and play until dinner is ready."

When she reached for the radio dial, Cuddy was reminded of something. "Momma . . . what's an anger alert?"

"You mean, amber alert?"

"Yeah. What's that?"

"It's nothing you'll ever need to worry about."

chapter 42

Deep space — present day . . .

Lorgue Prime Eminence Norsh was using a systematic approach to deal with the Gulk. He wasn't surprised when he arrived at the outer reaches of the sector that any threat from these disgusting green humanoids was determined to be nominal. There was slim indication that they were the same aggressive invaders Council Member Leshand had been so pre-occupied with. They were simply terraforming what previously were uninhabitable worlds—desolate rocks, drifting through space. But he had his orders, and, truth be told, his crew could use a little diversion.

Five days before, the *Pintial* joined with the Stalwart Fleet, consisting of twenty-three recently built, powerful Howsh warships. As he paced his command ship's bridge, Norsh nodded to himself. *This was how it was supposed to be.* A fleet of ships, each with remarkable capabilities, and manned by highly trained personnel.

"Prime Eminence, we approach the Gulk defensive parameter."

"Thank you, first . . ." Norsh said, staring at the display—at the closest blinking outer markers. Like large sea buoys, the strobing beacons were intended to send a not-so-subtle message to any approaching vessel. Conveying: Stay back, or risk being fired upon.

Beyond them, he saw the cluster of eight planets—each at a different level of progression in its terraforming evolution. The closest one was still in its embryonic state of change. Geo-engineering had barely altered that *other world*'s sheer and rocky gray surface. Progressively, the eight worlds showed signs of change—of burgeoning life. The farthest planets, that were more sustainable, were already beautiful—beckoning to be inhabited by adventuresome Howsh pioneers.

Some would consider what the Gulk were doing quite noble, even benevolent. But more accurately, it was only a means for the alien race to further their influence into deep space. Something the council regarded as a form of aggression. Norsh thought that was probably pushing it—the Gulk were anything but aggressive. A touchy-feely breed that only used violence as a last resort, such as protecting themselves against outside aggressors. The thought brought a smile to his lips underneath his snout. In nature, there was always an antagonist, and those antagonized. In the end, history would be chronicled by the victorious—not the wretched, vanquished ones.

Norsh knew that the Gulk's terraforming and later

settlement-building enterprises would have substantial security resources in play, such as a dedicated, constantly revolving, fleet of warships. This was a bigger enterprise than others that Norsh and his fleet had visited over the last few days. Most certainly, it would have more substantial defenses assigned to it.

"Thirteen heavy destroyers are approaching from directional coordinates 5668. Also, a smaller assemblage of ships, from directional coordinates 2144. All those are Angle-Fighters," the first officer reported.

"Talk to me about the worlds. Are any inhabited?"

"Three, sire . . . Four hundred thousand green vermin are populating the fully terraformed planets."

"Good! How about we deliver them a special message: A *Welcome to the sector neighborhood* gift. Configure it then let's go with high yields . . . say, an even hundred torpedoes. Distribute the offensive amongst the fleet. Fire at will."

"Yes, at once, sire."

The Stalwart Fleet was now passing the outer perimeter buoys. The nearest strobing beacon was so bright it was hard to look at. "Also, First, *rail-gun* that bothersome beacon . . . do it now," Norsh added.

Within moments, the beacon was decimated in a hail of brilliant rail-gun fire. Soon afterword, torpedoes were underway; each fleet asset sending off two, three, even five, of those lethal harbingers of death. Norsh watched as aft thrust fire, from the many rocket-like torpedoes, sped off toward their intended destinations. The projectiles would do little physical damage to the ginormous worlds, but Howsh scientists had perfected the payloads for both quick and irreversible effectiveness. The *Dirth* was the antithesis of terraforming—a biological scourge that would spread and kill organic life with blind abandonment. The beings inhabiting these new worlds would soon wish they'd never been born, dying horrific, painful deaths. It was a good day, Norsh figured. Perhaps Council Member Leshand did know best after all. This fiery diversion was just what he needed.

Small explosions soon exhibited on the various planet surfaces. There didn't seem to be any particular rhyme or reason for the frequency, or placement of the explosions, but actually there most assuredly was.

"Lorgue Prime Eminence Norsh ... the enemy fleet of heavy destroyers has arrived. We are being fired upon."

"Of course we are ... proceed ... engage the enemy. Return fire and bring shields up to maximum. And relay to the fleet not to underestimate those approaching Angle Fighters either. They're wily and highly competent. A desperate enemy is an unpredictable enemy. We've just initiated the eradication of hundreds of thousands of Gulk. They know this ... are fully aware what the Howsh have done to other enemies."

Norsh flinched, hearing the corresponding explosion on the nearest Gulk heavy destroyer. He took pride knowing that the*Pintial* had dispatched the killing ordinance.

Suddenly distracted, he noticed a commotion of sorts taking place at the coms station—his first officer reprimanding an obviously distressed crewmember. This was no time to be dealing with inconsequential drama, Norsh fumed. *We're in the midst of an important battle, for God's sake.* Angered, Norsh strode to the coms station, which had also attracted others from around the bridge.

"What is the meaning of this? Return to your posts! At once!"

The bridge crew scattered, like roaches caught in sudden light. The first officer remained, standing alongside the coms officer. Their expressions were identical. Both rattled.

"What is it?" Norsh barked.

"Something terrible has happened, Lorgue Prime Eminence Norsh." Obviously, they knew something he did not, which, of itself, was infuriating. "Tell me . . . *now*!"

"Your brother, Lorgue Sub Eminence Langer . . . has been killed, sire. I am very sorry to report this terrible news."

"Langer? No. You must be mistaken. He is on a special . . . very important mission for . . ." Norsh let his words trail off. Some part of him knew the report was accurate, he could feel it in his bones. His brother, the only being he even remotely cared about in this vast universe, was now gone. *Oh my.*

"Who did this?"

His first officer and the coms officer exchanged a knowing glance. "The First Officer on the *Dubon* reported it was the Humans; the same ones helping the Pashier. Led by Captain Cuddy Perkins."

Norsh let the news sink in for a moment. Taking in an enormous breath, he slowly let it out through exposed teeth. "Of course, it was," he said, staring unfocused toward the display; at the raging battle, taking place all around them.

"Prepare the fleet for departure."

"Eminence?"

"We will leave immediately . . . at once. Let the fleet know the change in orders."

"Sire . . . the ongoing battle . . . the Gulk . . . our orders from the council."

Norsh's eyes regained their focus—laser-like focus directed toward his first officer. With blinding quickness, he used an upward swiping motion—his right claw fully extended, like four protruding daggers. The first officer watched as his innards flopped out and onto the deck. Disemboweled, he died standing there, watching it occur, then crumpled down into his own gore.

chapter 43

Cuddy had no idea how the ones below would react to a spacecraft descending upon them from high above. There was far more he didn't know about the reclusive Howsh or, more accurately, the Jahin, than what he *did* know. Maybe they'd run around *crazed*, shouting *the sky is falling! The world is coming to an end!* Or perhaps they already knew of their ship's impending arrival; had been alerted via the empyrean expanse and those emerging from the heritage pods, or whatever the pods were called on Camilli-Rhine 5 in the Kwo System.

The small team had assembled within the airlock within the lower deck. Cuddy felt the *Farlight's* rapid descent in the pit of his stomach and reached out, grabbing ahold the bulkhead for balance. The others, Jackie, Kyle, and Tony, looked apprehensive. No one had spoken a word since Cuddy's earlier heated *words* with Marzon on the bridge. The giant Howsh had been adamant—not only demanding to be part of the team but to be armed, as well. Cuddy wasn't totally sure why he didn't want Marzon along, but perhaps it was due to Marzon's more violent nature. The upcoming visit was supposed to be a peaceful first encounter.

"Do you think we'll get him back?"

Cuddy glanced up to find Jackie staring at him. "Brian? I don't know. You heard Tow's words just the same as me. But some part of me thinks it's . . . I don't know, far-fetched, maybe?"

Jackie nodded looking resigned. "Me too, I guess." She diverted her eyes, staring down at the deck, as Kyle shrugged, uncommitted. Cuddy didn't want to mentally dwell on how close his brother was standing to Jackie. *Were they a couple?*

"If they are expecting us, I hope they've prepared something."

Cuddy shook his head, questioning—not getting Tony's meaning.

"Like a feast . . . or a barbeque. What do you think these creatures eat, anyway?"

"I've no idea, Tony," Cuddy said.

"Maybe they eat insects. If that's the case, forget it. They can do what they want with me. I ain't eating no fucking beetles, or*things,* like scorpions. No way!"

Jackie's lips twitched at his comment. Cuddy stole a look at her face for a few clandestine seconds. Standing there in the partial shadows in that particular moment of time, she had never looked more beautiful to him. Which only made things worse as more and more lost memories returned to him. He inwardly referred to those years as *the innocent years.* A time when he truly was innocent—forever age seven. Always none wiser, nor more informed, at least mentally, than he was on that fateful day when he fell head first to the barn floor below. What he now was slowly discovering was how much pain was embedded in those lost years. Short-lived pain, since—within a few short minutes—he'd forget everything. Like an automatic reset button, constantly pressed, the pain would quickly be gone and he was back to being age seven. Yesterday, Cuddy mentioned to Jackie some memories from *the innocent years* were returning. Not everything, but still a lot. Her reaction was immediate. Embarrassment. Guilt. *Maybe regret*? Today, it seemed *light years* separated them. He turned his attention to Kyle, hoping she hadn't relayed to him what he'd told her in confidence. Kyle didn't need to know. Things already were strained enough within the team.

Suddenly the landing thrusters noisily engaged. Within the confined space, they sounded intensely loud. Tony made a face, saying something undecipherable over the racket, and Cuddy found himself smiling though he didn't hear what was said—Tony was usually funny. The ship abruptly landed. When the outer hatch began to rise, he watched as the gangway was lowered through the partial opening.

Cuddy was just about to step forth, out into a whole new world, when another internal hatchway slid open. Spilor, entering the airlock compartment, wore a placid expression. "I have decided to join you. Would that be acceptable, Captain?"

Cuddy tried to come up with some reason to tell the awkward robot, "No," but couldn't think of one. Perhaps having it tag along would prove useful. Undoubtedly, Spilor could explain certain aspects of the world and its inhabitants. Cuddy, giving Spilor an unenthusiastic nod back, said, "Try not to draw too much attention to yourself."

First out of the hatch, Cuddy stood at the top of the gangway and surveyed the surrounding landscape. He'd decided earlier to land the *Farlight* approximately one-half mile from the small village, positioning the ship closer to the heritage pod, sited at the far edge of the village. Glancing around, he found no one waiting for them. As he descended the ramp, he momentarily questioned his own judgment about being unarmed. Nevertheless, in any event, would he be able to shoot—perhaps kill another being—as easily as Marzon could? He didn't want to even consider it. Soon enough, they'd know if his decision was the correct one, or not.

The surrounding terrain was certainly Class A. Somewhat earthlike, but with one significant difference: The smell. The scented air seemed somewhat bitter, like certain plants or trees were emanating a distinctive pungency. Not entirely awful, just different.

Cuddy waited at the base of the gangway for the others to descend. Everyone wore matching, light-blue jumpsuit-type, uniforms. On board the *Farlight* was something called the *fabrication berth*. Cuddy had briefly explored the large lower deck compartment days ago and found it both complicated and fascinating. Later, Spilor explained the area's main purpose. As its name implied, many things were fabricated in there—clothes, food stores, even the construction materials for ongoing ship renovations.

"No sign of any fur-balls?" Tony asked.

"Well concealed... but they are all around us," Spilor said.

Then Cuddy caught movement within neighboring trees. He wondered if what he would see would jive with his expectations and akin to Tony's comment: Fur-balls—large and lumbering.

Spilor, standing rigidly alert, looked off toward the *Farlight's* left. "There, coming from Camilli-Rhine 5's directional northeast, seven individual Rahin are approaching."

A definitive stillness blanketed the nearby woods.

"Maybe this wasn't such a good idea," Tony said under his breath.

"I'll second that," Kyle muttered, just as quietly.

"Look!" Jackie said, pointing at the arrival of a small contingent of Jahin. "Oh my God..." she expelled, wide-eyed in wonder.

Cuddy was speechless. Mentally acknowledging that the seven beings approaching were a similar species to the Howsh, judging by both size and basic form. But any other similarity stopped there. Beyond doubt, he'd never witnessed more beautiful creatures—either back on Earth, or anywhere else, for that matter. Whereas the Howsh were covered in a dense fur—typically matted and dirty—these Jahin's bodies were covered in perfectly straight hair—like shimmering manes. Their hair was at least a foot-and-a-half long, some the color of fawn, or as black as obsidian, and others so silvery they reflected back any in close proximity to them. Their facial bone structure was different too . . . far more refined, less bear-like . . . more something else.

The largest of the seven Jahin moved to the front of the group then proceeded forward while the others stayed back. There was no fear or hesitancy in his steady gaze. The presumed leader, a male, had magnificent silver hair. Cuddy wondered how the communication between them was going to work. Perhaps Spilor would be able to assist with that. *But were they even intelligent enough to converse?* he wondered.

"Where is the sprout?" the Jahin asked him disapprovingly, in heavily accented English.

chapter 44

Cuddy stepped forward. "I am Captain Perkins. May I ask who I am speaking with?"

"I am Dramin, leader of the Blue Forest clan. We have been expecting you."

"Then you know why we are here—"

Dramin cut him off, "Yes . . . of course. The emergence of the human-Pashier mutant." Dramin raised his snout, as if sniffing the air. "You are one . . . a mutant . . . as well."

Cuddy nodded in assent to his statement.

Dramin's attention turned to the *Farlight*. Again sniffing the air, he said, "Those savages are not welcome here . . . should never have come here."

"You speak of the Howsh? The ones onboard the ship?"

Dramin's nostrils flared. Abruptly thrusting out both claws, like a small toy being tossed aside, the *Farlight* skittered across the ground—ending up thirty or more feet from where it first landed. Dust billowed up all around the vessel.

Cuddy did his best to rein in his anger. Dramin's sudden

TK action easily could have fractured one or more of the ship's landing struts. He pictured Marzon inside, now readying to fire on the small contingent of Jahin. Cuddy raised an open palm in the direction of the ship and shook his head.

"I strongly advise you not to do that . . . or anything like that, ever again." Cuddy spoke with as much authority as he could muster, knowing his telekinetic powers were no match for this Jahin leader. But hopefully, Dramin didn't know that.

Ignoring Cuddy, Dramin said, "Send out the sprout. I wish to see that renowned ancient being for myself."

"Look . . . that's not going to happen," Cuddy said. "The sooner we retrieve our crewmember, the sooner we'll be out of your hair." Cuddy caught Jackie's eye, right after using that too familiar human colloquialism. Referring to the Jahin's hair was probably a bad idea.

"Interesting. You fear for the sprout's wellbeing, but here there is no need for that. She is safe amongst our kind. She is *Omnitoll* . . . a revered sacred being. Her presence is the only reason you can walk our land . . . breathe our air."

About to stand his ground, Cuddy noted he was already too late, as Haffan scampered down the *Farlight's* gangway. *Damn it!*

Excited murmurs erupted from the Jahin. Each—including Dramin—bent to their knees, bowing with lowered heads.

Haffan seemed not to know what to make of the spectacle. Hurrying over to Cuddy, she took his hand and stared up at him. "Why are they doing that?"

"Apparently, they know who you are . . . who you were in the past."

She stared at the group of genuflecting beings then noted, "They have pretty hair."

Like so many times before, Cuddy marveled at Haffan's odd mix of both childlike and adult behavior.

"How long are they going to stay all bent over like that?"

Cuddy shrugged, and Tony suggested, "Tell them to get up, Haffan. Ask them if there's anything to eat around here."

Ignoring him, she bent over sideways, trying to catch Dramin's eye. "Hello? You can get up now. You can stop doing that."

As the leader of the Blue Forest clan stood, the others followed suit.

Kyle approached Cuddy's other side. Keeping his voice low, he said, "Um . . . I don't know about you, bro, but this doesn't seem right."

"What do you mean?"

"It's too much about the kid. We're here only to get Brian then get on with our mission."

"Copy that, but we're in no position to make demands. I don't think Haffan's in any real danger. If her presence helps things to move along . . ."

"Yeah, I guess you're right. It's only that . . ." Kyle looked around, "this place creeps me out a bit. Like, it's not what it appears to be."

Cuddy couldn't argue with that.

"So what now?" Jackie asked.

Haffan, releasing Cuddy's hand, approached the clan leader. "Can I ask you a question?

Dramin bowed his head obviously star-struck by Haffan's near presence—a dramatic demeanor change evident from only moments before.

"Have we met before? You seem familiar. Perhaps at another time?"

Flustered, Dramin was momentarily speechless. "I did not presume you would remember. So much time has passed . . . so many different lives."

"You weren't very nice back then, I remember that. I hope you've changed . . . and for the better." The child's reprimand was acknowledged with a pained expression. What the little Pashier thought of the clan leader mattered very much to him.

What a strange situation, Cuddy thought. Most humans thought in terms of one life. One existence.

Jackie asked, "Haffan . . . how did the Pashier and Jahin . . . um, first cross paths?"

"Good question!" Tony said.

"There is a neutral dimension within the empyrean expanse. Most do not know of it . . . do not travel to it. Mixed sorts of beings are found there. Different races, breeds, from all over the universe. Not a place you'd want to be if you don't know your way around. It's where Tow recently connected with other Jahin, in order to set up this meeting. Twelve hundred years ago, I met this *Dramin*character. I wasn't impressed then . . . not so sure I am now, either. Just being *real*," she said with a half-smile, glancing at Tony. Undoubtedly, she'd picked up the phrase from him.

The Jahin seemed to be growing impatient. After the abuse afforded to the Farlight, Cuddy thought *screw-'em.*

Dramin, stepping forward, said, "The Constant Ritual shall commence soon."

To which Spilor leaned over and added, "That is the equivalent of the Ritual of Awakening, which you are familiar with."

The clan leader eyed the robot, as if noticing Spilor for the first time. "No technology! We do not welcome technology of any kind here. Send the metal man back to your vessel."

What an obnoxious attitude, Cuddy thought, having just about enough of it. Before he could respond in kind, Haffan said, "That's Spilor. You need to show him respect. Where I go . . . he goes."

"In your face," Tony said, barely loud enough to be heard.

Kyle said, "Cool it, Tony . . . I don't think we want to go up against these guys. Have you looked at their claws? Twice the size of Marzon's."

"You will come now . . . a feast is being prepared. The mechanical man can wait nearby . . . at the surrounding tree line to our village."

The group of Jahin headed into the woods, their long manes swaying back and forth in unison. The sight somehow reminded Cuddy of glistening, flowing, waterfalls.

* * *

Close to 200 beings were present. Apparently the same assemblage of Jahin they'd observed from the Espy table, back on the *Farlight's* bridge. Low tables were setup in the shape of a large U, and a telekinetic bucket brigade of sorts was being used to transfer big trays of food from another area of the village. The various aromas, coming off the platters as they passed by him, were tantalizing. Cuddy's stomach was already growling. Tony, keen to know what they'd prepared, reassured him there didn't appear to be any insectile dishes on the menu.

"I guess we sit on the ground and cozy up to the tables; it's kinda like a Hawaiian luau setup," Jackie said.

Cuddy wanted to ask her whether she knew that from personal experience. Thinking better of it, he decided he didn't want to know, if, or with whom, she'd ever gone to Hawaii. *Hell, until a few days ago, he'd never even think to ask her a question like that.*

Every villager was busy—with a specific job to do. No idle hands. Standing aside with his team, out of the Jahin's way, made Cuddy feel he should be doing something useful. Helping them out in some way. As an idea occurred to him, he wondered if it would be presumptuous of him to volunteer what he was thinking about.

"Kyle . . . can you help me do something?"

"Sure, what's up?"

"Come with me," Cuddy said, heading away.

"Where you guys off to?" Jackie asked, suddenly uncomfortable at being left alone.

"Can I come too?" Haffan called after them.

"Stay with Jackie and Tony. We'll be right back," Kyle yelled over his shoulder.

chapter 45

Cuddy nearly careened into the robot, standing idly at the tree line. "Stay here, Spilor. Keep watch over Haffan, Jackie, and Tony. Alert me if you think they're in any kind of danger. Any at all."

"Yes, Captain Perkins . . ."

Cuddy and Kyle continued their jog through the wooded landscape in the direction of the ship. Unless he'd specifically searched for them, Cuddy wouldn't have noticed the Jahin lurking in the trees. Most likely vigilant sentries, standing watch at the perimeter of the village while keeping a close eye on the *Farlight.*

They reached the ship and headed up the gangway.

* * *

Seated together at one of the low tables, Jackie tried to stifle her annoyance with Cuddy for being left alone with Tony. As usual, he was talking incessantly though mostly to Haffan. She gazed off toward the trees and thought she spotted Spilor.

Squinting, she was pretty sure of it but even that didn't reassure her.

"Did you hear me?" Tony asked.

"What? No, sorry," Jackie replied.

"I said, don't you think it's strange there aren't any little offspring . . . what do they call them . . . sprouts, around here?"

Hmmm, an interesting observation, she thought. Another item to add to the creepiness of the place. "What do you make of that, Haffan?" she asked.

Haffan shrugged, seeming unconcerned. "Sometimes it's just a preference, to return fully grown. Pashiers like to mix things up once in a while. A sprout one life and a full grown adult, or an adolescent, in another. But that's not the case here . . . you'll see."

"What age do you think you'll come back at next time?" Tony asked.

Haffan took several moments to answer him. "Right now, I'm making the best of this life, Tony."

There was new commotion at the center table—middle of the U—where the platters of food were being placed. Dramin leaned over every dish, in turn touching them, then raised his sticky claws to his lips—like he was passing on a kiss to all the offerings.

"Yeah . . . that's real sanitary . . ." Tony mumbled.

"It's obviously some kind of blessing," Jackie said.

Other Jahin were now starting to take their seats, an equal proportion of females to males. And once again, Jackie was struck with their beauty. Both elegant and dignified in manner, they certainly weren't gracious. Nary one had come over to welcome them to the festivities, though she certainly felt scrutinized, given a lot of sideways glances and stolen looks—murmuring between the female Jahin.

Until then, Jackie hadn't paid any attention to what the various food items were. Now, with the platters all laid out, each dish was easily distinguishable. Mounds of something, perhaps akin to rice, though the color and shape were off. Also heaps of different vegetable-looking dishes, maybe distant relatives of broccoli or cauliflower. But mostly set out were what appeared to be various stacks of meats. The similarities to a luau feast were growing. If she didn't know better, she'd swear she was looking at a platter-full of Kailua pig, typically cooked in an underground oven. At least on the island of Kauai where she'd experienced the whole Hawaiian luau-thing. Her mind flashed back to an intimate week in paradise, her first break from college, when Brian whisked her off to the islands for a romantic getaway. She thought about Brian—how he'd changed from the person she'd first known. Or maybe she hadn't minded his self-centeredness and arrogance back then. Being young and adventuresome, she just didn't care. She stared at the heritage pod in the shadows—not far from Spilor standing at the tree line. *Would Brian emerge from the pod different*? Would it matter, complicate an already confusing situation?

Startled, she didn't notice Dramin's approach until he loomed over her. "Where are the others? The feast is about to start."

"I think they'll be right back. Any moment now, for sure . . ."

Disgruntled, Dramin looked toward the trees, toward the heritage pod setting there.

"May I ask you a question?"

Without looking at her, Dramin replied, "Ask . . . I'll decide if I want to answer."

"How is it you speak our language? I can't think of when you would have the opportunity to learn it."

"Within the Empyrean Expanse, of course. I have met other humans there . . . those transitioning. Fascinating creatures. You are the first I have met on the physical plane. Odd, your kind is so forgetful about your previous life cycles. Even odder, you do not emerge from pods and, learning the particulars of how you are . . . born . . . a most disgusting process." With that, he turned and headed back toward the head of the table.

His few sentences gave Jackie something to think about—*much to consider.*

Table chatter increased dramatically when all heads turned toward the tree line. Jackie too did a double-take, watching as the familiar old heritage pod hovered several feet off the ground and steadily moved toward them.

"I was afraid of this . . ." Haffan said.

"What?" Tony asked.

"That Cuddy was going to bring out the heritage pod from the *Farlight's* hold."

"I'm sure he means it to be a nice gesture . . . a gift of sorts," Jackie said, appreciating Cuddy's thoughtfulness. She'd never considered the idea herself.

She studied Haffan. "Why wouldn't the clan . . ." *Oh no . . .*

was this a Jahin pod or a Howsh pod? Did Cuddy have a clue about the potential risk he was taking?

"This could be bad, huh?" Tony said.

Jackie didn't answer—just stared wide-eyed as the ancient heritage pod arrived closer to them, with Cuddy and Kyle not far behind. As the pod lowered onto a nearby clearing, silence fell over the crowd. Dramin, standing at the head of the table, stared with rapt attention, his expression unreadable.

chapter 46

Halfway back, Cuddy had the same realization as Jackie, that the pod might not be Jahin. His supposed a well-intended gesture could backfire. But there was an easy enough way to find out—and he had. He thought back to his brief telepathic conversation with Haffan:

Can you do me a favor?

What kind of favor?

The kind you say yes to and help me out. I need you to tell me if this heritage pod, the one from the Pashier hall exhibit on Darriall, is Howsh or Jahin.

What if it's a stupid question?

Just answer me, Haffan . . . we're nearly there.

Eight thousand years ago there was no distinction between the two. From my own recollection, the Howsh looked and acted far more like this Blue Forest clan than those sitting around within the Farlight now.

Brought back to the present moment, Cuddy gave Kyle an appreciative nod for helping him guide the pod over the last half-mile of terrain. He then walked directly over to the U-shaped grouping of tables. Coming to a stop he bowed his head, then stood up tall. "I bring you an ancient artifact. I apologize in advance if it is not to your liking, or if it represents to you some kind of insult . . . that is not my intention, I assure you."

Dramin, standing, was studying the pod with interest. He tilted his large head to the side, the way one did when appraising a potential new car purchase.

"You bring this to us . . . as a gift?" he asked.

Cuddy exchanged a quick look with Jackie, noting her concern.

"If you will accept it, yes?"

The Jahin leader moved around the tables and strode toward the pod. Cuddy realized how pathetic the old pod looked—especially compared to the one they'd just passed at the tree line. That pod stood perfectly upright—had wide, healthy-looking, leaf fronds. Thinking back, he and the other crewmembers never considered the old pod actually real, let alone alive. *This was a terrible mistake . . .*

Dramin dropped down onto all fours, bearlike, and crawled around the entire heritage pod—periodically sniffing certain areas before moving on to others. Eventually, he sat down beside it. No one spoke. No one moved. All eyes remained locked onto the Jahin leader. Gesturing with an extended claw toward Cuddy, he said, "Come . . . sit with me a moment."

Cuddy promptly did as asked, taking a seat on the ground next to the leader of the Blue Forest clan.

"I passed through this pod twice before. Once . . . 7,000 of your years ago . . . and once, 3,000 years ago. Did you know the older heritage pods . . . like this one, had names, Captain Perkins?"

Cuddy shook his head. "I didn't know that."

"This one is called Tammah Loth."

Cuddy repeated the words: "Tammah Loth . . . that's a nice name."

"It means, *go with fond memories*."

Cuddy stared at the pathetic-looking pod and wondered what it looked like a millennia ago.

"Our sacred rituals . . . the Reunite Ritual, is where we ascend to the stars. Next is our waiting time, where we pause and reflect. And then is the Constant Ritual, where we return to living life in a physical form. You are familiar with the Pashier versions of these events, called the Shain Rituals of the Rejoining and the Awakening, I believe."

Cuddy nodded his assent.

"All forms of organic life . . . throughout the universe . . . have their own versions of these cycles although not all organic life is aware of, or accepts, the basic principles. Some, such as the Howsh today, believe this recycling process . . . from physical form to pure energy form, then back into physicality again, and on and on . . . is purely tied to mythical, religious, or esoteric constructs. What they do not know, nor understand, or just refuse to accept, is that this ongoing cyclical process is very much a scientific one."

Cuddy wasn't very religious. Momma took him to church

on numerous occasions as a boy, but his brief recollections of those times were few. What Dramin was sharing with him now was nothing new, as he'd assisted Tow with the Pashier rituals numerous times before. Had seen individuals depart, and others return. If that wasn't scientific, he didn't know what else it could be.

"You have honored us today. You have honored me with this gift. And it is so much more than that, young Captain Perkins."

Cuddy looked at Dramin, unsure what to say to his remark.

"We came here with the hope of never being found. One of the reasons why technology, exhibited in your spacecraft and robot, are not permitted here. Technologies can be detected . . . can be tracked. Our very existence depended upon our not being found.*Ever*. But in retrospect, that was a naive expectation. But still, one made with earnest integrity . . . when we first arrived here"

"When was that?" Cuddy asked.

"Thousands of years ago . . . hard to keep track. We were fleeing the rising-up, hostile at that time, Pashier."

"How did you get here . . . cross the expanse of space?"

"Pashier elders, mostly. There were some both kind and sympathetic to us back then. We were refugees, of a sort, and needed help." His eyes sought, then found, the young alien. "The one you call Haffan was instrumental with that assistance. Her involvement has been told and retold to our young, to those reemerging, mostly in the guise of historical tales or fables, going back all the way to the beginning."

Cuddy, glancing about the grounds, said, "We wondered about that. Where are your young . . ." Dramin's abrupt eye closure stopped Cuddy mid-sentence, recognizing the leader was in a telepathic trance. *He's communicating with someone.*

When Dramin reopened his eyes they were full of amusement. "We are so very careful with our young sprouts. Until we knew your intentions, they could not be present here, put in harm's way."

"That makes sense. I understand."

Exiting then from numerous dwellings appeared the Jahin sprouts. Thirty or forty, different ages and sizes, came running into view. One by one, they hurried into the arms of their parents, where they were shushed and told to sit down quietly next to them at the tables.

Dramin rose to his feet and spread his arms wide. Good with picking up languages, Cuddy understood most of what the leader was saying.

"Eat and enjoy, everyone. This day is a momentous day. One that will be remembered, passed on to our young, then entered into the glorious Empyrean Expanse for all to know about."

Focusing only on Cuddy, he spoke in low tones. "There are those who only can return from the same pod they originally left from. In this pod are ancient life forms. It will be up to our own council whether or not to accept them here. I suspect they have been trapped in the Expanse far too long. Transitioning back to physical life will be . . . complicated. But we will see."

Cuddy looked at the throngs of Jahin, at the few humans

present, and the one Pashier. All were eating and openly conversing with one another. A true celebration.

"Join the others, Captain Perkins. I assure you, the food is quite good. We will talk more. And later, we shall bring the one called Brian back into physical form."

Cuddy watched Dramin's rapt attention turn away, refocusing back on the old heritage pod. Getting to his feet, Cuddy headed toward his friends. Jackie was speaking with a Jahin female, holding a young sprout on her lap. Tony and Kyle were laughing about something, their mouths full. Only Haffan watched him approach.

"We saved you a spot," she said, pointing across the table. Jackie, after giving him a quick glance, continued her conversation with the Jahin. As soon as Cuddy sat, a platter of food was placed before him. Looking up, he found the server to be one of the Rahil females who'd first greeted them at the ship.

"Peace and kindness. Enjoy . . ." she said, then left before Cuddy could say thank you.

"The food here is epic," Tony said, holding up what looked to be a large spare rib.

Feeling Haffan's gaze still upon him, Cuddy said, "What is it?"

"Nothing . . . just that you did a good thing."

"The old heritage pod? Not that big a deal."

"Not only that. You've started something new here. I doubt things will ever be the same for this tribe. It is clear they were ready."

"Ready?"

"To stop living in fear . . . from the past, or what the future might bring. Ready now to rejoin the cosmos."

"You could tell all that sitting over here . . . watching us?" he asked, taking a ginormous bite off one of the ribs.

"Who said I was sitting over here the whole time?"

Cuddy chewed, letting the amazing flavors fill his mouth, while briefly wondering what kind of meat it was. *What kind of game did they hunt on Camilli-Rhine 5?*

"You heard our conversation?" Cuddy asked.

"Only the parts I found interesting . . ." Haffan picked at the food on her plate, the way young kids liked to do.

So much he didn't know about this young Pashier. It occurred to him that she was far deeper than she outwardly appeared; far wiser than her young demeanor portrayed.

Eating together now, they laughed, learning each other's ways—their great differences but even greater similarities. As darkness fell upon the feast and celebration, Dramin stood, waiting for the crowd to hush and give him their attention.

"The time has come. I have contemplated long on this . . . spoken to our elders . . . and together we have decided that tonight there will be two Constant Rituals. Both heritage pods will awaken!"

The Jahin cheered—exuberant at the news. Not sure of the implications of such an announcement, Jackie leaned forward over the table. "Cuddy, was this your doing?"

"I don't think so . . . well, maybe, partially."

Jackie smiled and stretched her hand across the table. Reaching back, Cuddy took her hand in his. Warm, it felt good to touch her.

"I'm excited to see Brian again. I can't believe this is happening."

"Me too," he said, letting her hand go as she withdrew it.

chapter 47

The feast was completed—the empty platters of food, as well as the tables, were removed. A slight chill in the air, the Jahin had become quiet—suddenly introspective.

Dramin, making the rounds, spoke in low tones as he moved from one cluster—or family—of Jahin to the next. Cuddy wasn't sure what he was saying to them—probably words of encouragement; maybe a short prayer. As darkness fell over the village, it became evident that everyone, except perhaps the three humans, Jackie, Tony and Kyle, were *glowing*.

"Do you feel it?"

Cuddy was unaware that Jackie had joined him. Her arms were wrapped around her body, the soft light from Camilli-Rhine 5's two small moons twinkled in her eyes.

"What's that?" he said.

"The energy . . . the excitement in the air."

He did feel something too. Nodding, he replied, "I do."

In the distance, Dramin, along with several other villagers, could be seen heading toward the tree line. Jackie, moving in closer, faced away from him. "I'm cold . . . can you put your arms around me?"

Cuddy, on wrapping his arms snugly around her, felt her body lean closely into him. She clasped his hands in hers. Their closeness felt amazing—felt right. He could stand with her there forever.

"Where are they going?" she asked.

Cuddy watched Dramin and the others for a moment then observed the clan leader levitate the distant heritage pod up into the air. He figured Spilor must be there too—close to where they were standing—although in the evening dusk, he could no longer make out the robot's position.

"I'm not sure what to expect, how Brian will emerge. Be more of the same, or somehow different? And that other pod's so friggin' old . . . so decrepit-looking. Maybe some things should be left alone . . . I don't know . . . allowed to just wither away."

"Dramin sure seemed excited about it. I'm sure it'll be fine," he said.

"Yeah, until prehistoric gargoyles start pouring out from the thing . . ."

At that, they both laughed. She spun around—his arms still around her—and gazed up into his eyes. Her hands then came up and, pulling his face down to hers, kissed him.

"Get a room."

Quickly looking up, they found Tony and Kyle heading their way. Jackie slipped out from his grasp then was gone. Like the fading remnants of a dream, only the faint smell of her strawberry shampoo lingered behind, then that too was gone.

"Sorry, man… guess we stepped all-over your special moment," Kyle said. Cuddy couldn't tell if he was merely being sarcastic, though he didn't think so.

The other heritage pod, closer now, was high in the air—as if Dramin wanted to make a statement; have the pod give a special entrance. As the pod descended from high above, the gathered Jahin cheered, many slapping their upper legs—a form of clapping. Dramin, using TK, guided the heritage pod onto the ground not far from the age-old one.

The crowd slowly backed away, forming the familiar encircling ring around the pods. Cuddy scanned all the silhouetted shapes for signs of Jackie and Haffan and found them standing on the far side of the pods.

"They're over there," he told Tony and Kyle. Haffan, holding hands with Jackie, smiled as Cuddy hurried to her side then reached out with her free hand to take ahold of his. When Tony and Kyle joined them, they all eagerly waited together.

Barely audible at first, the Jahin began to sing a beautiful, albeit melancholy, song. The anticipation for what was to happen next grew in intensity. Jackie glanced Cuddy's way and winked, then turned to watch Dramin, standing between both pods. With his arms held high, his long mane of hair shimmering in the moonlight, the first sign of heritage pod activity commenced. Precisely, and at the same time, glimmering-spiraling fountains of light poured upward from the tops of the two heritage pods. Like two erupting volcanoes, sparks of light circled around them, then rose higher and higher into the air. The Jahin's sweet chorus of voices grew in intensity.

Cuddy never, ever, wanted to forget this swirling, magical, moment in time. Gazing upward, not one but two side-by-side spiraling galaxies of stars were taking shape above.

At the very top, the apex of the two pods where the fronds were the smallest, the leafy blades had begun to unfurl. Both pods opened in unison—like a choreographed dance, their movements were perfectly timed—synchronized. The Jahin's celebratory song reached a crescendo, and ended. An equally dramatic silence now encompassed the spectacle. The pods continued to unfurl until the last, the widest fronds, unfolded, lying flat upon the ground.

Cuddy knew now was the time to look up, where all shooting star-like life forces emanated from. They came at once—one from each swirling galaxy. Shot out from the heavens, they simultaneously flashed brilliant—one on the newer pod—one on the ancient pod, where two glowing physical forms now stood erect: One a Jahin, one a Human/Pashier hybrid.

The Jahin, acting confused, was quickly met by fellow villagers. Taking his arm, they guided him away. Yet the human/Pashier needed no assistance at all. Brian, walking off from atop the pod, seemed unfazed by his new surroundings. By then, Jackie was already running toward him, excitedly yelling out his name.

* * *

One by one, hundreds of shooting stars shot down from the

heavens. The Jahin rejoiced, seeing the return of many they'd known before, but eagerly welcomed the unknown ones too, returning from ancient ages, long since past. The adjustment for those ancient beings would be difficult; a whole new world lay before them. Cuddy wondered if they carried their old prejudices, their malice toward the Pashier, with them. Hopefully, their perspectives had elevated, since dwelling within the Empyrean Expanse, though he had no idea how any of that worked. A good question for Tow, Cuddy briefly wondered when he would see his old friend again, where he was right now.

Cuddy and Haffan stood back as their team members fielded rapid-fire questions at Brian. Indeed, he did look different now, like he did prior to entering the wellness chamber over a month ago. His once good looks mutated into something grotesque after spending far too long a time within the chamber. Even with the help of Pashier elders, he'd not looked normal again. But now Brian did—looking the way he *should* look. What Cuddy found more interesting was how he answered his teammate's questions. *Was he still an ass?* Yeah, he seemed to be, which was both disappointing as well as encouraging. Encouraging because showed he'd brought much of his old self back with him—it was still the same Brain they'd all come to know. Several times now, as Brian spoke, he looked beyond the others, making eye contact with him.

Tony asked, "So . . . were there any heavenly babes up there?"

Brian didn't dignify the stupid query with an answer.

Standing, he again looked Cuddy's way. "How 'bout we take a break from the twenty questions. I need to talk to Cuddy."

Momentarily, Jackie, sitting next to Brian, looked somewhat slighted, but recovered, saying, "Fine, if you'd rather talk to Cuddy . . . go ahead," and put on an *I couldn't care less* smile.

Brian headed away, motioning with his head for Cuddy to follow. When Haffan didn't immediately release his hand, Cuddy leaned over and asked her, "What is it?"

"Not everything Brian will tell you will be true. It may be real for him . . . but not necessarily true."

"Okay, I'll keep that in mind."

With that, Haffan was seven again. "Jackie, can you show me how to do that again?"

"A cartwheel?"

Haffan nodded, as Cuddy headed off in Brian's direction, into the darkness beyond. He found him standing alone at the edge of the trees, staring up to the heavens.

"It's good to have you back, Brian," Cuddy said.

"Cut the shit, Cuddy. I seriously doubt that's true. In any event, we have much to talk about."

"Like what?"

"Like how you need to get the team out of here . . . like right away. Like now!"

"Why . . . it's nice here. What's the big rush?"

"Survival, for one thing. Also, we need to dump the kid. Where she goes . . . trouble will always follow. Keep in mind I now have a far better perspective of things than you do. Remember where I've come back from. I've been to the very essence of consciousness. Climbed the mountain and viewed the world through the eyes of God . . ."

Cuddy stared at Brian, wanting to tell him he needed to take a few more trips up that heavenly mountain. Brian hadn't changed one bit, hell, maybe he was more arrogant than he remembered. "Haffan isn't going anywhere. You say something like that again and you are I are going to have a problem. But if you want to share whatever dangers you see lying ahead for us, then I'm all ears."

Brian chuckled. I've always underestimated you, Cuddy. But I've recently learned you're as dangerous to be around as that Pashier child. This mission of yours . . . of Tow's . . . to find the Prophesy of Harkstrong could very well get everyone killed. Take your brother, and that half-wit Tony, also the alien child . . . but not Jackie. She needs to come with me."

chapter 48

"I think you're forgetting what we're doing out here, about our mission, Brian. There's more at stake than any one of us, including Jackie, or have you forgotten that?" In the darkness, Cuddy couldn't see Brian's reaction, if there was one, then he wondered if he really had lost track of what they were doing here. Brian was right about one thing. The answers they were seeking weren't on Camilli-Rhine 5. He thought back, using his near-perfect memory recall, to one week earlier when Lorgue Supreme Eminence Calph was still alive, and their initial conversation together when they stood in front of the Marauder ship—the *Farlight*.

The elderly robed Howsh had said, "The world you call Primara... the Pashier Promised Land... will be attacked soon. An entire fleet of Marauders is being retrofitted with the very same technology. Earth may soon be next. Perhaps not immediately, but the Howsh are well aware of the ancient writings. The reference to an azure and emerald planet make Earth the obvious one."

"Why would Earth be of any interest to the Howsh?" Jackie asked.

Her query seemed to amuse Calph. "It isn't so much Earth . . . as it is you humans. A secular band of young humans, you are chronicled about in the ancient writings. A band of redeemers, is the more accurate phrasing . . . a small band of redeemers, dwelling on the third world beyond the yellow star . . . an azure and emerald planetoid. It is so written that the band of redeemers will deliver upon the soil of Primara a heritage pod and new Pashier life will thence reemerge."

"So, we're like famous?" Tony asked. "What else do those ancient writings say about us?"

"More than I can share with you at this time. Let me just say this . . . as the destinies of the Howsh and the Pashier are closely intertwined, so too are yours. But the final fate of the Pashier, as well as the Howsh, is not set in stone. Nor is yours. The decisions you make today . . . here and now . . . may very well have immense repercussions later on. I have been careful to let such decision-making be yours and yours alone."

"What's your angle in all this?" Brian asked. "What do you get out of meddling in everyone else's business?"

"As I said, we're talking about the fate of two intertwined civilizations. I simply am a warrior turned scholar. Their ancient past was inscribed onto animal hide scrolls. Or chiseled into stone tablets. So too is their future. The Howsh and Pashier civilizations may have come to their respective ends . . . a crossroads is now upon us . . . one where billions of lives lie in the balance. How could I not become involved with such an endeavor? What could possibly hold more importance for me . . . for anyone?"

"How long before Primara is attacked?" Cuddy asked.

"It could be days . . . possibly weeks," Calph said.

"And this quest of yours. How exactly does it help? Stop an attack?"

"By the dissemination of knowledge, human. As it presently stands, few Howsh know of their forefathers' true natural capabilities; that Howsh life forces too can re-cycle over many lifetimes, via heritage pods. Like the Shain Ritual of Awakening, of the Pashier. What you do not know, could not know, is the simple truth that the Howsh are dying out. Becoming extinct. They are unaware, as a species, of the need to re-cycle their life forces—the only solution to their impending demise as a people."

"You say certain Howsh higher-ups . . . elders . . . know about this," Jackie said. "That they've read the ancient writings too, and know about their commonality with the Pashier, right? I would think they would see it as a good thing; a way to save their species and live on forever having incredible telepathic and telekinetic powers. Why keep it a secret from the masses?"

"The answer is simple," Lorgue Supreme Eminence Calph replied. "Hatred."

"Hatred?"

"The Howsh elders . . . those who comprise the Howsh High Council . . . rule with an unforgiving power. They are a deeply religious . . . sectarian, bunch. They have followed a doctrine of hate for millennia. Where their differences with the Pashier have been an ongoing, timeless, drumbeat, the mere future prospect of developing a closer bond with their interminable enemy . . . well . . . that cannot be allowed."

"That's bogus," Tony said.

The others looked to Cuddy, who noted in all their glances that they would probably follow his lead. Even Brian. "I'll instruct Bob to pilot the Evermore back to Primara and deliver them the wellness chamber. Those here who wish to return to Primara with the orb, that's fine."

"Nah . . . I'm with you, kemosabe," Tony said, and Brian, rolling his eyes, said, "Fine. I'll come along," just as Kyle said, "Me too."

Jackie smiled. "Well, there's no way I'm letting Haffan go off with this guy without tagging along. So, Cuddy, I guess we're all going on this adventure together."

Back in the present moment, Cuddy contemplated how things had evolved since one week ago. Lorgue Supreme Eminence Calph was now dead. Cuddy and his crew had outwitted Calph, also the dead Lorgue Sub Eminence Lange, to acquire the ancient scrolls. They'd learned of some mysterious thing, called *The Prophesy of Harkstrong,* that Tow believed would, ultimately, hold the key to averting imminent demise of both Pashier and Howsh people . . .

"Brian, we're leaving here tonight. Jackie will not be going with you. She'd never leave Haffan behind, nor would I. We believe in this mission, Brian. Believe that the Howsh can be saved from their misdirected folly; that their winding-down evolutionary course does not have to come to a final end. If they cannot learn from the ways of the Pashier, they can learn from the Jahin—a race closer to their own kind. Accepting too that recycling of life is a necessary aspect to their ultimate survival; that the Pashier not only will survive but will also flourish, if the Howsh let them. But first, we need to complete our quest . . . find the Prophesy of Harkstrong. Come with us, Brian. Help us find this elusive Prophesy . . . and thereby bring peace and longevity to these two alien races, both now in dire peril of surviving.

"Come on . . . You don't even know where it is, Cuddy. Take a look up there," Brian said, gesturing to the stars above. "Billions of worlds . . . how on earth do you plan to discover just where this Prophesy of Harkstrong resides? The ancient scrolls you now possess will only take you so far."

"Because you will tell him where it is . . ."

Those words, spoken by none other than Tow whose glowing form appeared brilliant in the surrounding darkness. So happy to see him, Cuddy wished he could somehow embrace his ethereal astral projection. "Tow . . . you're here!"

Tow's gaze stayed on Brian. Cuddy had not seen such intensity in his eyes before, as

Brian stared defiantly at Tow. "Why is any of that my concern? If there is one thing I've learned traveling to the other side is that one must fend for himself. Watch for *numero uno* first."

"Brian . . . your time within the Empyrean Expanse was brief . . . mere moments, relatively speaking. You were alone, among life forces unaccustomed, and unwelcoming, to your presence. That mountain I heard you speak of earlier . . . sorry, but you have yet to take one step into the higher realms." Tow's words were harsh, though his expression remained kind, even compassionate.

Tow stepped closer to Brian, close enough that his ethereal glow reflected onto Brian's stony face. "Take time to realize that everything happens for a reason, even your death, then re-emergence on Camilli-Rhine 5. You have an immensely important choice to make. Certainly . . . you can do as you said: watch out for numero uno, or you can tell Cuddy, right now, what you learned from the only person you spoke with within the Expanse. I cannot intervene with your personal experiences there; that must come from you."

Tow stared at Brian for several moments before turning his attention back to Cuddy. "My time here, on the other side of Rah . . . here within *Tanthian* . . . is coming to an end. The same aspect of me you see will not appear to you again."

"But we need your help. I need your help," Cuddy pleaded.

"And you will have it, only not this way. Be patient with Brian. His is a relatively new life force. But there is much hope that he will make wise decisions."

"Will I see you again?" Cuddy asked, feeling his throat suddenly constrict.

Tow's eyes conveyed conflict . . . sadness peppered with good humor. "Do not worry, my friend.

Cuddy wanted to call out to him, get clarity on what he meant. But new distant, yet approaching, sounds gave him pause. *What is that?*

"They're coming. . . ." Brian said.

"Who . . . who's coming?"

chapter 49

Lorgue Prime Eminence Norsh's advanced fleet of new Marauder warships entered into the Kwo planetary system. Nine days had passed since he'd retired the *Pintial* and came aboard the *Raging Storm*, his new command ship.

Norsh had neither slept, nor eaten in days—not since he'd received the devastating news. To do so would insult the memory of Lorgue Sub Eminence Langer—his younger brother. Norsh's sorrow was so great it exhibited itself physically—a congestive pain. His huge sense of personal loss gripped his heart—at times he felt it was being ripped from his chest.

Norsh's arrival at the obscure, totally inconsequential small planetary system was nothing short of a miracle in itself. The odds of finding the murderous band of killers—those humans who'd stolen poor Langer's life—should have been astronomically improbable against such a possibility.

But a miracle had occurred. Aboard the stolen Marauder, the *Farlight*, was a true patriot. With a series of clandestine, interstellar messages, she single-handedly managed to bring forth justice even to a cold, harsh galaxy. She would be rewarded. Perhaps, he would allow the old cow to bed with him . . . but then, probably not.

But his good fortune hadn't ended there. As far back as he could remember, he'd heard stories—more like fables—that there was a Howsh-like society, living an enigmatic existence somewhere out in the vastness of space. A weird and dangerous people, they held an ideological perspective that threatened the status quo, dangerously mirroring the Pashier—and unbelievably, here too were more fucking heritage pods.

As Norsh stood at the red railing on his new vessel, he savored the prospect of what was about to come. *Vengeance.* The opportunity to make an example of that wayward clan of Howsh, or whatever name they called themselves.

A new rush of adrenalin coursed through the Howsh leader's veins as he took in the constantly scrolling tactical readout near him. Indeed, there were indicative signs of biological life within the sixth planet of the system—the Kwo System. The highest concentration emanated from Camilli-Rhine 5—their destination.

Along with the new command vessel came a new crew. His First, Mongere Sub Fhat, was an old space brawler, fifteen years his senior. His matted fur was the color of trampled ice sludge and his milky eyes appeared nearly colorless. He moved, more like waddled, around the bridge with slow, determined conviction. The experienced Fhat could have had his own command decades earlier, but he was not ambitious. Norsh heard that what he lacked in ambition he made up in loyalty. *We shall see.*

Mongere Sub Fhat approached the red railing. "Sire, as you ordered, the fleet will split into three squadrons." He spoke in a low gravelly voice that hurt his ears. "Squadron one will begin surface-level exploration of Camilli-Rhine 5 at once, based on the rough coordinates provided in the last communiqué coming from the *Farlight*."

"You find even the most primitive collective of life forms down there . . . any kind of community at all . . . torch it!" Norsh let his words fully sink in before continuing: "Before we leave the Kwo planetary system, we will ensure that nothing larger than a house fly survives. I am talking total eradication. Do I make myself clear, First?"

"Clear . . . yes, sire. If total eradication is what you seek, then that is what you shall have," Fhat said, his voice emotionless.

"One more thing. Do not forget . . . our prime directive here is to destroy the *Farlight*; bring that band of humans to a quick, and just, end. If they manage to escape, then no one on board here should ever expect to return home. If you know anything about me, you know my executions are not quick. Nor painless."

A junior officer approached, waiting to be acknowledged. Norsh gave him an impatient glare. "What is it?"

"Sire, squadron one has zeroed in on a small village. Intelligent life. Sensor readings tell us the genome characteristics are nearly identical to those of the Howsh."

"And the *Farlight*?" Norsh asked.

"Still looking, Lorgue Prime Eminence Norsh. But there are telltale energy signatures that could only come from an advanced spacecraft. We are close… it is only a matter of time."

"Carry on with your previous orders. Clear the village and the nearby surroundings," Norsh said, watching for a reaction from Fhat. *Something wasn't right about the old bag of bones.* Norsh turned his attention to the primary display, watching as bright energy bolts rained down on the dark landscape below.

chapter 50

He saw their running lights in the far distance—mere pinpricks of illumination miles away—no fewer than seven or eight vessels were approaching in their direction. Moving slowly, yet making steady progress, they were flying low over the black terrain evidently searching for something. Cuddy's thoughts turned to the *Farlight. Would the vessel's stealth capabilities hold up against certain scrutiny by that approaching fleet?*

"We need to get back to the ship!" Cuddy said.

Approaching them, rapid footfalls could be heard. Cuddy stared into the darkness, instinctively balling his hands into tight fists. Spilor came into view and stopped in front of them. Cuddy hadn't thought the spindly robot could move like that.

"Captain Perkins . . . the enemy approaches."

"Get back to the *Farlight*! Have Marzon fire up her drives . . . we'll be right behind you. Go!"

Brian's expression turned both smug and condescending. Cuddy didn't have time for him and set off at a dead run, heading back toward the village. As he approached the clearing where the two heritage pods had begun a slow, but progressive, closure process, the glowing Jahin, stared toward the horizon at the approaching vessels. At the one thing they feared most—the destructive technology the ships brought with them.

Cuddy found Dramin directing his people to get to their dwellings and to stay out of sight. Reaching him, and very much out of breath, Cuddy said, "No! You need to get your people into the woods . . . scatter! Your village . . . will be the first thing they hit."

Dramin stared back at Cuddy. The leader of the Blue Forest clan, clearly afraid, was unsure he should trust the alien human, or not. Quickly turning to the cluster of fellow Jahin around him, he ordered, "Do as he says. All of you . . . hasten into the village and instruct everyone to leave their homes. Tell them to hurriedly collect their sprouts and leave everything else, their possessions, behind. That there is only time to hide and to hurry into the woodlands!"

"I'll do everything I can to draw them away. We must go . . . I'm so sorry." Cuddy wanted to offer more, but what else could he say? He'd brought the approaching calamity upon this small enclave that were peaceful—not a threat to anyone. "I'm sorry . . ." he said again. Spinning away, he yelled out, "Jackie! Kyle!"

Cuddy recognized his brother's voice, shouting in the distance, "We're over here!" And four silhouetted figures could be seen, running across the village's central clearing area and heading for the distant tree line—toward the *Farlight*.

Cuddy ran flat out. The sound of low-flying ships, mingling

with low-frequency vibrations, came up through the ground and into the soles of his shoes. His mind raced, a hell-storm of disjointed thought. *Would they make it back to the ship in time? Where was Brian? Would he decide to join them after all?* His most dominant concern revolved around the imminent, unavoidable coming battle. He wondered if there was a possible way to avoid violence—avoid any killing. He thought of Tow, who undoubtedly would choose to sacrifice himself, even his people, in place of reciprocity and violence.

Sprinting now, Cuddy was almost upon the others. He saw Jackie steal a quick look over her shoulder, while young Haffan had to take two strides for each one the others took just to keep up. In that moment he knew the answer to his internal turmoil. He would kill anyone—every last one of the approaching enemy—to protect those he loved.

Cuddy soon took the lead, dodging one way then another, around tree after tree. Twice, low-hanging branches smacked him in the face, causing blood to trickle down his cheek. *Where's the damn ship!* He didn't recall leaving it this far back into the woods. *Is that weapon fire I'm hearing behind us? Oh God . . . the village.*

Cuddy, at hearing the *Farlight's* propulsion system start to wind-up, slightly altered his direction. Relieved at seeing it—barely visible in the nighttime shadows—he slowed, then stood aside, motioning for the others to hurry up the gangway. Taking a quick last look around, he shouted, "Brian?" Waiting a few seconds, he followed the others up the ramp.

Entering the lower-deck airlock, Cuddy heard the ship's

alarm klaxon bellowing above. Running, he made his way into the lift then onto the bridge. Marzon was there, standing at the Espy table.

Turning at Cuddy's arrival, he looked more than a little exasperated. "Can we lift off now?"

"Most definitely! Get us up in the air," Cuddy said, joining Marzon's side, viewing the scene now taking place on the Espy. Seven Marauder ships, virtually identical to the *Farlight*, could be seen circling, periodically firing upon the Jahin village, which was already ablaze with high-reaching flames. Cuddy noted the level of destruction that had already taken place.

"We cannot go up against a force of that magnitude. We are far outnumbered," Marzon said.

"And TK doesn't seem to have much effect on the bastards . . ." Brian added, stepping up to the far side of the table and looking contrite. "I tried . . . wondered if I was losing my touch. But Marzon tells me those advanced Marauders are protected against those kinds of intrusion."

Cuddy was happy to see Brian. Happy in spite of his obnoxiousness that he'd decided to stay with the team. "That's right. We can't affect the ships directly, nor their crews. Special shielding. But we can affect what's near them." Cuddy then pointed to a rocky ridgeline adjacent to the village, just beyond a large cropping of trees. "Those boulders—"

Brian cut him off: "Better if I can see them first hand."

Cuddy directed new orders to the Howsh crewmember, sitting at the helm station. "You heard him . . . get the *Farlight* into position. Keep low over the treetops and double-check our stealth mode and that our running lights are turned off."

Cuddy and Brian moved to the red railing and faced forward toward the large display screen. Bright energy bolts coursed through the air. Cuddy didn't want to think about the loss of life below. How the Howsh were systematically firing on the defenseless Jahin, scattered about in the trees. It wouldn't be long either before the *Farlight* was detected. No ship, no matter how well shielded, was totally invisible. Not when the enemy was so close.

"I see them. They are . . . huge!" Brian exclaimed, pointing to a cluster of enormous light-colored boulders.

"I can try to help," Cuddy offered, acutely aware his TK abilities were pathetically inadequate compared with Brian's.

"Just shut up and let me concentrate. You . . . at the helm . . . keep the damn ship steady!"

Cuddy closely watched the huge rocks along the ridgeline and below it though nothing could be seen happening. Maybe Brian's trip into the Empyrean Expanse affected his abilities . . .

The others, Kyle, Tony, and Jackie, who was holding Haffan in her arms, were now standing at the Espy table.

"Put me down," Haffan said to Jackie. Complying, Jackie watched the alien child run to the red railing to stand with Brian and Cuddy.

"I can help loosen the boulders from the cliff . . . but nothing else," she said.

"Do it, Haffan! Hurry up, kid!" Brian said.

Gazing up at Cuddy, Haffan's expressive eyes locked onto his, silently asking if that was what he wanted from her too. Almost imperceptibly—he nodded.

chapter 51

The three stared intently at the display—at the wall of rock, looming hundreds of feet high and completely filling the screen. As they exerted their individual TK abilities, Cuddy picked up on the strained cadence in Brian and Haffan's breathing—the tremendous stress put on both. The cacophony of plasma fire continued. *How many more Jahin have died in just the last minute?* Cuddy wondered.

Suddenly aware of Jackie standing right behind him, he heard her whisper in his ear: "Help them, Cuddy . . . you're more powerful than you know. Don't hold back, not this time. It is . . . okay . . . for you to do this."

Cuddy's eyes locked onto one of the massive rocks he'd arbitrarily selected and he briefly wondered if that exposed gray slab of cold sedimentary rock was like an iceberg. Only the tip visible, its true mass lay submerged beneath the sea—below the ground. Focused inwardly, using TK, he pulled with everything he had within him. Mentally commanding his entire self—each hybrid human Pashier cell, the nucleus of each cell, their constructing molecules, the very atoms comprising the entity of Cuddy Perkins—to forge together in that instant. Unite. Committed. Unwavering. Cuddy watched as the massive slab began to tremble in place. In a sudden outward explosion of dirt and rubble, it came free.

Cuddy heard Jackie's quick intake of air. The rock levitated momentarily before it was whisked high into the inky-dark sky above, but not before it careened into three attacking Howsh Marauder warships. Cuddy paid no attention to the explosions that ensued, his attention focused again on the boulder-strewn cliff. The next house-sized rock shook free, momentarily levitating, waiting for Brian's TK ability to do its destructive bidding. Another three warships, like bugs splattering against an oncoming windshield, were then eviscerated.

Marzon said, "The movement of ten more Marauders had been detected leaving high orbit. Soon those vessels will be inbound . . . headed our way."

Cuddy stared at the ragged cliff. Additional, far smaller, boulders had now come free, providing more TK artillery for Brian. He knew that was the work of Haffan.

It was time to end this. Cuddy figured there were no fewer than a couple dozen boulders embedded in the bedrock slope. He didn't allow himself to think or consider the ramifications of his next course of action. Knowing it would be easier, from this point on, since he'd figured out the mental mechanics: How to raise his TK abilities to a level he never thought possible. Using both hands this time—in a rapid pulling motion—whatever was left of the cliff came free with that one simple movement, crumbling into itself, becoming little more than a great mound of pebbled dirt, while huge slabs of rock—enough to shape a small mountain—remained motionless up in the air. Suspended—waiting.

Cuddy's work was done—the rest now up to Brian, who was clearly up to the task. One by one, the ginormous projectiles shot toward the next wave of incoming ships—ships which had zero chance of avoiding them—or of surviving.

The bridge instantly quieted. Only when Marzon spoke did Cuddy bring his eyes away from the display.

"The signal is almost undetectable but there are others."

"Others?"

"Still in orbit, Howsh Marauders. Ten . . . could be fifteen," Marzon said.

"Keep a close watch on them. Right now, I'm more concerned with survivors." Cuddy turned away, joining the others at the Espy, where Kyle was at the controls, zooming in on various location sites in and around the village.

Jackie said, "It's horrible. We brought this misery upon them. We facilitated their massacre."

Kyle responded, "Well . . . it could be worse. Not that things aren't bad, but I'm seeing survivors. A lot of them."

"Can you tell who is who? Like . . . could you tell if Dramin is still . . ."

"I have been following the Jahin leader with my own sensors, Captain Perkins," Spilor interjected. "He is alive. Thirty-five Jahin were killed in the attack. One hundred and ninety-seven are still alive."

Cuddy continued to watch the 3D Espy that was morphing and changing shape as Kyle changed location points. He was shocked seeing one of the heritage pods billowing smoke—flames had completely engulfed the backend and curled fronds. Cuddy felt sick to his stomach. Then, looking to the other pod, the ancient one, it was seemingly unharmed. *At least there was that.* Kyle finally settled on a close-up view of eight to ten Jahin, standing together along the outer rim of the village. He recognized the way one figure moved, the gait of his walk. It was Dramin.

"We need to tell him we're sorry. Offer him our assistance," Jackie said.

"He doesn't want that. He wants us, all of us, just to leave here," Haffan said.

Jackie wiped her moist eyes. "So . . . we just leave? That seems so heartless."

Cuddy shook his head. "Not just leave. We first need to ensure they have nothing more to worry about of what still remains of that Howsh fleet. We finish the battle."

All eyes leveled on Cuddy. He knew what they were thinking. That he had never spoken such things before, of advocating violence.

"So the man-boy from Woodbury, Tennessee has finally grown a pair. Finally," Brian said mockingly.

Cuddy didn't respond.

Brian continued, "Which one of you did that to the cliff side? Offered me up those colossal rocks?" Staring at Haffan first, then at Cuddy, he asked, "You did that?" After waiting several beats and not getting an answer, he whistled, "I don't think I could do that. Impressive. Remind me to stay on your good side, Cuddy."

Cuddy was not proud of his actions, in fact, he felt sickened by them. He'd facilitated in the destruction of close to twenty spacecraft. The death toll could easily be several hundred.

Tony clucked his tongue. "Um . . . I think we're all out of big rocks now to toss around. Any thoughts on how we're going to go up against those remaining Marauders?"

* * *

Lorgue Prime Eminence Norsh stared at the display in rapt horror, watching his second wave of Howsh Marauders come to the same grisly fate as the first. How had those highly advanced vessels succumbed—not by another, equally technologically advanced enemy, but by nothing more than a few humans hurling massive stones through the air? His vessels were indeed immune to the direct influences of telekinetic powers, but not, obviously, from the indirect effects caused using such powers.

Norsh, feeling beaten and out of options, contemplated his next course of action, when Mongere Sub Fhat cleared his phlegmy throat. "If I may be so bold, Sire . . . I may have a solution."

"Spit it out, Fhat . . . now is not the time for formalities."

"Stealth is far more difficult for our assets when entering the world's atmosphere . . . the disruption of surrounding air currents, and all the countless other minute influences that the *Farlight* can pick up on."

"You are not telling me anything I do not already know, First."

"We must wait for them to come to us, here in upper orbit," Fhat said. "The void of space will keep what remains of our fleet invisible to their sensors. One rogue vessel will be no match for the destructive power of fifteen Marauders."

"I see your logic. But the *Farlight* will be just as invisible to us as we are to them. And what's to keep the *Farlight* from simply moving on . . . disappearing into the cosmos? No, what we need is our unknown Howsh patriot to assist us one more time. For her to subversively broadcast the ship's coordinates to us, once the *Farlight* leaves Camilli-Rhine 5's atmosphere."

Norsh thought of his sibling. *Perhaps I will avenge your death after all, young brother.* "Tell me, Mongere Sub Fhat, can you find a way to contact her? You do that and I assure you we will bring victory to this nearly decimated fleet of ours; bring honor to the Howsh. A rise in rank will be in order, perhaps your own command. Name it, anything, and it will be yours."

Fhat seemed to ignore Norsh's attempt at blatant bribery. "Contacting her is not the issue, which can be accomplished easily enough. The issue comes from the resulting broadcast, which will focus attention back on her; her treachery to her shipmates. It would, most likely, result in her immediate execution. She would know that too, most certainly."

Norsh considered his words. Execution would be far too lenient a punishment for anyone in his crew even contemplating such treachery. No, he would need to trigger her emotionally; inspire her allegiance to a higher calling—her Howsh lineage.

The officer on Tactical sat up straighter and said, "Sire, there is a disturbance, undoubtedly caused by a propulsion wake. The*Farlight,* most definitely, is on the move."

A smile crossed the Howsh leader's lips. He knew just what to say to Fhat's patriot. Quickly striding toward the coms station, he would reach out to her himself. It's not clear who the female is that they're talking about.

chapter 52

"We're being hailed by the *Raging Storm*, Captain Perkins. It's Lorgue Prime Eminence Norsh . . . himself," coms officer Ganther said, sounding somewhat awe-struck.

Clenching his fists, Cuddy thought about the recent attack—so many dead Jahin. Thirty-five gentle souls mercilessly picked-off at the hands of the same lunatic commander; also the destroyed village, and the destroyed heritage pod. Cuddy had little experience feeling hatred, but he hated the vile sadist responsible for such cowardly acts.

"Go ahead, put him up on the primary display," Cuddy said, turning away from the Espy and moving back to the red railing at the center of the bridge.

Lorgue Prime Eminence Norsh's video feed snapped into view. Strangely, it showed a wide-angled shot of the Howsh ship bridge, of the bridge crew all lowered to one knee, their heads lowered too. Norsh was at the red railing and, like the crew, had lowered to one knee, his head bowed.

"Lorgue Prime Eminence Norsh," Cuddy said.

A moment passed before Norsh slowly looked up. His face spoke volumes: Distraught—crestfallen—ashamed. "We . . . I . . . am at your mercy. All I ask is that you spare my crew . . . a crew only following orders of their superior."

"What is this all about?"

"Our surrender, of course. Within moments you decimated two-thirds of my fleet. Obviously, we are outmatched."

Cuddy, on scanning the feed, noticed the precise location of the enemy's fleet was not showing up on the tactical readout—instead giving only a broad bandwidth of *probable* coordinates. Still relatively close, they could pretty much be anywhere out there.

Surrender? How was he supposed to deal with something that huge? Cuddy's mind raced. *What would he do with them, anyway?* It wasn't like they could squeeze so many prisoners into the *Farlight*, or even escort the fleet somewhere else. The pacifists dwelling on Primara certainly would have no interest in such a prospect. He briefly contemplated escorting them back to Earth but never Earth's battle, he knew that was a *stupid* idea.

"You will have to destroy them," Marzon said, loud enough for Norsh to hear.

Norsh stood up, "Fine, but I have one request . . . if that is to be our fate. "Let me say goodbye to my niece first. With the recent loss of my brother, she is my only remaining family member. A crewmember on your vessel, I believe her duties are performed somewhere within Engineering. Her name is Min Sub Pith."

Cuddy was reminded of Norsh's relationship to Lorgue Sub Eminence Langer, who'd succumbed to that vile curse. He mentally pictured the younger Howsh leader—the countless small heads sprouting all over his furry body. *Still, it was a strange request.* Quietly informed by the helm that the *Farlight* had reached lower orbit, he quickly eyed the tactical readout. Although they were fairly close, no specific coordinates showed the fleet's exact whereabouts—a fleet outnumbering them fifteen to one.

Marzon said, "This is an obvious trick. Do not trust him, Captain. I don't like it."

Cuddy saw Jackie moving beside him, standing directly to his right. "Who exactly is this Min Sub Pith?" she asked Marzon.

Looking annoyed, Marzon replied, "She is just as he stated. Min Sub means an entry-level position. Her duties deal with the *Farlight's* propulsion system."

Jackie spoke just loud enough for Cuddy to hear: "Maybe we should see what she has to say about her . . . uncle, or whatever he is to her. What could it hurt? It's not like we have a lot of choices here."

Cuddy looked from Jackie to Marzon. Due to certain circumstances, both were now first officers: Jackie's was a carryover position from the *Evermore*, and Marzon, stationed here on the *Farlight*.

"Let's go ahead then and bring her up to the bridge," Cuddy ordered. While they waited, Cuddy quietly watched the display, taking in the bridge confines of the opposing vessel. Although similar to the *Farlight,* it didn't have the same alterations directed by Lorgue Supreme Eminence Calph. Alterations Cuddy was still pretty much oblivious about—what they either were, or did. He scrutinized the opposing Howsh bridge crew. No one had moved yet. Except for Norsh, all were still bowed down on one knee.

Being escorted in, Min Sub Pith looked nervous as she approached. Cuddy noted she was indeed young, also tall. Her six exposed teats were small and firm, different from the few other, older, Howsh females aboard the ship. Approaching the red railing, her eyes darted from Norsh on display then up to Cuddy.

"Thank you for coming, Min Sub Pith. Look . . . you're not in any kind of trouble here. You can relax. It's come to our attention you are the niece of Lorgue Prime Eminence Norsh. Is that true?"

Pith's eyes went wide, looking ready to bolt.

Cuddy glanced around the bridge until he found Spilor. He raised his chin in a summoning gesture the robot understood, and then he waited.

When he arrived, he said, "Yes, Captain Perkins."

"Is it true, what Norsh claims, about the two being related?"

"Most definitely, Captain." Min Sub Pith threw the robot a hateful glare back.

"Lorgue Prime Eminence Norsh once had a sister too; dead now for ten years. This is her offspring," Marzon said.

Upon seeing her, Norsh lifted a hand, as if he expected his niece to somehow reach through the display and grab it. "Little

Pith . . . it is so good to see you again. It has been too long." A smile, perhaps only a reflexive response, momentarily flashed across her lips then was gone.

"Enough . . . he has seen her, Captain. We must remove her from the bridge—"

Marzon's words were quickly drowned out by Norsh: "I know you are a patriot, Pith, have proven to be so. You are loyal . . . to the Howsh and to me . . ."

Cuddy realized that very moment that Marzon was right. This was a mistake.

Yelling now, Norsh demanded, "Read me the *Farlight's* set of coordinates, there on the readout to your right! Do it now, Pith . . . do it now!"

Young Min Sub Pith, nodding enthusiastically, did as asked: 44.234.555.641112! The feed went black, but it was already too late. She'd given her uncle the *Farlight's* exact coordinates.

"Enemy ships are coming alive! God! . . . so close . . . they're powering up weapons!" Jackie called out, sitting now alongside the tactical officer.

Cuddy noticed the *Farlight's* sensors had indeed locked onto the *Raging Storm,* as had the other fourteen warships. Each enemy ship exhibited a faint, ghost-like outline on the primary display. "Get us out of here!" Cuddy yelled, though he knew it was already far too late.

The display, now showing nearby space, suddenly came alive. Countless bright-red streaks of energy fire highlighted the screen as fifteen ultra-powerful warships all fired at once. Holding his breath, Cuddy reached for the railing and gritted his teeth in preparation for the impending impact. But none came. The warships had fired in the wrong direction; toward coordinates not their own.

Marzon calmly said, "Return fire, sir?"

"Yes! Fire at will. Fire everything we have!" *Why was Marzon suddenly so calm?* Cuddy watched Min Sub Pith offer Marzon an apologetic smile then turn and give Haffan a really wide grin. *What the hell is going on?* Cuddy wondered.

"We have a lock . . ." the tactical officer next to Jackie yelled. "Torpedoes away!" The *Farlight* shook with each torpedo deployment, as the ship's multiple plasma cannons also continued to fire non-stop.

"They see us now, that's for sure. Incoming!" Jackie shouted. Immediately, the *Farlight* shook violently, receiving three massive staccato jolts.

"Shields down to thirty percent," someone yelled out.

An immensely bright flash filled the display—then another—and then another. Three Howsh Marauders had exploded.

"Shields at twenty percent!"

Cuddy wanted to do something, *anything*, wishing he could take over the helm's controls. Standing around, just barking out orders, was not his forte. He realized theirs was indeed a valiant effort, but with their shields failing, and only three of the enemy ships destroyed, they were in big trouble.

"Incoming!"

Cuddy saw Brian step in front of the red railing, a few paces away from the display. *Didn't he remember?* "Those Marauders are protected, Brian. TK has no effect—"

Brian threw up a hand. "Shush! I'm concentrating," just as Haffan hurried over to his side—joining him at the railing.

What the hell? Cuddy thought.

No less than a dozen torpedoes were now inbound toward them, fired from two, or more, warships. Enough to easily take down what still remained of their shields. Haffan, glancing over her shoulder, dramatically waved for Cuddy to join them.

What's the point? he thought, but did as asked, hurrying around the railing to join Brian and Haffan. Now, studying the display, he watched in bewilderment as the first incoming torpedoes began to change course—were separated from the rest of their arrowhead formation. *Although the Marauders were immune to TK, their torpedoes apparently were not, at least not to the same degree.*

Cuddy quickly focused on the rest of the warships, at their respective locations. Concentrating then on the incoming torpedo formation, he selected five from the trailing edge of the cluster. Entering into the hidden realm deep within him, he found the same inner quiet he'd tapped into before when he mentally excavated that huge cliff side of its giant boulders. Now, and with far less effort, he began to turn the five torpedoes away. Their trajectory moved along in a wide arc until they came around 180degrees. He noticed Brian and Haffan had also maneuvered their selected torpedoes into their new trajectories, as well.

Cuddy thought of Tow, of his simple pacifist ways, and could only imagine what his friend would think of him now . . . in the process of committing an incredibly violent transgression against other beings.

Haffan, without looking at Cuddy, telepathed, *If you don't shove them along . . . add your own push to them, what happens is not on you . . .*

So you're reading my mind now, Haffan?

Your expression told me exactly what you were thinking.

Cuddy, unsure if Haffan's logic really rang true, took extra care not to send the five torpedoes any unbidden nudges. Instead, he gave each one of the fast-moving projectiles a new separate trajectory.

"Shields are down!" Jackie said. "We cannot take another direct hit."

As the torpedoes closed in on their individual targets, Cuddy micro-adjusted their courses one final time. He remembered reading—some technical specification—that the *Farlight*'s weakest, most vulnerable point of contact was along their underbelly. Approximately five feet in from the aft thrusters, making a direct hit there would be cataclysmic. He was fairly sure the same would be true for the enemy vessels. He smiled . . . *Drop the mic . . . turn out the lights.*

But the first Marauder to explode was not one that Cuddy targeted. Haffan screamed out, "Got it!" Then another two of the Marauders that she'd targeted were also eviscerated. Next, came Brian's. Like Cuddy, he'd also picked five torpedoes. Unaware of the same technical specs, only three of his five warships were completely destroyed.

Two seconds later, Cuddy's five redirected torpedoes did

find their marks. Coming in through various outer bridge windows, the flash of the synchronized explosions momentarily turned the *Farlight*'s bridge a blinding white.

chapter 53

Seven years ago . . . Woodbury, Tennessee

Momma slowed, cranking the steering wheel around all the way to the left. The old Maxima turned down the sloping driveway, avoiding the all too familiar potholes, lying along the left and right sides of the dirt drive. As she brought the car to a stop in front of the house, a trailing cloud of brown dust encircled the car then quickly dissipated in the late afternoon heat.

Kyle, with Jackie right behind him, hurried from the house. Both looked scared, trying to peer inside the bug-splattered windshield.

Cuddy waved. "Hey look . . . Jackie's here!" He fumbled with the seatbelt till Momma swatted his hands away, saying, "Just let me do it, Cuddy!" She was annoyed with him and he wasn't sure why. Wasn't even sure where they'd just come from. Before opening the car door, he looked into the back seat.

"For goodness sakes, Cuddy, Rufus is right there… over on the porch," Momma said.

Sure enough, there he was. Cuddy opened the door and scrambled out. But before he could take his first step Jackie was right there, throwing her arms around him and pulling him in tight. She hugged him like that for several seconds, awkward for two twelve-year-olds. When she released him she looked angry. "You should have kept up with us?"

Kyle, his hands buried deep in two front pockets, was far less accusatory. "Sorry, little bro … um … we heard you got abducted. Hope nobody did any weird shit to you."

"Kyle!" Momma barked, coming around the front of the car. "No one did anything to anyone … you know that's how rumors get started."

"Sorry, Momma. So Cuddy … did old man Slatch really take you to see Pa? Did you see him? How was he?"

Red-faced, Momma stopped on the top porch step then spun around, "Kyle! You know he won't remember … already too long ago. Drop it … never bring it up again … not ever!" With that she opened the screen door, letting it clap loudly behind her. A moment later, the screen door clapped again as Kyle went inside too.

"I'm sorry, Cuddy," Jackie said.

Giving Rufus a pat on the top of his big head, Cuddy said, "There's nothing to be sorry about. You're my best friend, Jackie … you'll always be my best friend."

Years later, somewhere amidst many deep-space

adventures, Cuddy would recall that exact precise moment—the way she smiled back at him so lovingly—and the burgeoning pain he'd noticed just behind her pretty blue eyes.

chapter 54

Deep space — present day . . .

As the overhead klaxon continued to bellow, Cuddy stared at the display. The myriad of crisscrossing energy strikes had gone with no more incoming. What remained outside was a virtual scrapyard of space debris. One of the few remaining, somewhat intact Marauders, slowly spun on its axis, a constant misty spray of gasses escaping via a small hull breech.

"Any signs of life?" Cuddy asked.

Spilor, standing at one of the now-redundant stations, said, "There are some survivors . . . most have injuries."

"What about the command ship? What about Norsh?" Jackie asked.

"The *Raging Storm* is unaccounted for."

"Are you telling us Norsh escaped?" Cuddy asked, an edge to his voice.

"The *Farlight's* AI will have that data," Marzon replied, and proceeded to speak in low tones to a complex-looking panel two paces away from Spilor.

Cuddy turned his attention to Min Sub Pith, who appeared nervous, standing quietly on the bridge. "Explain yourself. What was that all about?"

"Don't be a bully," Haffan said. "It was my idea. Pith and I are friends."

"Since when?" Jackie asked.

"Since I first came aboard the *Farlight.* That's when I found out who she was related to."

"What exactly did you two do . . . come up with?" Jackie asked, continuing her interrogation.

"I couldn't tell you. Knew you and Cuddy wouldn't approve," Haffan replied somewhat defiantly.

"Approve of what? You're evading the question," Kyle said.

"Well, I knew about it, too," Marzon said, looking somewhat pleased with himself.

"Knew about what? Could you just tell us what happened here?" Cuddy asked, glancing at Pith, who clearly was getting uncomfortable with the questioning.

"For the last week, we've been sending secret communiqué's to the *Raging Storm.*"

"You what!" Cuddy and Jackie exclaimed at the same timc.

Haffan's first reaction was to smile and then, unsuccessfully, to hold back a short nervous laugh. "I told you . . . sometimes I get subtle nudges. This time it came to me in the dream state. I had a glimpse of the future. A future that included our same battle with the Howsh fleet." Pointing to

Cuddy, she added, "A battle between you and Lorgue Prime Eminence Norsh."

For the first time, Tony—standing back and leaning on the Espy table—interjected a comment into the conversation. "I'm fucking confused," he told them.

"It's not that complicated," Pith said, seemingly surprised by her own boldness. "Haffan can sometimes see little bits and pieces of the future. After she learned who my uncle was . . . she tracked me down in Engineering. Asked me if I wanted to save everyone onboard the *Farlight*. Told me only I had the unique capability to do so. It took some convincing . . . but she's smart, and . . . well, I believed her."

"So what did you do then?" Jackie asked.

"I knew I'd need help," Pith said. "I didn't know enough about the ship's coms system, which meant I'd need to bring my boyfriend into the mix." She looked over to the giant Howsh.

Everyone else looked at Marzon.

"You and Pith . . ." Jackie queried.

Marzon shrugged. "Whom I bed with is no one else's business."

"And you went along with their, whatever this was . . . this caper?" Jackie asked him, dismayed.

"In my own defense, I wanted to tell Captain Perkins," Marzon replied, looking at Cuddy. "I was talked out of it. Told you needed to be totally surprised; that you wouldn't be able to play the part if you knew how things really went down. I am sorry."

"So you exchanged back and forth covert communications

with the *Raging Storm*? Convinced the Howsh, Norsh, you were . . . more loyal to them than to your own crew here?" Jackie asked.

"Basically, yes," Pith said.

"That's where my inner nudges came into play," Haffan said. "I saw Pith . . . in my dream. She was yelling, giving spatial coordinates of the *Farlight* to Lorgue Prime Eminence Norsh."

Cuddy said, "That's actually pretty ingenious. You get them . . . Norsh . . . to totally trust Pith, then, when the time comes, she blurts out the *Farlight's* position, only it's the wrong position . . . wrong coordinates."

"And when the enemy fleet began to fire, it gave away their own hidden location!" Jackie exclaimed, looking astonished.

"So you're not mad at me anymore?" Haffan asked, turning to Cuddy.

Before Cuddy could answer, Brian, who'd stayed out of the conversation thus far, cleared his throat in such a way that caught everyone's attention.

"You have something to add?" Jackie asked.

Brian studied Haffan with a bemused expression. "Are you going to tell Cuddy the rest of it? Or should I?"

The alien child's happy expression froze, turning to something else. Mild panic. Glaring at Brian, she said, "Let me guess, you discovered my secret from your time within the Empyrean Expanse."

Brian nodded, holding his tongue.

Again, Haffan turned toward Cuddy. "It's not that big a deal. We still have an important mission ahead of us . . . right, Cuddy?"

Cuddy nodded. "Sure, we still have to track down the Prophesy of Harkstrong . . ."

"So what now? Where to?" Tony asked.

Before anyone could answer, Spilor turned away from his console, saying, "The *Raging Storm* left the area approximately halfway into the battle. The AI tracked the vessel's movements well into the next planetary system, where it jumped to FTL."

"Good riddance," Jackie said.

"No . . . Norsh lives to fight another day. Destroying the *Raging Storm* should have been our first priority," Brian said.

Half listening, Cuddy's thoughts were still on Tow; the realization he would never see him again. Feeling an unavoidable sense of loss, he wondered how he would get past it? His eyes moved over to Haffan—the young alien, so animated—so engaged with everything going on around her. *What a small dynamo she was.* It then occurred to him that perhaps the only way to move past losing Tow, perhaps a *father figure* in his own life, was to become one, himself.

Haffan caught his eye. *Am I in trouble?*

Yeah . . . maybe . . . a little . . .

Can I still stay here? With you and Jackie?

Of course, this is your home . . . if you want it to be.

Haffan smiled. Then, as if something important had just occurred to her, she quickly rejoined the conversation. "I just remembered something. Something in those old scrolls."

"Something about the Prophesy?" Kyle asked.

"Uh huh . . . the Prophesy of Harkstrong. Harkstrong is actually a Howsh word, not a Pashier one. We took it to mean a place . . . maybe a location, like a distant city, on another planet. But Harkstrong, in the Howsh language, means something else completely . . ."

"It means peak, or high tower," Marzon interjected. "A place high above everything else."

"That's kinda cool, Haffan, but it doesn't really help us," Kyle said.

Haffan shot him an annoyed expression. "You're not getting it! Marzon, what's the highest point on your home planet . . . on Rahin."

"That would be the Citadel of the Dead."

"And what is that?"

"It is located on a distinct small mountainous continent, called the Barren. A place no one is allowed to go to—sacred, well protected, highly guarded," Marzon said, sounding more than a little proprietary.

"You're thinking the Prophecy is there . . . in this citadel place?" Jackie asked.

Haffan nodded. "Yup . . . could be."

Jackie glanced at Cuddy. "Find the Prophesy and we'll save two races of people . . . billions . . . you said it yourself."

Cuddy didn't answer right away, noting the anticipation on each face. Even Brian looked ready to go. Finally, he offered up, "It'll be dangerous. We'll be entering a world where we're despised. If discovered . . ."

"We're screwed," Tony said.

"Then it's settled . . . we're going to Rahin . . . right?" Jackie asked.

The End

Thank you for reading The Simpleton Quest.

If you enjoyed this book, PLEASE leave a review on Amazon.com—it really helps!

. . . And yes book three of the ***simpleton trilogy*** *is already on the way! To be notified the moment all future books are released—please join my mailing list. I hate spam and will never, ever, share your information. Jump to this link to sign up:*

http://eepurl.com/bs7M9r

acknowledgments

First and foremost, I am grateful to the fans of my writing and the ongoing support for all my books. Can you believe it? Seventeen books published thus far. I am truly blessed to have the people I care about most rooting me on. I'd like to thank my wife, Kim, she's a good sport putting up with my strange working hours and even stranger scifi *what if*... questions. I'd like to thank my mother, Lura Genz, for her tireless work as my first-phase creative editor and a staunch cheerleader of my writing. A special 'thank you' goes out to L.J. Ganser, who produces the audiobook versions of my books. Anyone looking for a truly immersive—not to forget 'fun'—reading experience, with all his wonderful character voices, will have to try the audiobook version. Others who provided fantastic support include Lura and James Fischer, Stuart Church, and Eric Sundius.

Made in the USA
Middletown, DE
23 June 2018